DEATH ON THE

Copyright © 2017 by Eric Horridge

All rights reserved.

Cover photo: Eric Horridge
Book design by Eric Horridge

No part of this book may be reproduced in any form or by any electronic or mechanical means including information storage and retrieval systems, without permission in writing from the author. The only exception is by a reviewer, who may quote short excerpts in a review.

This book is a work of fiction. Names, characters, places, and incidents either are products of the author's imagination or are used fictitiously. Any resemblance to actual persons, living or dead, events, or locales is entirely coincidental.

Eric Horridge

To Rebecca,

Whose encouragement and love inspired me to write this book

Prologue

She knew she was going to die if she did not take her chance.

She knew that it would come at some point, a single chance, maybe in a split second. She needed to be ready for it.

She kept her eyes closed and tried to think only of the routine, the process they were following. When she felt there was an opportunity to run, she would try to take it.

When they had first carried her here, she had tried to scream but each of them had either their hands over her mouth or had hands around her throat. Eventually, they had stuffed a handkerchief into her mouth, upon which she tried not to gag.

It was painful too. Each of them in turn clumsily thrusting themselves into her, encouraged by the others, until they had been satisfied inside her or had ejaculated upon her.

Initially, she had tried to fight, but that had only increased their aggression and their threats.

Her only hope was the youngest one, who had been unable to see it through, to participate in violating her. The one who had been unable to bring himself to perform, unlike the others.

Despite encouragement and baiting from the rest of them, the youngster had only been able to make a feeble attempt to enter her, but he had no desire, no will. After pretending to *come* he had rolled off her, his face covered in dirt and sweat.

After initially tasting the forest dirt, he vomited his disgust into the grass surrounding the clearing, his eyes streaming with tears, the jeers of his friends assaulting his senses.

The moon struggled to break through the scudding cloud that was low across the treetops of the woods, but it cast just enough light to show silhouettes and shadows in a macabre dance of the prone figures. The cold she initially felt when they had pushed her to the ground no longer mattered and she did not feel the chill of the November night anymore. She had no feeling at all.

Her clothes were dirty, torn, dishevelled, her jeans discarded a few feet away from her where they had thrown them, mocked her semi-nakedness. She was confused, scared, and angry with herself. So different from how it had been only a few hours before.

The concert she had been at with her brother, was even better than she had expected. One of her favourite bands, who sang all the songs she wanted to hear.

The *hits*, the atmosphere! The fun of a night out. The joy of meeting a boy she fancied while standing near the stage, and who was there with his friends, made the night seem magical. It had been a real struggle with her father to let her go to the event. He had initially said no, but he had finally relented as long as her brother remained in tow.

She was not happy about being chaperoned. She was 18 now for God's sake and she could do what she wanted. She didn't need to listen to her older brother, didn't need him close like a shadow hanging over her. She had eventually told him that she would get home herself, that she would get a lift, that she didn't need him to mollycoddle her. That her father could "go to hell." Kylie Clarkson could stand on her own two feet!

How she regretted that now. How she longed for her brother.

"We've got to stop this," shouted the youngster. "This is so wrong," he pleaded.

The others looked at him vehemently. The one who had failed in the eyes of the rest of them, the one who had already had his chance.

He sat slumped on the ground shivering, face stained with dirt and streaked with tears, his eyes averting the scene in front of him. Barely 17 and the baby of the group he had at first thought the whole idea was a joke, a bit of fun. She had teased them all and the thought of a grope in the dark had excited them all, but this...this was something he couldn't comprehend.

"Shut up," a snarled reply. "Shut the fuck up!"

The response was harsh, brutal, just like the act he could see in the cold grey night before him. The words spoken were more like a growl, filled with power and threatening violence. The rebuke was meant to intimidate and indicate who held the power over the group.

He received the message, loud and clear, understood it. It made him feel small, insignificant, useless and cut through him like a Stanley knife across the flesh of unguarded fingers. Shivers rippled through his body, bile rose again in his throat, and he felt the warm acid in his mouth.

He turned his face to the ground to vomit a second time. The others though were like a pack of dogs, a silent pack, a few grunts as they reached a climax, the occasional unnecessary thrust of victory.

They knew that with the main road less than half a mile away and a few farmhouse lights shining through the trees around the clearing, they had had to be careful about where they had stopped and parked their car and how to keep the girl quiet. Now, this no longer seemed relevant, they had lost all sense of perspective. It was now about lust, power. They didn't care about the danger.

The third member of the pack was rolling off her and as he did so the fourth, released his grip on her right arm, ready for his turn. As he stood up to loosen his belt, in his eagerness he tripped and lost his balance on the damp undergrowth and collided with the one holding both her legs. For a split second before the one holding her left arm was able to grip her right shoulder to press her further into the dirt, she realized her legs were free.

She kicked out and caught one of them high in the chest. He fell backward crying out more in shock than in pain. She tried to turn her body so that she could release her arms but found the strength of the one holding them, way too strong. She tried to cry out in frustration and fear, but only a muffled sound escaped from her mouth, caught on the handkerchief still in her throat. She realized that the opportunity had gone.

The last of the men threw himself onto her back, expelling the air from her lungs. She struggled to breathe. Her face was ground into the damp foliage as the men organized themselves, making sure she had no further chance of moving. She struggled to take in any air through her nose. She felt like she was going to faint, realizing she was losing consciousness as she felt the cold, dark, damp soil invade her nose and eyes.

The last man was the *pack* leader, the one whom she had thought was cute and who she had fancied at the concert. He was the one who had danced with her, had held her, sang all the band's songs with her, and had offered her a lift home. It was he who she had trusted, and for whom she had turned to her brother and told him to "get lost." It was he, who had jumped on her back as she tried to escape. And it was he, who shouted at the others to hold her down, to hold her *face-down*, and *"don't fucking let go."*

The others had entered her while she was lying on her back. She had felt their heads next to her own and saw their faces looking down at her, enjoying themselves as they penetrated her, clumsily, angrily.

They had grinned, salivated, spat at her. She had tried where possible to keep her eyes closed, but had sensed their eyes looking into her face. She had smelt their breath and felt their hungry mouths on her lips.

She had also tried to ensure that they had not been able to kiss her properly, by grinding her teeth together, her lips becoming a thin line of defiance. However, with the handkerchief in her throat, she had found it difficult to breathe. When she couldn't take it anymore, she had needed to get as much air into her lungs as possible, and so she had needed to open her mouth as wide as she could.

All of this, they had not noticed in the darkness. They did not care. They had not seen how she was struggling to get air into her body, to them, their actions were about their own personal release, personal pleasure only.

The last of them, the leader of the group, the boy she had fancied, and the reason she was now fighting for her life. He was different.

It seemed he was determined to hurt her. With his left hand, he pulled her hair back so that her face was a few inches off the ground. She tried to cry out but as her shoulders were pinned down by the other men, she could only take a few quick breaths through her nose, before he pushed her head down into the soil again. As he did so, she realized he was going to enter her from behind. She felt him lift her hips slightly and then, almost without warning, she felt the raw, terrible, pain. It spread through her like a wildfire across a remote tinder-dry forest.

She knew of anal rape. In her confusion, she had a strange thought about what happened to men in prison, about how prevalent this was, in men-only environments when they are locked up together.

She hadn't realized how brutal it could be, how humiliating, how degrading. She tried to struggle again, but the pressure of the hand on her head became more intense. Each thrust of the man on top of her grew more violent and as it did so, her face was pushed further and further into the dirty, soil. Into the soft damp ground.

She could barely hear anything other than her pulse pounding in her ears but she sensed the other men had all gone quiet. She sensed that they were staring at him, this leader of the pack, as he lay above her. She sensed the tension between them, a realization that this was going too far, but that they were powerless or too scared to say anything, do anything.

Her lungs began to scream for air as he continued thrusting into her. She gagged as she tried to open her mouth, but all she could take in through her nose was the dirt. Saliva mixed with mucus in her throat, but no oxygen entered her body.

She sensed that she would soon blackout.

She hoped when she regained consciousness, that she would be alone. And then she couldn't feel his thrusts anymore. The pain was receding, the sounds were distorted, even when she opened her eyes for a brief second she couldn't see anything at all. She could not even see the black dirt that her face was being pushed into, that she had previously tasted.

She had no taste in her mouth now, no sense of anything.

Her mouth and nose were clotted with soil, mucus, and vomit. Her face embedded deep into the floor of the woods.

An odd thought flashed through her mind. A random, useless thought. If this is how people died from asphyxiation, then she could understand why hanging was no longer a capital punishment. Her mind wandered, thinking that it was horrific that people could die slowly like this, perhaps thinking of what they had done in their lives, what they still wanted to do, but no longer would do.

She began hallucinating, thinking of her family, thinking of their mistakes, her mistakes, thinking of a future that would no longer be hers to live.

It was the very last thought she would ever have.

TODAY......................

Chapter 1

The alarm pierced his subconscious.

He had been dreaming, and the crossover from fantasy to reality confused him for a second. The dreams always did that. They weren't a regular occurrence but when they happened, it always seemed to take longer to gather his senses together. The beeping continued. Finally, he recognized it was the alarm on his phone, his regular 4:30 am wake-up reminder. He felt a tightness across his shoulders until he realized it was Michelle's arm that she always seemed to drag across him every night when they slept together.

Michelle stirred, barely awake, "God is it that time already?" she mumbled. "Turn it off for heaven's sake!"

Mike Cannon reached over to his phone. Still not quite awake, he pushed the necessary four numbers on the keypad and slid his finger across the face of the phone to stop the ringing. He dropped the phone back onto the bedside table, then with a sigh, lay back onto the warm sheets. For a few seconds he lay still, silent, seeking the willpower to get going. As he rubbed his eyes to wake himself up to the day ahead, Michelle rolled over onto her left side, her back to him, pulling the sheets over her shoulders, clearly intent on another few minutes of sleep.

Cannon sighed again, ever since Michelle had moved in, well semi-permanently anyway, Cassie had become even more distant, and he knew that the tensions that existed between Michelle and his daughter were something he needed to address. It was an issue that was affecting his sleep, but it wasn't something that would resolve itself overnight, nor something he could address immediately either. He had too many things to consider and Cassie was only due back tomorrow, anyway.

He rolled off the bed and headed to the bathroom knowing that most of his staff in his small stable had already been up for at least 30 minutes and were hard at work starting the day with the routine of feeding the horses, and preparing them for what was to come that day, either training or racing. The yard which he had set up some four years before, just outside the small Oxfordshire village of Stonesfield, was now his life, its acquisition and development his sole focus ever since Sally had passed away from breast cancer seven years before.

He hadn't been there the night she had silently slipped from her deep slumber to that place from where she could never return, and he regretted it so much.

It had been a long six-year battle, in and out of hospital, so many times. Days and weeks of ups and downs. Times when it seemed like the battle had been won. Times when the hours were so dark that it felt the night would never end. Yet, there were times he now looked back on and occasionally wished that he could go back to, as, despite all the heartache and the finality they brought with them, he remembered the good times with fondness.

Eventually, as with all things, time passed and denial of the loss eventually turned to acceptance and he knew that he could not live in the past. He had needed to move on, and so he had. He had decided to pursue his passion and do what he knew he should have done years before.

So far, so good.

It was colder than expected for early October but at least it was dry. The nights had been clear over the past few days resulting in the lower temperatures making the ground a little harder. It was something he needed to think about when he considered where to run any of the 25 horses under his care. Too hard ground could easily damage the horses' legs when they jumped the fences that he trained them for.

He shivered while he stood waiting for the water in the shower to run hot and he subconsciously noticed the swirls of steam rising from the shower floor.

Lost in thought, he immersed himself inside the cubicle under the invigorating spray and then turned his mind to his dream. He could only ever recall the same few elements, the same three of four components that constituted a narrative somewhere in his brain as he slept. It was a mixture of fact and fiction. A kind of twisted reality that was somehow brought to the fore and put onto a loop like those on a modern roller coaster ride that never seemed to end. The police psychiatrist had told him just before he left the Force a few months after Sally's death, that the past was always there and would at times come back to visit him.

As he soaped himself down and washed his thinning shoulder-length hair which had the odd grey streak here and there across the crown and just above the ears, he relaxed his eyes for a minute and reflected on his dream. The dream and variations of it always brought him to the same place, his *past*, his former life. How it had meant so much at the time and how the *job* had become his *life.* How living the job had impacted his relationship with his daughter and how being true to its' ideals had meant missing out on many of the key milestones of Cassie's childhood. Her growing up, from her first steps to her first school and into her teenage years. All that time lost and yet more importantly, more regrettably, not being there when Sally needed him most.

He knew it was the same for others and that some of his former colleagues had struggled while on the job – alcohol abuse, divorce, suicide, affairs. He knew much of what happened to them was brought on while under stress, with the pressure of the job. Pressure to meet numbers, reduce cost and achieve more with less. It was not something he had expected when he had first joined the Force. It came later. All the ideals of protecting the community, catching the bad guys, doing what was right, were noble. However over time and as one progressed 'up the tree' one saw those ideals thwarted, change, become less important, and cynicism and anger become more prevalent. Over time, a long time, and despite any attempt to put the issues to one side, ignore them, *pretend* they were not there, they did start to impact you. They did start to make you question things. Question your own values. Eventually, question the whole point. Eventually… move on!

Once out of it, once you had broken the link, once you no longer needed to live that life and were away from some of the *shit* that you saw, the low life's, the abusers, the scum of society, surely you were in a better place and your mind would free you from it all? Well, perhaps he was wrong. The dreams he had or at least the parts he could remember, he knew were of incidents from the past. A mixture of what was real and imagined. He had been out of that world for some years now, yet despite all attempts to forget it, he had baggage and he did not like it. He managed it the best way he could, often ignoring it, but he was always aware of it.

He brought himself back from the past, gave himself a mental slap, and noticing the water starting to cool, he turned the hot water up a little so that he could complete the task at hand.

Once he had finished showering, he tried his best to address the stubble on his face. Standing in the bathroom, a towel around his waist, looking himself in the eyes through the fogged-up mirror, he scraped away at his chin. Finally, but without conviction, he shrugged his shoulders, and decided he had done the best he could do. He cleaned the razor and stepped back into the bedroom, dropping the towel as he did so on his side of the bed, and turned on the bedside table lamp.

Michelle didn't stir. He looked across at her as he dressed. She had pulled the duvet up around her chin, and with her back turned to him he could only see the long dark curls of her hair cascading on the pillow and across her face. Her breathing was slow and rhythmic, and she had fallen back into a deep sleep. She didn't need to leave until 7:30 in order to get to school so once he completed dressing, he turned off the light, closed the bedroom door, and headed off to the kitchen to make some tea. He would wake her at six for breakfast after he had done his rounds of the stable.

The first *lot* of horses walked around in a circle.

The blankets on their backs were the sole protection from the cold. That and the small racing saddles used by the men who controlled these half-ton creatures as they ran across the gallops that were part of the shared land used by many of the trainers in this part of rural Oxfordshire.

Just west of the small town of Woodstock and the famous Blenheim Palace, Cannon had found a small run-down farm with a set of stables that was on the market, part of an estate of a former member of the landed gentry. It had been neglected for several years as it was far away from the main house and sat beside a copse of land and a small forest just off Combe Road. Because it was quite some distance from the main house it had been a case of *out of sight* and thus *out of mind*.

Eventually, when the landowner had died and the estate sold off by his children who had no intention of living in the country, Cannon had been able to acquire the place at a very reasonable price. Though still mortgaged, his lump sum from his service in the police had allowed him enough to obtain the property and to fix up most of the stables, acquire the necessary equipment and have a little leftover to survive on until he had managed to procure a few clients and some reasonable horses.

To obtain the necessary training licence, he had worked with another local trainer, Charlie Barnes, for a few years, learning the ropes, understanding the way horses behave and how to get the best out of them. It had been an apprenticeship and friendship built on mutual admiration. Charlie had been a friend of Sally's family for many years and Cannon had met him when Cannon and Sally first began dating and ultimately married. Charlie was over 70 when Sally died, so when Cannon approached him to help turn Cannon's hobby into a new career, Charlie was only too happy to *'take him on'*. He agreed to help him move through the stages from punter to stable-hand and ultimately to assistant trainer over a couple of years until Cannon was able to go it alone. For that, Cannon was eternally grateful.

"Ok, off you go," he called out, and the dozen horses making up his first string were pulled out of line by his head lad and headed off in a slow walk towards the small track that led to gallops just about 200 yards from the property's perimeter.

Cannon watched them go. The light from the kitchen window on the west side of the yard dancing slightly on the horse's flanks and the peaks of the jockey's caps and stirrups as they rambled away from him, the sound of their hooves breaking the silence as the sun struggled to rise. The morning was still. Dawn was still another hour or so away. There was no movement in the air and the darkness and the cold exacerbated the breath of the horses as they sneezed and shook their heads from side to side. They knew where they were going, they knew what they were going to do, the anticipation of their primal urge to run reflected in their gait as they jogged on their *toes*.

Cannon was thankful for these men, boys really, given their physical stature, and to the single girl who made up his team. Thankful that they entrusted him to provide them with a job that they loved, notwithstanding the physical labour involved, and the antisocial hours it entailed.

His head lad, Richard 'Rich' Telside, had been with him almost from day one. Rich originally from Exeter and nearly 18 years younger than Cannon, had been with Charlie as well, but when Cannon decided to go on his own, Rich approached him knowing that Charlie was soon to retire, and asked Cannon if he could join him. Cannon was delighted and the relationship had grown from there. Cannon trusted Rich implicitly and both men had become good friends over the subsequent years. While they could have been father and son, they had a solid professional relationship and as a result, maintained healthy mutual respect. This allowed the necessary forthright discussions to take place when needed and at times, fortunately not that frequently, they could turn into no-holds barred arguments. Generally though, common sense would ultimately prevail, peace would return and no matter who had 'won' the argument, no grudges were ever held.

The darkness along the track that took the horses from the stables to the fields a half-mile away, quickly enveloped them and they were gone. He would go up later in his Land Rover to see the second string on the gallops.

The first string were the younger horses that still had to be schooled over the jumps, so they were being sent out just to run at various speeds, jog, canter, and then finally gallop. This was all about getting them fit, not about how to jump. That technique would be taught later.

When it was lighter in an hour or so, the horses ready to race soon would be taken from their stables for their exercise, and over the subsequent seventy-five to ninety minutes, be put through their paces and then return to their stalls.

Cannon went quickly into the house to wake Michelle. She was still asleep when he sat on her side of the bed having turned on the bedroom lights.

"Hey," he said ruffling her hair with his left hand, "Time to get up Miss Ward, the kids won't take kindly to *teacher* being late." His emphasis on the word *teacher* resulted in Michelle opening her eyes and with a slight struggle sitting up, her back against the headboard.

"What time is it?" she asked, rubbing her eyes.

"It's just after six. The first string has just left. I am about to have breakfast. What would you like?"

"I think I'll just have the usual, bit of toast and some coffee if that's okay?"

"No problem," he said, standing up. He kissed her on the head and noticed as he turned to leave the room that she was kicking off the duvet as she started to make her way to the ensuite. Out of the corner of his eye, the fact that she always slept naked no matter the time of year was apparent as she tiptoed across the carpet. The glimpse he had of her slim body made him smile. *How lucky*, he thought, that he had found someone to love again.

Cannon gathered all the items necessary for breakfast and put them together on a kitchen cart in one corner of the room. The room itself had once been a scullery but when Cannon had bought the property, the stables, and the living quarters as they were, one wouldn't have called the place a house at all.

It was more a small cottage of three rooms, probably initially built for a groundsman and his family, he had surmised. A place for someone to live who looked after the grounds or who would have looked after the horses used to work the land many years before. It had needed extensive renovations.

Over 18 months and with the help of Rich, the stables had been brought up to standard and likewise, the living quarters had been slowly turned into a proper house. *Get a good set of plans drawn by experts, get a good builder and it was amazing what £70000 could do* he had realized at the time.

The rustic charm of the 18th-century building with its darkened sandstone and thatch roof was completely renovated and modernized. The integrity of the building and the brickwork outside were maintained and expanded but the inside and the roof itself were completely revamped.

As it had been a bargain buy, it meant that Cannon had enough money and needed limited borrowing to get the place as he wanted it. However, what he really needed now was more owners and more horses to earn a decent living. Being an up-and-coming trainer was great but it didn't pay all the bills. Thank goodness for Michelle's income and the fact that he used public gallops. He had no money yet to buy or build his own.

The coffee machine gave a short *puff* of steam as the water finally filtered through the pod Cannon had inserted into it a minute or so before. Michelle walked in, her long dark auburn hair was still damp and the curls that looked like ringlets throughout, cascaded around her face. She had dressed but had not yet attempted to put on any makeup. Not that Cannon thought she needed any. She was in her late thirties, slim, with a body that had not been challenged to cope with babies.

She wore dark trousers. In the kitchen light, they seemed black but were actually dark navy. They accentuated her narrow waist and contrasted with the light grey blouse she had on under an unbuttoned navy cardigan. A silver chain with a small onyx insert in the shape of a star, about an inch across, dangled from her neck.

Her green eyes still showed that despite the shower she had taken, she still had not fully woken up. She yawned showing teeth that were not quite straight, not quite perfect, but were certainly looked after. Her face was open, slightly oval, reflecting a willingness to be engaged. Her nose was small, her skin pale almost milky white, yet had a hint of beige that somehow made her look healthy. As a teacher at a local high school, she was often the talk of the boys in their final year as being *'fit'*.

"Just what I needed," she said, as Cannon took the cup from the base of the machine and handed it to her. "God, did I sleep well? How about you?" she asked.

"Oh not bad" he lied, thinking back to his dream. "What have you got on today?"

"Same old, same old," she answered, "but at least it's nearly weekend. I can't wait until tonight. You?"

"I have a couple of things to sort out later. Need to send off some declarations for Leicester, Warwick, and Newbury for next month and follow up on those I plan to run at Cheltenham next week and Southwell later this month."

"Sounds like 'same old, same old' to me," she said somewhat sarcastically as she sipped her coffee. "Oh and by the way, is Cassie home tomorrow?" she enquired "or is she still planning to go to her friend's place once they get back from the school trip?"

Cannon knew that the past week at home had been the calmest it had been for quite a while. Cassie being away on the school trip to Europe had been a Godsend. It had allowed the tension between the three of them to evaporate a little. Cassie had reached that age where she was fourteen going on forty. She had opinions about everything, which in some ways was good. At least she had a brain. Unfortunately, the tongue wasn't always connected to it.

One of her strong opinions was that her father's choice of partner was a bad one. Cassie's view was that a teacher from her school being her father's lover was not a good idea. She felt that she was always under the eye of school authorities, and accordingly, everything she did, was being fed back to her dad. She felt that she had no freedom and needed to be constantly on her toes. As such, she felt that any boy she might be interested in, would shy away from her knowing that she was always under some form of scrutiny. It was a misguided view of things, but try telling a teenage girl that.

"I don't know," he said. "I think she's staying at home. In fact, I hope so," he added, "I want to hear how it went."

Michelle did not reply. She drained her coffee. Her face remained impassive

"Well, I better get finished," and with that, she put her empty cup into the dishwasher

"What about your toast?"

"Oh, I'm not hungry, I'll get something at school in the staff room" she replied, as she left the kitchen.

Cannon sighed. He went over to the machine to make himself some toast and put the kettle on. When he eventually left the kitchen having satisfied his hunger, Michelle had almost finished getting ready. He called out to her to have a *'great day'* as he walked out of the house through the front door and climbed into his Land Rover. He sat for a second before he turned the key to the ignition.

I guess I need to have a chat with Cassie tomorrow, he thought to himself, *if I don't, I'm not sure how long it will be before Michelle and I end up with a problem that will have gone too far for the relationship to last.*

"Shit," he said out loud as he whacked the steering wheel with the palm of his right hand, "as if I don't have enough to worry about?"

As he sat in the car contemplating how to talk with Cassie and what to say, he realized that it was now almost time for the second string to be exercised. The sky had lightened and dawn was breaking in the east. Tiny fingers of red and amber could just be seen over the fields to his left.

There were still another twenty minutes before the sun had officially risen, but the effects of the encroaching day were just beginning to show.

The clouds that had drifted softly into the area over the past few hours could just be made out in the ever-lightening sky, their edges reflecting colours of orange, reds, and blues. The old adage of the *red sky in the morning* and its associated warning did not sit comfortably with him, as he knew it was a sign of a cool and potentially wet day ahead. Not what he wanted.

The lights of Michelle's car coming from his right pierced the morning greyness that still lingered at ground level. A kind of shadow neither black nor blue but that obsequious colour between the dead of night and early morning. Her car wheels crunched on the gravel driveway that ran from the garage to the road. As she passed him, she blew a kiss. He could just make out the gesture and he smiled.

The second string of horses, another twelve, circled each other nose to tail, walking on the soft grass of the gallops. The riders including Rich, who also schooled the horses each day, chatted quietly to their charges offering encouragement with a click of the tongue, a soft word, or a pat on the neck.

The horses' flanks and heads constantly changed colour from the deep bay or brown to a rust colour where the sun's rays fell across them from various angles as they maintained their discipline and continued in the never-ending circle.

This process was to loosen the muscles in their legs, stretch and flex the tendons and ligaments. While a horse's heart and lungs give it the capacity to run, and the brain sends the primeval signal to the rest of the body with the desire to win, the legs are a racehorses' lifeline. Any injury, be it a muscle tear, a chip in a knee or even a damaged hoof could spell the end of a racing career or even the end of a life.

Cannon knew that most owners who had entrusted him with their animals loved them like any other pet they may have owned.

Some however did not.

Some owners bought a racehorse for prestige or to make money. It was, however, a known fact in racing circles, that to make your first million you needed to start with two million. Yet despite this, each owner of Steeplechasers or Hurdlers usually has a vision that one day, the horse they owned, would win the Grand National or the Gold Cup or the Champion Hurdle and because of this, their beautiful *investments* had to be protected.

With the first string having completed their work just as the sun rose above the horizon, by the time dawn had turned the night into the cool crisp morning the first lot of horses were already back in their boxes having been hosed down from their exertions, fed, watered and given fresh bedding to lie on. The only thing they would see of the world for the rest of the day was the inside of their stables.

Occasionally Cannon would allow the top half of the stable doors to be opened for an hour or so in the afternoon if it wasn't too cold or wet for the inhabitants to enjoy some fresh air, but only if he or Rich were at home. While he had never had any issues himself since he had started training, burglaries, theft of farm implements, tools, tractors, livestock including horses, while infrequent, still occurred in the area. Cannon's intuition from his past had always been to *'be safe rather than sorry'*.

Cannon stood about ten yards from the circling athletes and looked across at the field that contained the rough sandy track and the five fences that the second string of horses were schooled over. Two of the fences were basic hurdles, the other three considerably larger obstacles, specially built for the steeplechasers. The incline from where he stood to a ridge about 800 yards away to his right was approximately 12%, enough to give a good workout for any horse, especially when one added the 200 yards of the track away to his left. This, in addition to the jumps that each horse was required to navigate. Two of the horses would be covering that distance on this particular training run at least five times, while the others only ran three.

"Ok, Rich," called Cannon, "could you please take *Mr. Scarecrow* around the track five times, please? We have entered him at Cheltenham in just over a week. Take him at a half pace for the first couple, then at three-quarter pace for the next two. Really push him for the last round. He's pretty fit already so I just want to get a few more miles into his legs and then we'll start tapering him off over the coming few days."

"No problem boss," replied Rich.

Cannon smiled to himself. He still struggled with being called *'boss'*, especially by Rich. To him 'Mike' was the only label he attached to himself. Even as a Detective Inspector he was never happy with 'Sir' or 'Guvnor' and he always tried to make light of things when he was introduced as DI Cannon. He hated labels.

"Oh and Angela," he said to the red-headed girl aboard the horse walking behind Rich, "could you do the same with *Aeon's Ago,* please? Try to keep up with Rich but if the horse struggles a bit near the end don't whack him, just try and complete the distance even if you have to ease him down. I don't think he will give you his best just yet. He still needs a bit more work in him."

"Right you are," replied Angela, in her soft Lincolnshire accent.

The other riders were given their instructions and then Cannon leaned back against his car and watched the horse's wheel away from him as they began their respective circuits.

As they did so Cannon took a pair of binoculars that he had draped around his neck and followed each of the horses as they strode along the track and jumped their respective first fence of the day. The hurdlers over the smaller fences, *Mr. Scarecrow* and *Aeon's Ago* clearing the larger fences. Cannon noticed the pace begin to increase as the first circuit was finished, the horses moving past him in a cascade of snorts, pounding hooves, and steam released from flaring nostrils. The riders sat stock still with their legs tight against the horses' flanks, their bodies leaning forward so that their heads were directly above their mount's shoulders. The rise and fall of the horses' necks almost crashing into the chins of the riders.

He was pleased.

At the end of the session, it was clear that all the horses had enjoyed the exercise. The hurdlers had completed their work a good few minutes before the others and had pulled off the track to watch them complete their task. Once all the work had been completed the group was drawn together and then came across to where Cannon was still standing. As they walked slowly towards him the chatter from the riders became more audible. Previously each time a circuit was completed and the horse and riders passed Cannon all he could hear was either expletives from the riders or grunts and shouts of encouragement as they cajoled their mounts to increase the pace.

"Good work everyone," Cannon exclaimed, "Any issues?"

The mixture of accents all rolled into a single cacophony of sound, as the riders began to share their views about how their mounts had travelled along the track or met and jumped the respective fences

"Nearly came a bloody cropper here on *Katmandu* on the second circuit," said Sean Creezey, in his Dublin sing-song voice. "But I think it was my fault, I got too close to the fence before I asked him to jump," he said. "After that, he felt great in my hands and finished it off well. So no harm done and he's in good shape boss."

"Thanks Sean. Tim?"

The last of the riders Tim Emery was an extremely lightweight jockey from the tiny village of Wooton just about 4 miles to the northeast. Tim looked about fourteen but was actually twenty-nine, touched his riding helmet with his whip, and relayed his view of his ride, *Belle o' the Ball*.

"I think she's got the hang of it now boss. She never put a foot wrong and she was strong at the end. I think you've got a good one here," he said.

"Yes, she seemed to travel very well. The owner will be pleased. She's down to run at Southwell in just over two weeks. A bit more experience and perhaps a little bit more work over a little longer distance and she could turn into something very useful. OK everyone, let's give them a slow walk once around the track to cool down then let's get back home. See you back at the yard."

Cannon watched the group walk off together again, the steam from the horses mixing with the breath of the humans. The sky that only two hours ago had been clear with a few clouds had now completely clouded over with a grey/black tinge of menace. While it did not threaten rain in the short term, the recent dry spell could very quickly become a distant memory. The wind had increased and the temperature felt much cooler than it had been when Cannon had first arrived upon the gallops. He pulled his open jacket tighter to himself, a habit he had developed and one he did without thought, and jumped into the driver's seat of his car.

As he settled down to make a few notes of the exercise he had just been watching, he noticed his smartphone that he had left on the passenger seat, showed there was a text message for him. It was from Michelle. *'Please call me urgently'* it read. He also noticed that there were a couple of missed calls on the phone as well. The last, just ten minutes beforehand. He looked at his watch, it was now just after nine. *She should be starting her first class now*, he thought, but he decided to call anyway seeing as she had tried to get hold of him a couple of times.

"Hey," he said as she answered the phone almost immediately after the first ring, "what's up? Is everything okay?"

"Oh God," she replied, "Oh God, Mike...." her voice trailed off as if any words she wanted to say were stuck in her throat.

"What is it?" Cannon exclaimed, panic rising up from his stomach "What's going on? Has anything happened to Cassie?" Dark thoughts filled his mind as he realized Michelle had only been at school for about forty-five minutes, and any news of a school trip running into trouble would have likely been channelled through the school first before any of the parents were notified.

"No, No," Michelle countered, "nothing to do with Cassie," she hesitated just for a second, just enough to make Cannon's heart sink "at least not directly..." her voice trailing off on the other end of the phone.

Cannon looked out of the car window but saw nothing, his mind fixed on trying to get to the bottom of what was going on. "For God's sake Michelle, what is it...?" He realized his voice had risen almost to a shout.

Finally, after what seemed like an age Michelle spat out what she needed to. "It's Cassie's best friend Wendy. Her father, Simon Crabb. He, He.....He's been murdered!"

Cannon could hear her start to sob down the phone, he could feel the waves of emotion pouring out of her. He tried to make sense of what she had just told him. After what seemed like a minute but was only seconds he said "Okay, I'm on my way, I'll be there in 15 minutes. I'll meet you in the staff room."

Chapter 2

The car park at the school was small but large enough for the Head, his deputy, and the twenty or so teachers and administrators who martialled those pupils attending each day, through each stage of their secondary education. It wasn't full as some of the staff were away with the pupils, like Cassie, on school trips.

Being in the country, halfway between Charlbury and the beautifully named village of Shipton-under-Wychwood, just off London Lane, the school buildings sat on a small hill with an elevation that gave it incredible views of the stunning scenery of the North Cotswolds. The hills and valleys spread out like a quilted carpet before it.

Farms with crops of winter wheat, and other cereals like barley as well as dairy, pig, and poultry farms stood like the squares of a chessboard across the plain towards Gloucester and Cheltenham to the west.

The autumnal colours of the trees that surrounded the grounds with their bright reds and yellows stood in contrast to the sky above which had darkened even more since Cannon had left home. As he walked from the parking lot towards the school reception in the administration building, the dark, muddy clouds swirled above him bringing with them the threat of rain. He pulled his coat tighter around his body again, as he did habitually. A sudden gust of wind trying to lift its edges created flapping wings around his legs.

Cannon entered the relative warmth of the building, its modern design inside indicating a different mindset to education than that portrayed by the exterior of the building, with its Tudor cottage style of pseudo-thatch, steep arch gables, and arched doorways, all common features of the area.

There was no sign of any of the school staff in the reception area. The only person Cannon saw was a boy, about twelve years of age, his hair uncombed and his shirt hanging out below his blazer. A backpack was slung across his left arm as he tried to tuck the shirt into his trousers as he shuffled along a passageway leading to what Cannon assumed was the boy's classroom.

He walked straight past the reception desk and headed to the staff room. He didn't worry about trying to let any one of the staff know about his arrival. By pressing the requested bell on top of the reception desk and waiting, he would be wasting time, and he knew where the staffroom was anyway. He had collected Michelle many times from the school even before her moving in with him. In addition, he had been *'asked'* to attend there on several occasions when Cassie had gotten herself into trouble with her *'attitude'* over the past 18 months or so. This had become more frequent in recent times.

He arrived at the staff room door, knocked, and entered. Given the issue at hand, he wasn't going to stand on ceremony.

The room was light and airy, indicative of the rest of the school design. A modern ethos, the same modern look as the rest of the inside of the building. The school took pride in portraying, *'modern thinking in a modern world'*. The building's overall interior looked like a cubists' wet dream with how it was put together. It seemed out of place in a rural setting. The contrast was something he never lost sight of, but he knew it was a good school providing good education, and that was what he wanted for his daughter.

There were single seats spread around the edges of the room, and several two-seater sofas in a dark beige patterned fabric of faux leather. In addition, there were other three-seater sofas positioned in what looked like pods. Altogether, there were enough chairs to seat around twenty-five to thirty people. Cannon always thought the modern look was similar to an IKEA showroom, but he kept that view to himself.

Michelle was sitting with three other people, two women and a man, cups of half-drunken tea stood on a small table between them. Michelle stood up as she became aware of Cannon's arrival and within a few seconds, she had her arms around him, hugging him fiercely, her face pressed against his neck. She sobbed gently. He held her for a few seconds, almost embarrassed by the fact that the others in the room looking on at them, none of the three uttering a word.

"OK, OK," he said, his hand caressing the back of her head. "Let's sit down and tell me what's going on."

He gently unwrapped himself from her arms and led her back to the seat she had occupied so that she could compose herself. As she did so, Cannon introduced himself to the three others.

"Joseph Crabb, nice to meet you," said the man, standing and shaking his hand. "Sorry that it's under such terrible circumstances," he continued. "I'm Wendy's grandfather, and this is my wife Irene." The woman he had nodded towards as an indication of which of the two women he was referring to, remained seated but offered up a sad smile. Cannon nodded acknowledgement in return.

Joe Crabb was clearly the head of his household. He was in his mid-sixties, about five feet nine tall, with short dark hair in almost a crew cut style, very military. He stood straight-backed and was extremely well dressed. He obviously liked his branded clothing. Cannon noticed the logos on the dark blue sweater and the well-pressed fawn-coloured casual slacks that he wore under the black overcoat that sat loosely around his shoulders. Irene Crabb was effectively the bit player in the relationship. She was a neat and tidy woman. Similar in age to her husband, but extremely demure, almost to the point of being a non-entity. She sat with her hands in her lap, her grey hair cut in a pageboy style. She wore a pink print dress under a deeper pink cardigan all hiding under a dark grey mohair coat. Cannon noticed the obligatory pearl necklace was thankfully absent.

"And I am the Reverend Eunice Fountain," announced the last of the three. "From St James' church in Stonesfield," she added, holding out her hand which Cannon took, noticing how limp it felt in his own. "Likewise, Mr. Cannon," she stated, "I also wish it was under better circumstances."

"Can I suggest we all sit down please?" Cannon proposed, "and tell me what is going on? What's all this about a murder?"

An odd silence filled the air for a few seconds after they all sat down. Teacups were then emptied, giving the impression that only when the liquid had been consumed would it give people a voice, and what needed to be said, could be.

Joseph Crabb broke the silence. He spoke directly to Cannon.

"My son….Ahem, *our* son," he motioned to his wife who remained silent, stoic, her face set in stone. Cannon noticed her eyes shimmering with tears that somehow she refused to be let out and cascade down her cheeks, as many other mothers would do. "Is…sorry was, Simon Crabb. He is, umm, was," he corrected himself again, "the golf pro at the Kirtlington Golf Club, which is about twenty minutes from here, on the other side of Woodstock, near Bletchingdon "

"Yes, I know of it."

"Well, last night according to our daughter-in-law, Rachel, his wife, he didn't go home. This morning around five-thirty we received a call from the police that our son's body had been found."

"And why was that Mr. Crabb?" Cannon enquired.

"Sorry?" came the confused reply.

"What I meant was why did the police contact you and not your son's wife? The normal procedure would be to advise the next of kin first."

For an instant Cannon stopped and took stock of what he had just indicated to the older man. He realized that his mind had taken him back to another world, another time, a time since past, yet its effect was still being felt, lying just under his skin, resting in situ somewhere in the deep recesses of his mind. No wonder at times his dreams took him back to those days.

"Forgive me," he went on, "I used to be a D.I. up until a few years ago …" He saw confusion in the older man's eyes but let the silence linger for a few seconds before continuing. "A Detective Inspector," he emphasized. "So I have a reasonable idea how investigations like this start and the procedures that are followed."

"Oh," responded Crabb. "Rachel is away you see, up in Edinburgh at a conference. She's a lawyer, a corporate lawyer"

Cannon was sure the old man had pushed out his chest slightly to indicate to everyone how important he felt his daughter-in-law was in the world.

"Anyway," Crabb continued, "the police told us that they had tried to contact her once they had found Simon's body. It seems his wallet for some reason had not been taken, so the police had his ID and have been trying to use whatever means they could to get hold of Rachel. They came to us because they said when they went to their house, there was no one home"

"Which make sense," interrupted Cannon. "And your granddaughter is on a school trip, yes?"

"Precisely," agreed Crabb.

"Have you tried to get hold of Rachel since the police told you of your son's murder?"

A small sniffle escaped from Mrs. Crabb, who had remained sitting silently until that point, almost forgotten. Reverend Fountain gently put her arms around her in comfort.

"Yes, Mr. Cannon, we have," went on Crabb, "but unfortunately we were only able to leave a message on her mobile phone for her to call us. We called her the moment the police arrived. It was just a couple of hours ago, though it seems like a lifetime ago," he said sadly. "When she called us last night, she said she was worried," he went on, "as when she is away, she always phones home to see how Wendy is and how Simon's day has been. You know, the normal things we all do …" he let the sentence drift.

"And when she called, he wasn't home?"

"That's right. So she called us and asked if Simon had perhaps come to our house for dinner. Which obviously he hadn't."

"And what time was this?" Cannon enquired.

"About 9:30."

Cannon was thoughtful for a second then asked, "So if he wasn't home, was your daughter-in-law worried about anything specifically?"

"Well," responded Crabb. "She was more concerned about the fact that she had called him several times on his mobile and he hadn't called her back, despite her asking him to do so"

"Was that unusual?"

"Mr. Cannon," said Crabb, somewhat indignantly, clearly not used to being questioned. Cannon could see that he was a man much more comfortable being the one who issued instructions, asked questions, and has his demands met rather than having to respond to inquiries about other people's lives. "I don't check on my daughter-in law and my son, and I don't know if it *is* unusual or not. All I know is that my daughter-in-law is only due back from Edinburgh late tomorrow night. Her conference runs until two in the afternoon and then she is driving back afterwards."

He went on. "When Wendy arrives home tomorrow morning, we have already arranged that we would collect her here from the school and take her to our house. Rachel would then collect her from there and then take her home."

Crabb's voice continued to rise in volume though remained controlled, only the tremor in his voice displaying emotion. He continued saying. "So all I do know is that the police have told me that my son is dead and we," he nodded towards his wife, "we need to make sure that when Wendy arrives back from her trip tomorrow that all of us ensure that she is cared for in the best way we can!"

"We understand Mr. Crabb," said Michelle, conscious of how the atmosphere in the room was becoming more strained. "Please accept our condolences, and please rest assured we will do everything we can to help Wendy get through this ordeal. I will speak with the headmaster shortly and once we have discussed our plan of action, I will advise you both"

"Thank you," he said, taking his wife's hands in his own, the first sign of affection towards her that Cannon had seen since he had walked into the room. It was clear that despite how things looked between them to a stranger like Cannon, there was a deep love between Crabb and his wife.

"Mr. Crabb," went on Cannon, more sympathy in his voice than previously. "May I ask you a couple more questions?"

"Go ahead," came the reply, his voice reflecting a level of resignation. It was as if he knew he would have to endure a lot more questions at some later stage when the police began their investigations in earnest.

The older man then sat more upright in anticipation of what Cannon wanted to know.

"I'd expect the police will be asking your daughter-in-law or yourself to formally identify the body as soon as possible. Given she is in Edinburgh and at a conference and currently out of contact, I assume they will ask you to do so. Are you okay to do that?"

"Mr. Cannon," chimed in the Reverend. "I have already spoken with Mr. and Mrs. Crabb, and advised them that I will be with them as much as is necessary should they require any support at that point in the process, or at any future time," she said, continuing. "After all they are members of *my* congregation." The Reverend then gave a sad smile before adding, "It is at times like these that while we don't understand why things happen in the way that they do, it's important that we remain together as a family in Christ, support each other, and believe that something positive will come from this tragic happening."

Cannon noticed the resignation in the Minister's voice. The words seemed almost robotic and while he admired her sense of resilience in the face of the tragedy, he reflected inwardly the familiarity of the words she had spoken. They were precisely the same as those he had heard at Sally's funeral.

"Thank you Reverend," said Cannon with as much sincerity as he could muster. He had never been much of a churchgoer, nor much of a believer. To get him to marry in church had been the subject of many a debate before Sally had overruled his preference for practicality and being married at a registry office. It was a *'wedding in a church or not at all!'*

He looked quickly at Michelle feeling a slight sense of guilt as Sally's image popped into his mind. He hoped none of his thoughts were mirrored across his face. Michelle's eyes and facial expression urged him to be both sympathetic and quick. It was obvious that her concern was for the older couple and for what needed to be arranged and put in place for when Wendy, Cassie, and the other kids arrived back from France the next day.

"Just one last thing Mr. Crabb, if I may?" he went on. "Did the police say where your son's body was found?"

"Yes, they did," came the reply.

"Where was that?"

"The police said they didn't want to say too much, just that he had been found on the golf course. He was apparently found by a man walking his dog early this morning, that's all they would tell us."

Chapter 3

The rain that had been threatening, had arrived about an hour ago. Dark clouds still mottled the sky above, and the wind whipped at the rain, sending it in a multitude of directions. Sometimes it was almost parallel to the ground, at other times in sheets at 45 degrees, then changing again within seconds to nearly vertical. With the rain came the cold. The clear sky of dawn just a few hours before was now a distant memory.

"Sod it," said Skinner to no one in particular.

He stood almost ankle-deep in the puddle of water that had formed at the bottom of the bunker where Simon Crabb's body lay. The tent that had been erected and surrounded the kidney-shaped golf hazard, flapped and shook as the wind and rain tried to lift the entire flimsy structure, and hurl it across the golf course.

"Somebody get this bloody thing sorted," he shouted through what was the front of the tent. "Before we know it, every bloody potential piece of evidence that may be around here will be washed away."

The two scene of the crime officers and one forensic pathologist in their sodden paper suits continued with their investigation and ignored Skinner. DCI or not, they had been in much worse circumstances than this before. He could shout at his own underlings if he wanted to, but not at them.

The SOCO's had their job to do. They would find what they could, the forensic lab boys would analyze it, the pathologists would work out time and cause of death and the detectives could solve who did what and why. The defending of turf was often an issue that caused many a problem between the various bodies within the police, and sometimes it got in the way, resulting in hindered investigations and finger-pointing when things went *belly up*.

They hoped this wasn't another one of those times. If it was, then so much for cooperation across the force!

It was easy to see how Crabb had died.

He lay on his left side almost in a foetal position, his eyes wide open, his face contorted in an expression of surprise. The back of his skull was smashed-in and congealed blood matted his sodden hair and grains of sand from the bunker mingled with it. The rain had turned the sand around his head, a deep rust as it diluted the blood.

Surprisingly, just a few inches from his hand was his mobile phone, where it appeared to have fallen during the attack. The fact that it was where it was and assuming it hadn't been deliberately placed there seemed to suggest it was being used at the time he was struck.

Skinner made a mental note to get it checked out the moment it was formally bagged and made available as evidence.

A few feet away was what Skinner expected would be confirmed as the murder weapon. He bent down to take a look. The golf *club*, Skinner thought to himself, being a poor amateur Sunday golfer himself, had clearly lived up to its name. The handle lay facing away from the body where it had been casually thrown, the shaft appeared to have some grey matter along its underside and the clubhead lay closest to the body.

Skinner hoped for fingerprints somewhere on the weapon but doubted any would be. Murderers hardly made it so easy nowadays.

Fortunately, DNA analysis was now the main tool used to obtain evidence and Skinner hoped that despite the weather and the conditions in which the body had been discovered, the chances of finding something useful was still possible.

"How long you going to be?" he barked towards the two SOCO officers. The younger of the two ignored the question, not seeming to hear, and continued taking photographs of the dead man and the immediate area around the body. The older man carefully stood up from bending over the corpse.

"Detective," he replied, "it will take as long as it takes. You of all people should know that. We've only been here about an hour and with all this rain about we need to take care to get as much as we can. The area has already been compromised as you can see from the footprints around the edge of the bunker." He pointed to several small indentations in the grass as well as to some in the bunker itself, including some paw impressions. Some of them were not just those of a dog or dogs, either. He guessed that the others could be those of a fox or some other nocturnal animal, though at first glance there was no sign of the body having been being used as breakfast.

It was also going to be a challenge trying to get any evidence from the lawn itself due to it being very short grass with restricted '*play*'. The fairway had been cut low and the recent frost had made the ground very hard, a level of firmness that was not helpful. This limited any potential impressions that may have been made by anyone in the area who had walked upon it recently. Mix this with the time the body had lain where it was, and the impact on the area by the man who had found the body left the environmental circumstances the SOCO's found themselves in, not those one could easily follow the textbook on.

Adding to the challenge was the now persistent rain. Hence why they were not happy being questioned by the DCI.

It was a real mess and the older SOCO sighed loudly.

In frustration at the stupid question he was asked, he said, "The body is already stone-cold, has been for hours after last night and you," he continued, pointing his finger towards Skinner, "are not helping. So piss off! We'll let you know when we're finished!"

Skinner's reputation was known across the local area as being that of a lazy detective. A dinosaur. He had been in the force now for almost 37 years. Somehow he had survived the changes over that time. He was not particularly popular with his peers or his seniors, and the more junior members who didn't have to work with, or for him, desperately tried to steer clear.

It didn't mean he hadn't had success over the years. He had solved many cases, none particularly high profile, but he had been involved in some significant busts over the years.

He had done his job, or at least been seen to have done it, but not without incident.

He was a plodder now, nicknamed *'PC Plod'* in the station and at the local headquarters of the Thames Valley Police. Deemed reliable, steady but flawed, with a slightly unsavoury history. Definitely not dynamic, a reasonably safe pair of hands, but *someone who walks to the beat of his own drum,* was how he was described by the local commander.

"Charming!" exclaimed Skinner sarcastically as he left the tent and walked out into the rain, "Fuck you as well," he said under his breath.

His mood did not get any better as the rain lashed his face, causing rivulets to run down his neck and under his collar.

"Hey Constable!" he shouted at the uniform who stood on the other side of a cordon of blue plastic tape, encircling the tent standing over the bunker. The tape fluttered angrily in the wind. At times appearing to stretch almost to breaking point, nearly snapping from the stakes that it was attached to that had been hastily pushed into the ground.

"Yes Sir?" replied the Constable, his voice trailing off as the wind caught it.

He was a big man who dwarfed Skinner by a good six inches at least, his yellow waterproofs protecting his uniform from a soaking. Skinner looked on enviously, his own casual clothes now wet through, his coat offering little protection from the elements.

"Get your mate there," he pointed to another Constable who was busy walking towards them from the clubhouse across the course "to help you tie down the sides of that tent over there with something will you?" He pointed towards where the SOCO's were working. "And be bloody quick about it!"

He then added as an afterthought, "Oh and by the way."

"Yes Sir?" repeated the Constable, annoyed at the arrogance of the detective.

"Once you've done that, bring me a cup of tea, I'll be in my car," he pointed towards his blue Nissan sitting in the clubhouse car park, where he had parked it forty-five minutes earlier. "Milk and two sugars," he said, as he walked away.

The steam from the tea curled up from the Styrofoam cup, like little genies from Aladdin's lamp. Skinner sat inside his car. He wiped the condensation from the windscreen with his left hand, being careful not to spill the tea. The rain had finally started to ease, but the wind still blew in gusts throwing some of the leaves of the trees that abutted the car park across the bonnet of the car and onto the putting green that stood to their left. Some of the hardy golfers who had picked their tee-off times and hadn't cared about the weather, lingered in their disappointment huddled in a small group near the now-closed pro-shop under bright umbrellas. Skinner pointed them out.

"Guess that's ruined their day," he said, "no eighteen holes for them."

"Guess so," echoed the man sitting next to him. DC Andy Quick had never cared for golf or indeed for golfers. He had never mentioned it to Skinner but he had always considered them pretentious pricks and the private club mentality was anathema to him. Give him Leicester City and the Premier League any day.

A career policeman, he sat in the passenger seat, the window to his left steaming up as he spoke. He wore a heavy black leather jacket that would strain at his stomach if he ever tried to zip it up. He was a big man in every way, six foot four in his socks, with size thirteen feet. He always seemed to fit inside a car but never seemed to be able to properly stretch out and relax. It always seemed to others that he was bent over whenever anyone saw him inside a vehicle.

He was thirty-eight years old, had two children, and a wife of similar proportions to his own. His face was shaped like a full moon, round and open. He had a decent size nose for a man with such a big head.

He wore a full beard that was well trimmed and that covered his pockmarked face from years of teenage acne. His shoulder-length hair was curly, a light chestnut colour, though currently looked much darker given how wet it had become during his wandering around near the first tee.

He had been looking for the club captain, or whatever it was that he had been told they called the man who ran the operations of the clubhouse each day. He had needed to advise him to close the course and keep everyone away from any areas the police needed to restrict while they undertook the investigation.

Quick continued, with a slight nod of his head to where the SOCO's looked like they were starting to conclude their work. "What do you reckon boss? A fight over cheating on the scorecard?" His attempt at humour didn't particularly please Skinner who remained silent gulping down the last drop of tea and throwing the cup onto the back seat along with the other detritus that had piled up over the past week or two. A few newspapers, some takeaway boxes from various pizza and burger outlets, and a couple of empty lager cans.

"Not sure Constable, but what I can tell you is that I've had enough of this waiting. Those buggers are taking forever. Slow bastards." he spat." And where is that bloody morgue van you called for half an hour ago?" he said accusatorily as if Quick was solely responsible for the speed at which traffic from Oxford could get to the golf club.

The Constable picked up his phone ready to dial the mortuary again when along the driveway that snaked from the main road to the clubhouse, a mud-spattered combi style vehicle came into view. Looking very much like a ten-seater mini-bus the driver expertly stopped about thirty feet away from where they sat and undertook a rapid reversing movement so that the doors at the back of the van were facing towards the bunker and the nose of the vehicle towards the way it had just arrived.

"About bloody time," said Skinner as he opened his door to get out. The air was fresh after having been inside the Nissan. The rain had now totally stopped, though not for long, Skinner expected.

The driver and his assistant alighted from the van and opened the doors at the back. Inside, stood two low-level trolleys ready to receive the latest victim. Skinner wondered why mortuary vans always carried blankets on the beds. It wasn't to keep anyone warm as the *stiffs* didn't need them. Normally a sheet was all that was needed to cover a body. '*Maybe it's for the van staff themselves*' he thought to himself '*perhaps they have a kip when it's not too busy?*'

He chuckled to himself, as he and Quick walked over to explain the situation.

"Right Sir," said Skinner addressing the club Chairman as they sat in the boardroom of the Golf Club. "Thank you for making yourself available. I appreciate this is not an easy time for you, the club, or indeed your members. However, I am sure you will understand the need to investigate the incident overnight which resulted in the death of Mr. Crabb as quickly as we possibly can? Time being of the essence."

"Yes Inspector," agreed Dale Simpson with a slight nod of his head, "I do indeed." He was a short man around five foot seven who seemed particularly intimidated by the size of DC Quick who sat to the left of Skinner who was at the head of the table, while Simpson sat to the right. The introductions had been brief.

Skinner looked at his watch and noticing it was almost three pm wondered where the time had gone.

After ensuring the murder site had been properly secured and the body had been carefully removed and despatched to the mortuary, the two policemen had set about trying to piece some of the previous evening's events together. Their lunch would have to wait. It was likely to be in a pub somewhere on the way back into Oxford.

They had established that being a Tuesday night, the club had been well attended as it was a weekly quiz night and the dining room had been well patronized up until about eight o'clock. Thereafter through to closing time around eleven, the bar had been pretty busy with the regulars, the visiting guests having left at various intervals during the evening.

While they had waited for Simpson to arrive, Skinner had managed to confirm that the club had a bank of closed-circuit cameras, which were located at both the front and back doors to the premises.

Establishing the comings and goings of patrons and staff the previous evening was therefore expected to be much easier than they could have hoped for. The building itself was not particularly large but had a somewhat unusual design. It was effectively an oblong shape with wings at both ends. These wings protruded away from the main body of the building and both contained a passage towards changing facilities, men's toilets and storage facilities on one wing and women's toilets and other facilities, and the boardroom where they now sat, along the other.

The wings seemed to envelop the green of the eighteenth hole.

Between the two wings were a lounge area, a small restaurant, a kitchen, and a bar. The bar area looked onto the fairway through large glass windows where drinkers could watch those players tackling the last.

"So Mr. Simpson…."

"Dale, please…Inspector. Call me Dale," said Simpson cutting off Skinner. "The formality makes me nervous and besides 'Mr. Simpson' was my late father," he added somewhat sheepishly.

"Ok…Dale, no problem," responded the Inspector with a cursory raising of his eyebrows towards Quick. "You will have noticed that while we were trying to locate you Sir…err….Dale, we have requested your events manager…a…."

"A Mr. Winton," interjected Quick, looking up the name from his notebook.

"Yes…Mr. Winton," said Skinner acknowledging Quicks' interruption. Continuing, he said, "Who we understand was here most of the evening and indeed was the last to leave the premises and lock up. Would that sound about right to you?"

"Yes, Inspector that makes sense. The normal process is that once *'last drinks'* have been called and the bar closes, the staff tidy up as guests leave. They collect the glasses, the empty bottles, that kind of thing, and then while they put everything into the dishwashers, Mr. Winton…Jack," indicated Simpson, who being a social person was on first name terms with most, "would cash up along with one of the other bar staff. Once that's done, the staff would all leave around the same time…"

"What, around midnight say?"

"Yes, about that. And then Jack would take all receipts and put them away."

"You mean in a safe of some sort?"

"Yes, we have a small safe in a room behind the bar counter."

Quick made a note in his notebook as Skinner continued.

"And nothing was taken?"

"No, inspector, the safe hasn't been touched. I checked with Jack when I first arrived and he told me that there was no sign of anything having been taken."

Skinner considered this for a second, concluding that a robbery gone wrong appeared not to be the motive for what had happened to Crabb, but it was something that still needed to be looked into if there was no obvious alternative.

"Ok," he continued, "but just for the record, as this is not a formal interview, we will need to take statements from you, and all those here last night. I assume you have a guest list of sorts?"

Simpson shifted uncomfortably in his chair, conscious of the impact the murder could have on the club, its clientele, and visitors if they were dragged into a police investigation.

"Well," he said forlornly, "our members are supposed to sign in their guests when they come into the bar or use the restaurant, but," he hesitated, "I can't say if it is done all the time, every time."

Skinner turned to Quick. "Constable, could you get hold of the visitor's book, please? Now!" he emphasized.

Quick sighed to himself, stood up, and went in search of Winton to find the applicable register.

Turning back to Simpson, Skinner continued, "How many staff do you have here at night, especially last night? I assume it's a different bunch to those who work during the day?"

"Well, again it varies. Last night we would have had a full complement of around nine including the kitchen staff. I'm sure I can get you all the details inspector"

"Thank you, Sir...err... Dale."

Shit thought Skinner to himself, *this will be a bloody nightmare having to interview a bunch of waiters, barmen and cooks, and bottle washers.* His experience was that they were always so busy with customer orders that they could hardly remember their own names at times, let alone what was going on around them. Then his natural instinct kicked in and he smiled internally as he realized that he wouldn't have to do it himself. Some other sod could do all that paperwork. He would review the statements once they were all done.

"OK, thanks again," he said. "You realize though that we will likely need to keep the club closed for the rest of the day and possibly even tomorrow as we take statements from the staff. Obviously, we will try and conclude this initial phase of our investigation here as soon as possible. Thereafter we may need people to come down to the station as required. This may be over the course of a few days or even longer."

"I understand Inspector," responded Simpson. His face and demeanour giving away his real feelings.

It was clear they weren't those of a happy man.

Indeed, Skinner noticed, it was clear that Simpson was highly pissed off.

Chapter 4

Skinner had decided to leave the scene as soon as he finished with Winton, and had relayed to Quick that he would see him the later the following morning, at the station.

There was nothing else to be done once the body had been removed, he had said. Forensics would eventually pack up and take everything they needed, including their tent, and for Skinner, there was a nice pint in his warm local waiting for him.

Despite the investigation needing the get going, Quick knew it would only be around midday before Skinner would eventually turn up. Old habits were hard to break, and Quick knew that Skinner had no intention, of breaking any of his.

In the interim, the process of taking initial statements from the on-duty staff from the night before took Quick and one of the PC's who had been onsite, several hours to complete. They had been able to track down six of the staff who had come in for their evening shift during late afternoon, not knowing that the police had shut the club for the day. The other staff members would be contacted directly and asked to come into the police station on Monday, to give their statements.

While Quick was busy with the interviews, the visitor's register had been taken by one of the SOCO's and bagged as potential evidence and would be tested for DNA and any useable fingerprints.

A list of all visitors along with the members who had signed them in would be collated and passed on to Skinner within 24 - 36 hours. A hard copy of each page would be made and would be consolidated with the visitor's list and the staff list for Skinner, so that each and every attendee and their movements, actions or otherwise, could be reconciled with what was recorded on the CCTV footage.

In addition, they had dusted the area and looked for fingerprints on and around the safe, as well as on the cash registers situated at the bar counters. Quick had also arranged for a member of the regional IT security team to come down to the club and make a copy of the film and store it on disk for review once the investigating team had been set up. The original recording was also removed as evidence and for further analysis.

Creating the team to work on the investigation and getting things moving was always critical. Time was always a commodity that few ever had enough of, and a murder investigation always seemed to start like it was stuck in quicksand before it could gain traction and build momentum. With Skinner as the Officer-in-Charge and resources being stretched with other cases being worked on, Quick knew that Skinner would make some noise to get what he needed, but he would also play the game.

He knew if things took their time to be set up, then so be it. This was how Skinner worked. It always frustrated the hell out of Quick, but he knew he would never win the argument.

By the time Quick was ready to leave and the rest of the team had packed up it was already dark. It was just after six and the rain had stopped again after several downpours over the past few hours.

As he and the Constable who had helped him take statements came outside, the clouds hung low across the treetops. The wind whipped around their shoulders, swirling around their legs and freezing their faces.

The strength of the breeze had taken what little warmth there had been during the day, and left a cold damp residue floating in the air. A mist seemed to seep from the ground. Moisture curled upwards into a fog and then disappeared like silent wraiths.

The moon peeked out from a break in the clouds for a brief second but was immediately swallowed up again, as if it had never been there in the first place. The lights of the car park, now almost devoid of any vehicles other than that of Winton and the police car that Quick would get a lift home in, threw elongated and dancing shadows across the ground.

The contrast of the orange sodium lamps of the car park reflecting off the cars' roof, to the bright spotlights above the entrance to the clubhouse, and the warm glow of the lights within the building that Winton was in the process of turning off, sparked something in Quicks' mind.

"Wait here Constable," he said, indicating to the junior policeman to stay where he was.

Quick frowned as he began to walk around the building.

With a torch that he had borrowed from the Constable, he walked firstly down the left-hand side of the premises, the beam shining left and right as he scanned the ground. The remaining lights inside the building provided illuminated oblongs along the ground as he trod carefully and slowly, occasionally looking upwards and then backwards from where he had started.

He turned to face the way he had come, looking towards the bunker where the body of Crabb had been found. He continued walking backwards until he reached the end of the building where the dustbins and the doors to the kitchen were.

Something wasn't right, but he couldn't understand what it was. He turned to face forwards again and slowly continued to traverse the building perimeter watching his footing as he did so. As he continued walking, undertaking a slow inspection of the ground looking for anything that may have been disturbed or dropped, the inside lights of the building were turned off, the oblong of light that had been ahead of him disappeared, leaving only the thin beam of the torch to illuminate his way.

Finally, he was back at the front entrance as Winton was locking the door.

"Everything all right?" Winton said to him.

"Umm, yes Sir, thank you," he replied though there was something inside him that niggled. "Have you set the alarm?" he continued.

"Absolutely."

"Good. Well let's get going Constable!" he called out, as he turned to the slightly bemused junior officer who was still standing where he had been asked to wait.

The feeling inside Quick began dissolving slowly. The concern he felt, and that he tried to retain, slowly disappearing as the reality of the days ahead and the procedural requirements of the investigation began to enter his consciousness.

"Thanks again Mr. Winton," he said, "I'll be in touch in the morning."

The evening stables inspection over and the horses all bedded down for the night, Cannon felt the warmth of the house as he entered.

Michelle was busy in the kitchen putting the final touches to their evening meal together.

"Goodness, that smells nice," he said as he walked into the room. The aromas from the casserole Michelle had made, permeated the air.

Michelle remained with her back to him as she washed some utensils in the sink. The silence between them was palpable and Cannon noticed the slight trembling of her shoulders. He walked up behind her, gently putting his arms around her.

"Are you okay?" he said gently, as he nuzzled her neck and kissed the top of her head.

For a second he sensed her reluctance to respond, then unexpectedly she turned and threw her arms around him. She cried silently into his shoulder.

"My God," she said, "what a mess. What are we going to do?"

"What about?" responded Cannon, somewhat confused.

"About Cassie, about her friend Wendy. The school is going to have to let Wendy know about her father," she exclaimed. "We think Wendy may need some counselling, and I suspect Cassie may well be affected too."

"Okay, well perhaps it's best that when they arrive back tomorrow, that I am there?"

Michelle considered this for a second and then agreed that it was a good idea.

"Yes. I think you're right. Though I'm really worried about Wendy."

The rest of the evening was muted. During dinner, they hardly spoke. The mood ruined by the happenings of the day. Both of them spent time, lost in their own thoughts.

For Michelle, the relationship with Cassie was difficult enough, and with the added stress of trying to manage that, along with Cassie's best friend's father's murder, she could only imagine how the relationship between them could develop.

While she felt sympathy for Wendy she also knew that she couldn't get too involved. She was a teacher and that was her job. She wasn't a counsellor, she was more a confidant of the girls in her class, and she needed to keep her perspective. She knew though that the next few days were going to be difficult, and that it could potentially push her relationship with Mike to the edge.

Sitting on the couch, the TV flickering away with the sound low, she looked at Cannon now dozing next to her. It had been a long day. Normally he was in bed and fast asleep by nine but now it was nine-thirty and he hadn't made any attempt to get off the couch.

His head lolled to the left, resting on his shoulder. Michelle moved to shake him awake when suddenly the phone rang. It was very unusual to receive a call so late in their evening, and she immediately thought it would be a wrong number or a call from some Indian call centre trying another scam. Calls like that seemed to be happening more frequently in recent times.

Cannon woke up with a start, and by the third ring was completely awake. He crossed the living room and picked up the receiver, ready to vent his annoyance on the caller.

"Hello," he shouted into the mouthpiece, "what the hell do you want at this time of night?"

For a few seconds, the caller at the other end of the line was silent, somewhat taken aback by the unexpected tirade.

"Mr. Cannon?" the voice asked. It sounded familiar to Mike, but he couldn't initially place it.

"Yes," he replied, "who is this? And how did you get my number? It's a bit bloody late to be….." his voice trailing off as his head cleared away the fog that had clouded his brain while he had slept. He had recognized the voice from earlier in the day.

"So sorry to bother you so late in the evening," came the reply, "but I was hoping to catch you before you retired for the night."

The voice of Joseph Crabb was unmistakable.

Cannon felt a twinge of annoyance. He didn't like the man and hadn't warmed to him earlier in the day. He mouthed to Michelle who was on the line as she looked anxiously to find out who it was, and then he gestured to her a sign of drinking tea. Michelle nodded. She left the room to go and make some for him in the kitchen.

"Oh hello there Mr. Crabb, what a surprise," said Cannon. "Again my condolences to you, and your wife," he said. "What can I do for you so late in the evening?"

As anticipated, Crabb's response was direct and business-like.

"Mr. Cannon, I am seeking your help and I have a proposition for you that I would like to discuss."

"Right now?" said Cannon indignantly, thinking that after the morning they had both been through, to be talking about training a horse for Crabb, was both unusual, and under the circumstances of his son's murder, was particularly distasteful. "Can't it wait until tomorrow?"

"Yes, I suppose it can," came the reply, "however for your information, what I wanted to talk about, is to do with your previous line of work, not what you do for a living today," he said.

Cannon almost burst out laughing, but was able to swallow the thought before it could surface. The way Crabb had expressed himself, the use of old military-style language seemed so old fashioned, and yet something about the tone with which he spoke, suggested a seriousness and a focused intent.

"Well, Mr. Crabb, before this starts getting silly I need to advise you of some practicalities. Firstly, trying to get me involved in any investigation about your son's murder, I think you need to understand, is just not possible. The police have all the skills and capability to find out what happened, and who the perpetrator is. I am sure they will bring whoever it was, to justice," he said, "and anyway I am not sure what you have heard about my past, but that part of my life is over. Gone!" he emphasized.

Crabb was silent for a moment as he contemplated what he had just heard.

"Nevertheless," Crabb said eventually, after what had seemed like a full minute, but was mere seconds, "I would like to talk to you about this in more detail tomorrow. Perhaps we can meet before the girls get back?" he went on. "I certainly would like your help, Mr. Cannon. Something is going on that I can't quite explain, but for the sake of Rachel and Wendy, I really need to find out the truth behind my son's death."

Cannon let out a deep sigh, just as Michelle came back into the room.

"Okay Mr. Crabb, if you insist. I will see you tomorrow but I doubt I will be able to help. Anyway, shall we say around 10:30, at the school?"

"Thank you," came the reply down the line, and with that, the connection was broken as Crabb instantly put down the phone.

Cannon rubbed his temples as he replaced the receiver on the stand.

"What did he want?" enquired Michelle, holding out his tea for him to take.

"A good question," came the reply. "I don't know, but I think Joseph Crabb has somehow lost the plot!"

The rain of the previous day had not returned, but the same dark clouds still hovered overhead, leaving one with the impression that a deluge of water from the angry grey mass that stretched across the sky from east to west, could engulf everyone at any time.

A piercing wind had whipped up as soon as daylight had broken, and while the morning exercises had been uneventful and both lots had worked well, Cannon's mind was restless.

He hadn't slept well, tossing and turning throughout the night.

He had suffered again with the dream that refused to leave him alone and continued to bring back the past. Another variation of it, but one that this time seemed more realistic, closer to home, closer to today.

When he awoke and his mind had cleared, he put it down to the previous evening's phone call. Somehow his former life was still haunting him.

Perhaps he needed to speak to someone?

Michelle had left as normal and was already at the school. They had spoken briefly as they got ready for the day.

Their communication had been muted, strained. It was clear that life and teaching needed to carry on as normal. Despite preparations needing to be made by the staff to provide support to Wendy once the news of her father's murder had been relayed to her, Cannon's concern however was for Cassie, and how she would react.

In recent months her behaviour had been erratic, changing almost hourly from a sensible teenager to an out of control, spiteful bitch. Cannon knew it was natural and understandable given Cassie's age and the physical and emotional development that occurs during that time, but he wasn't really equipped to handle it.

He also realized that it was unfair on Michelle to take the burden of easing Cassie through this difficult period. Cassie wasn't her child, yet he admired how Michelle at least tried to act as a de facto parent and a mentor to Cassie, offering her help, guidance, someone willing to listen to whatever troubled his daughter.

Arriving at the school, he knew that Joseph Crabb would be waiting for him.

As an ex-military man, Crabb clearly valued efficiency and timeliness and as Cannon parked his car, he saw Crabb sitting in his own vehicle some distance away from where the majority of the other cars were parked.

As Cannon got out of his car, the wind swirled across the parking lot. Old sweet papers, dead leaves, and plastic crisp packets flew into the air like they were being sucked up into a tornado's funnel. He noticed Crabb gesturing to him through the window of his car to join him. Cannon ducked his head against the wind and ran across the tarmac. Jumping into the passenger seat, he quickly closed the door to keep the warm air inside.

"A crappy sort of day," he said, to break the ice. "Have you been waiting long?"

Crabb looked straight ahead as if the weather was irrelevant, replying almost disdainfully, "About twenty-five minutes."

Cannon let the slight sarcasm in the comment slide by.

While they had agreed on the time the previous evening, the vagaries of running a stable didn't always allow one to be precise in every detail of timekeeping. Timings applied to how horses ran, not to how they settled down in their boxes after exercise or the process of cooling down and grooming thereafter.

If his horses showed signs of injury or discomfort, then that was what needed to be focused on first. The welfare of the animal was his main priority. In addition, if vets were needed, then so be it. That could take up even more time than expected and everything else could wait.

As it was, he had his head lad take over from him, to complete the morning routine. Which, by the time Cannon had left, had not yet been fully concluded. Being only ten minutes late Cannon believed that he had done well to get there when he did.

Cannon waited for Crabb to speak but the older man stayed silent far longer than felt comfortable. It was as if he was contemplating how best to issue an order to be followed while knowing full well that what he was considering could quite easily be rejected out of hand by Cannon. If that occurred, Crabb himself would have no obvious recourse.

"Forgive my tentativeness, Mr. Cannon," he eventually said, "but as an ex-military man, I'm not used to negotiating these types of things. I'm used to saying 'jump' and people ask 'how high?'"

"I understand. Being in the police I did receive and give my fair share of orders as well, you know."

Cannon smiled to himself.

Crabb visibly relaxed, his demeanour now more settled. The hands he had placed on the steering wheel when Cannon first got into the car and that he seemed to hold with unnecessary force, were now resting in his lap.

"How long were you in the forces?" enquired Cannon.

"Thirty-six years," came the reply. "Made it up to Colonel, though most of my time was spent in administrative duties, not field command…" his voice trailed off for a second. "Anyway that was a long time ago and we are not here to talk about that."

"So what are we here to talk about?"

"As I said last night, I want to make you a proposition and one that I hope you will give careful consideration to."

"I'm all ears Mr. Crabb, but as I said last night I'm not sure I can or indeed want to help."

Crabb ignored the inference and inflection in Cannon's response.

"Mr. Cannon, I love my granddaughter very much. I'm sure you will understand that, being a father yourself. Likewise, we love Rachel, but recently we have been very concerned about her. She has been acting a little strangely …"

"Strange?" interjected Cannon, "what do you mean?"

"Well, she has been away quite a lot recently, travelling for her job, and has not always been clear about when she was expected to return home."

"You mentioned yesterday that she is a lawyer. Does she travel away often? What type of legal work does she do?"

"She does corporate work, contracts, that type of thing."

For the first time, Cannon noticed that Crabb wasn't so sure of himself. It was as if private practice law was something so foreign to him, that as he knew so little about it, though undoubtedly he knew military law, it was something he couldn't get his mind around.

"And this gave you reason for concern?"

"No," said Crabb, "the concern has only increased recently due to our inability to get hold of her when we have needed to. It's almost as if she doesn't want to be found at times."

"Maybe she was so busy, she needed to concentrate on her work?"

"Perhaps?" contemplated the older man. He stared out through the windscreen with eyes that looked unfocused. A sense of indignation seemed to ripple through him as if his own judgement was being questioned, something he was obviously not used to.

Silence filled the air between them for a few seconds, just the wind buffeting the car could be heard like a soft groan.

"Where is she now?" said Cannon, bringing the other man back to the present. "Have you been able to get hold of her since last night?"

"Yes, yes," came the reply. "We left a voice mail on her message service last night and she called earlier this morning, around 7 o'clock. She's on her way. She said she would leave as soon as she could, so I expect that she will be here in the next hour or two. I guess it depends on the traffic."

Cannon was intrigued and couldn't help notice himself being more interested than he should be. He tried to pull himself back from being so keen.

"Look, Mr. Crabb, I am really sorry for your loss, but I think the police can handle this for you. I think it best that they investigate the murder, and if there are issues related to your son and his wife that they uncover, then I am sure they will be able to get to the bottom of them."

They sat in silence again for a few more minutes, the windows of the car steaming up from the warmth within, and the cold outside. Eventually, the old man reached into his jacket pocket and pulled out a handkerchief to wipe the windscreen and the driver's side window. As he passed it to Cannon to do the same on the passenger side, he spoke again.

"Wendy told us that my son and Rachel were arguing a lot recently. That she had overheard them talk of divorce but she didn't know what the reason was." Crabb paused for a second, gathering himself as he spoke about a subject that he was clearly very uncomfortable with. "She told us that my son had said some very ill-advised things ….."

"What kind of things?"

The older man, who to Cannon seemed to have sunk a little into his seat, paused for a second then continued.

"Oh, stupid things, off-the-cuff taunts about other women, about their personal lives…about their…" Crabb took a deep breath, "their sex life. That sort of thing." He turned to face Cannon with eyes that appeared moist, yet defiant. Cannon could sense the internal struggle within the old man.

Regaining something of his composure, Crabb continued. "I don't know if any of these things I have mentioned are as serious as Wendy made them out to be, or were just told to us in fear by an upset teenager. She could have exaggerated them, as they often do at that age. But what I do know, is that she seemed genuinely upset, and my granddaughter, despite her age, has always been sensible and confided in us whenever she has needed to. So in my opinion there may have been something in what she said."

"Did you ever ask your son about this?"

Crabb shot back a look that indicated that it was a dumb question being asked of him.

"Of course not, we don't interfere. My son is…was…quite capable of working through any problems he may have had with Rachel. I think all relationships have ups and downs. Wouldn't you agree Mr. Cannon?"

Considering his own position and his relationship with Michelle, Cannon knew there was nothing to say, other than just nod in agreement.

"So Mr. Cannon, having said all I have so far, let me explain my proposition to you."

"Sir," Cannon replied, "I still think….." He cut himself off almost as quickly as he had started, as he noticed the older man had raised an open palm towards him as if to say '*stop!*'

"I know you still think the police would do a better job than you in following this mess up," he said, waving his hand towards the windscreen as if gesturing to the outside world, "and you may be right" he continued, "but I don't want all that I have told you to be out there in the public domain for all the world to see," he said. "Oh, I know the police have processes and procedures to follow, statements to take, and the public at large to protect, I understand all that. But at the same time I know that things leak, any salacious detail or innuendo soon finds its way out and what was perhaps just a private internal family matter can very quickly become gossip, rumours. And that is something I want to avoid," he concluded.

"Well with today's social media, that's not always possible Mr. Crabb."

"I know," he replied, "and that's why I want your help. It's my wife you see. She would be absolutely devastated if this..this...tragedy, resulted in the family name being dragged all across the papers, that Facebook *thing*, bloody Twittering or whatever it's called, and any other places of such tittle-tattle. No!" he reiterated, "I want this investigated quietly. The police can continue with what they do, that's fine, but I would like you to conduct a more discrete investigation in parallel. To be honest, I have more faith in you than I do of that DCI they have put on the job, Skinner I think his name is. He has a reputation I understand, of being less than thorough."

"That may be so. But the police do have a lot more resources than just DCI Skinner," retorted Cannon.

"True, but they have too many cases to work on as well," came the reply somewhat offhandedly as if that line of discussion was closed. "Look, Mr. Cannon, I know this is an unusual request but just hear what I have to say....please."

Cannon considered things for a moment.

He thought of the various people in his life that were already impacted by the murder, even if they didn't know it just yet. Cassie, who would be home shortly, and Michelle, who he knew was already struggling with what had happened.

He realized that his past, his history, had never really gone away. The dreams, the nightmares he had occasionally, reminded him of that. It was as if his heart wanted to move on, but his mind took him back at times to a place where he didn't want to be.

The conflict he held inside himself and the desire to protect Michelle and Cassie from where this matter could lead, but could also help bring closure, made him hesitate.

He knew he should say no. He knew he should leave well alone, but he also knew if he did so, the question would remain – *'what if?'*

What if the killer struck again?

What if another murder could be prevented?

Would Cassie ever forgive him if something happened to Wendy's mother or indeed Wendy herself? What would Cassie feel or how would she react, if she found out that he had refused to help?

While he wrestled with his thoughts, Crabb interrupted him. "I know you have a relatively successful stable and though it's small I assume you make a reasonable living from it? You seem to have done quite well for yourself in just a short period of time," he said, "especially in an industry normally dominated by the big players. But I'd guess," Crabb paused, as if for effect, "that you could always do with more horses, more owners, more patrons?"

"Yes, that goes for everyone in this game, but I have a reasonable lifestyle."

"Well, I've made some inquiries, and from what I hear you are quite a talented trainer."

A gentle smile crossed Crabb's face, the first time Cannon had seen a softer side of the man he was sitting next to.

"You may not know this, but I have had a keen interest in racing ever since I can remember. I've owned a few horses in the past but basically as part of a racing syndicate. They were all on the flat, and we had limited success, unfortunately. Being in the army meant that I rarely got the opportunity to see them race live and since my retirement, well I've been more an armchair spectator," he went on. "So what I want to propose to you is this. If you help me with finding out what happened to my son, I will invest immediately in three horses to be chosen and trained by you and they will remain in your yard with you for their entire racing career. In addition, I will give you a 50 percent stake in each of them."

For a few seconds, the silence between the men was deafening. Eventually, Cannon responded.

"That's a very generous offer, Mr. Crabb, indeed way too generous. What's the catch?"

The older man turned towards Cannon and with incredulity in his voice answered, "No catch. I just want to highlight how serious I am about this Mr. Cannon...or may I call you *Mike?*"

He held out his hand highlighting both intent and integrity while softening his demeanour. He was a man confident in himself yet aware of the need to be engaging if he needed to be.

This was one of those times.

Cannon gripped the other man's hand in his own. "I can't give you a 'yes or no' straight away, but I will consider it," he promised. "I appreciate the offer and you have my word you will have my final answer shortly. In the meantime, I think you need to work out how best to break the news to your granddaughter about her father, and I need to figure out how best to handle Cassie. I don't think for either of us it is going to be easy or pleasant."

Crabb sighed loudly, disappointed that Cannon had not accepted his offer immediately. "I agree," he said. "I just hope Rachel gets here before the kids arrive."

Rachel Crabb phoned her father-in-law to let him know that she was "not too far away," half an hour before she eventually drove into the school car park.

By the time she parked her car at 12:45, and with the bus expected around one o'clock, the spare spaces in the school car park were nearly all occupied with the cars of the other parents who had arrived to collect their progeny from the trip to France.

Fortunately, one of the last available bays free was just three cars away from that of Crabb.

Since their conversation, Cannon had left the older man alone and gone inside the school to talk with Michelle about what he and Crabb had discussed. They had managed to find a quiet spot in the staffroom. As they spoke, teachers and staff came in and out at various times to collect documents or teaching materials, acknowledging Michelle with subtle nods of heads or slightly awkward smiles. They knew that what she was facing was not going to be pleasant. Eventually, he had returned to the car where Crabb had waited since Cannon had left.

They spent the next few minutes discussing what Cannon and Michelle had shared. As they chatted, they watched Rachel Crabb alight from her vehicle. Crabb, followed by Cannon, then left the warmth of the older man's vehicle, to greet her.

As both men walked towards her, Crabb slightly ahead, arms outstretched to embrace his daughter-in-law, Cannon's eyes swept over the advancing figure. She was dressed in a dark two-piece suit. Black, as befitting a lawyer, he thought. The hemline of her skirt sat just below the knee. Despite the cold, she wore no coat. The beige blouse she wore under the jacket was straight-cut, with a square neck and complemented by a pearl pendant that sat between her breasts. Her shoes were clearly expensive, with two-inch heels, patent leather, *not* Cannon thought, *very useful for driving in.*

This was a stunning woman. At around five feet eleven, slim, with narrow hips, she seemed almost too thin, almost boyish. It was however her face that Cannon noticed, more than anything else. Under short-cropped hair, that was cut around her ears and stopped just about an inch above her collar, she had deep brown eyes under barely noticeable eyebrows. Her skin was clear, almost off-white in colour. Her nose was small and delicate. She didn't smile, but when she spoke, Cannon noticed how white her teeth were, and how, if she did smile, it would light up any room.

"I am so sorry darling," said Crabb, as he hugged his daughter-in-law, holding her tightly to him.

Cannon stayed back, noticing tears flow from Rachel's eyes. She had them tightly closed, as she held him firmly to her. Holding him as if for dear life.

Eventually, they released their embrace. Noticing Cannon for the first time, standing stiffly in the cold just a few feet away and observing them, she turned to reach for a tissue inside the handbag that was slung across her shoulder. As she wiped away the tears and blew her nose, Crabb took Cannon by the arm and introduced them to each other.

Cannon took the hand extended to him. The fingers were long, thin, and recently manicured, the nails shone in the dull light, a vibrant deep red.

"Nice to meet you, Mrs. Crabb," he said, "I wish the circumstances were different. Please accept my condolences."

"Yes, thank you," she replied, her voice cracking with emotion. "I don't know what's going on, but I want to see my husband." She turned to her father-in-law and put her head on his shoulder, tears flowing again down her face.

"There, there, you will soon," responded Crabb, as he held her to him, "come on, let's go inside and get out of the cold. The bus will be here shortly and we need to be ready for Wendy."

Rachel did not protest. She nodded her head slightly and appeared happy to be led away from the car park. The three of them entered the school building and were allowed to go into the staff room where they were offered tea by one of the school administration staff.

As the tea arrived, Michelle joined them.

She had been advised that the bus was running about an hour late due to a delay of the Eurostar and that the children would only now be arriving around 2 pm.

In the seconds of silence that surrounded them, each sat quietly with their thoughts, contemplating what had happened.

Eventually, Cannon took the opportunity to speak.

Addressing them both he said, "Mrs. Crabb, umm….Rachel, I know this is a very difficult time for you, indeed for both of you, and it is likely to be doubly so in the next few days as the police ramp up their investigation, but I think it is important that the immediate issue we need to focus on is the impact on Wendy. She is going to find things extremely challenging, so it is pretty obvious that we consider how best to help her, as well as yourself Mrs. Crabb, through this ordeal."

Rachel lifted her eyes towards Cannon and then looked at her father-in-law, "I agree," she responded, "what are you suggesting? Do we need to arrange a counsellor?"

Michelle jumped in to answer the question. "The school can offer counselling if needed Mrs. Crabb."

"Rachel, please," she answered.

"OK, Rachel…..but I think that may be a little premature just yet," said Michelle. "Perhaps we can talk about what we discussed with your father-in-law earlier to see what you think?"

"Sure, okay," came the reply. Rachel's eyes acknowledged the old man. "Go ahead."

Cannon began to outline the next steps. "Firstly," he said, "with Wendy and Cassie being best friends, basically inseparable at times, we thought that it may be a good idea over the next few days for them to stay together so that Cassie could be there for Wendy if needed."

Rachel opened her mouth in slight protest, almost ready to put the idea down in its infancy, her body language giving the impression of being affronted that she, as Wendy's mother, wouldn't be there for her daughter.

Sensing her mood Cannon continued, "I know Mrs. Crabb that you may feel a little aggrieved by the suggestion, but please hear me out, ok?"

A single nod of the head was given.

Cannon continued, "A short while ago, Mr. Crabb and I, had a discussion. Your father-in-law made two proposals to me. The first one was in relation to my past. He asked me to investigate your husband's death as he was aware that I was previously a DI in the police. Initially, I told him, and I still believe this, that the best way this case will be solved will be by the police themselves, not one man acting alone. However," he went on, "your father-in-law can be quite persuasive and he has some specific issues concerning your family's privacy that he thinks will be best served by someone like myself. So, I have agreed to help, but I will do so when I can, given my own business commitments. At times though everyone needs to understand that whatever I learn, I will need to share with the police. After all, my involvement here is not in any official capacity. I hope everyone is clear on that?"

Cannon paused for a second, as Rachel Crabb considered what she had just heard.

"In addition," he went on, "your father and mother-in-law have a deep love for your daughter and are very concerned as to how Wendy will react to the news of her father's death. I am sure you feel the same about Wendy, Mrs. Crabb." It wasn't a question, just a simple statement

"Absolutely," came Rachel's reply.

"So, the suggestion is, that Wendy and my daughter, given the upcoming weekend and half-term break next week, stay at your father-in-law's place for the next few days to hopefully keep Wendy's mind off things. Especially during the next few days, which will be quite traumatic for everyone." Cannon said. "It will also mean the police, as they will need to, won't be meeting with yourself, Mrs. Crabb, while Wendy is around. This should help keep Wendy far away from any official contact the police will require of you."

Pausing, he studied her face intently looking to gauge her thoughts. "What do you think?" he continued.

Before she could answer, the old man jumped into the conversation, "Of course Rachel you can stay with us as well if you wish, but I know your work is so intense currently. I know you always seem so busy. I don't even know if you will be here or needing to be elsewhere for the next little while, will you?"

Rachel considered this for a second, "Yes you're right Joe. Maybe it's for the best, for Wendy, for...for...all of us. But I want to see Simon, I need to see him. Seeing him is more important than my job at this stage."

Then suddenly, and without warning, she let out a wail and burst into tears, once again reaching into her handbag for a tissue.

Joseph Crabb again provided comforting arms, while Cannon and Michelle looked on. After a few more minutes of tears, Rachel finally composed herself.

Once ready, they discussed and agreed on the formalities regarding what the two girls upon their return would be told, by whom, and where they would be taken that afternoon.

Cannon also advised them what the police process would likely be, and that Rachel could expect to be interviewed within the next 24 to 48 hours.

Eventually, the bus carrying the girls arrived. The vehicle disgorged a heaving mass of teenagers who seemed to be permanently laughing and giggling. Heads full of thoughts of sharing their recent adventures with parents and friends.

Cassie and Wendy came down the bus steps one behind the other. Both of them looking around as they did so, for their respective families. While all the teenagers had mobile phones, they had been banned from use on the bus and had been stowed away in the luggage hold which was kept in the compartments along the side of the vehicle. Accordingly, neither girl was aware of what had happened to Wendy's father.

Before either was able to collect their suitcases, they stood in the line that had formed alongside the bus. The line consisting of the rest of the girls and the teachers who had been on the trip, all of whom were eager to get what was theirs and then rightly move on.

Eventually suitcases in hand, a spring in their step, and despite the cold, still dressed as they were when they left France, each of them sought out their families.

Cassie immediately saw Cannon standing about 20 yards away from the bus. He waved and gave a wry smile when she called out to him. Wendy saw her grandfather standing next to Cannon, and squealed with delight.

The next few minutes saw the girls' emotions change from the disappointment of being back from the trip, through relief of having being met by their loved ones, to the harsh reality of what had happened to Wendy's father. The two close friends both reacted in the way teenage girls can often do and as expected. All thoughts of immediately sharing their experiences in France were shelved for the time being. It took the use of a spare office in the school administration area, and a lot of patience of all four adults to normalize their behaviour, until eventually, the girls were ready to travel back with Wendy's grandfather, to his house.

As they left the school buildings, rain began to fall softly, but the wind became stronger. It blew in gusts whipping the debris of old newspapers and tin cans around the car park. The girls ran to Joe Crabb's car, Cannon carried the suitcases of both girls, dropping Cassie's off next to his own vehicle, while Michelle opened the doors with her electronic fob key, and put Cassie's bag on the back seat.

Joe Crabb eventually caught up with the girls and unlocked his car. Rachel likewise jumped into her driver's seat and opened the boot from the inside, using the fob on her keyring.

Cannon reached Rachel's car as the rain started to come down harder. He lifted the boot lid as high as he could, dropped Wendy's suitcase into the empty boot, and slammed the lid. Then he ran to his car as quickly as he could, to save himself from too heavy a soaking.

"My God," he complained, "what a bloody mess."

Michelle turned to look at him. His hair lay in streaks across his head, his shoulders were damp, and his trousers were wet below the knees.

"And I'm not talking about this…," he said as he pointed to his clothes and the rain now hitting the windscreen hard.

As he turned the key to start the engine, he noticed in the rear view mirror, the cars of Joe and Rachel Crabb drive away.

They had agreed that Michelle would go back to the house with Cannon, drop off the suitcase from the trip, collect some things for Cassie that she needed, and then take them to Joe Crabb's home. Likewise, Rachel would take Wendy's suitcase home and bring to her fathers-in-law, everything Wendy would need for a few day's stay.

Rachel would also stay at her father-in-law's that evening. She could then spend time with Wendy and be able to re-arrange her diary for the coming week. She would call her boss the moment she got home and then would attend the local police station first thing in the morning, along with Cannon.

There was so much she was unaware of, such as when would they release her husband's body to her?

Why would someone have done this?

More importantly…. who?

Chapter 5

Strangely, Cannon had woken up the next morning at his normal time of 4:30 am without confusion. No dreams, no agitation. He had slept like the dead, and it surprised him. As he surfaced from a deep sleep, his mind appeared to be clearer than it had been in recent times.

Perhaps it was due to today being something different from the routine that he had been engaged in and focused on for months?

Perhaps it was the excitement of the challenge he had agreed to, though not knowing where it would all lead?

Perhaps it was the thrill of the chase? Just like jockeys putting themselves in danger each time they climbed up on a horse. Knowing that this race could result in a win, a failure, or indeed their last ever ride. The adrenaline rush of what lay ahead.

It was somewhat surprising to him that he felt the way he did, as he and Michelle had stayed up talking far longer into the evening than normal. Their usual bedtime had come and gone as they discussed the events of the day. Cannon was still reluctant about what he had agreed to do. He was conscious of how these things tended to escalate, to suck you in. His life was that of a racehorse trainer, not a D.I. anymore. He had obligations to his staff, to his owners, to Cassie and Michelle, and he did not want to lose that focus. Yet, the tug of his past did not want to let go. As he had drifted off to sleep, something had already begun to niggle at him about the day he'd had. Something he knew was important but was just out of reach.

The building on Hensington Road, in Woodstock, looked like many others in the village from the outside. The brown walls and red roof, gave the impression of a rural bed and breakfast establishment, rather than of a police station.

The road that ran past the front of the building was bordered on both sides by low stone walls that stood at the end of the pretty gardens throughout the village. He had managed to find a small parking area where he had left his car just a few hundred yards away behind the local fire station, and he had walked past the local library towards the building.

The sky still had a dull grey hue to it. It was dry and the wind had died a little so the gusts of the previous day were less frequent or intense, yet occasionally a cold blast from the east would shake the trees and the few remaining leaves would drift down across the pavements and roads.

Now, as he stood in the reception, waiting for Rachel Crabb to arrive, he looked around at the once-familiar surroundings. He immediately recognized the contradiction.

Earlier that morning he had done what he loved. Watched his horses on the gallops, and seen the steady improvement he had hoped for in *Mr. Scarecrow* and *Belle o' the Ball,* but he was somewhat disappointed in the work of *Aeon's Ago.* All three were due to race during the next two weeks. It gave him such pleasure, such freedom, to be working with beautiful animals and amazingly dedicated people. People like his head lad who he could hand over the running of his yard to, knowing full well, that he could trust him to do the right thing, by the horses and by Cannon himself.

Yet here he now was. Back in a place where lack of trust, and lack of decency between people, resulted in the need, even in small villages, for everyone to be on their guard.

This was a place where human failings that had gone beyond what was considered acceptable in society, began their journey into a dark realm. Failed relationships that turned to anger, to violence, even to death. Neighbourly friendships that turned to disputes, to property damage, to accusations and counter-accusations. All of this would come through this building. A police station was never really a happy place, and he was glad he had gotten away from the Force when he did.

The noise of a buzzer and the door next to the charge desk opening brought Cannon back to the present. DC Andy Quick poked his head from around the door, obviously looking for someone.

He did not see Cannon standing where he was.

"Typical," he said to himself under his breath, "bloody typical, no one here."

As he was about to turn back into the building, Cannon called out his name, at which Quick came out from behind the door, sliding the rest of his body into view.

"Oh hello Mike, how are you?" surprise in his voice "I didn't expect to see you here. To what do we owe the pleasure?"

They shook hands warmly.

The Constable on the desk was given an unfriendly look by Quick as if to say why hadn't he let him know that a former colleague was in reception? The Constable turned his back, mumbled to himself, and started to pick up some papers, to look busy.

Cannon noticed the interaction, and nodding towards the desk he said, "Oh I told the lad on the desk not to say I was here to anyone until the person I'm waiting for arrived, so....give him a break will you Andy?"

Quick smiled.

"OK," he said, "no problem. So why are you here anyway?" he continued, "And who is this 'other' person you are waiting for? It's an odd place to meet someone."

Cannon considered his response, "I know. It might sound a little strange and I'm not sure myself if I've done the right thing, but I've been asked to help in a matter that I am sure you are across, and I wanted to be upfront about it with whoever is leading the investigation."

"And which investigation is that?"

"The Simon Crabb murder."

"Bloody hell!" exclaimed Quick loudly, making the Constable on the desk flinch. "You don't mess around do you, Mike? The man's been dead less than 48 hours and you...," he pointed his finger at Cannon's chest, "you of all people are getting involved."

Cannon noted the exasperation in Quick's voice, and tried to raise his hands in a gesture designed the say, '*let me explain*'.

However, Quick carried on. "Mike, that investigation is a police matter now, for a real policeman not one for an ex copper," the emphasis on the '*ex*'. "Skinner will have your guts for garters mate. You know what he's like!"

The Constable on the desk tried to pretend he was not listening.

Fortunately for both men, there was no one else in the reception area to overhear what was being said, but Cannon raised a finger towards his lips in a silencing motion, took Quick gently by the shoulder towards the furthest corner from the desk, and said quietly, "Look Andy, I'm not going to interfere in the investigation. God knows why I even allowed myself to say I would help at all, and I have *told* those involved, that it's a matter best left to the police."

"So why?"

"Look," Cannon emphasized, "Simon Crabb's daughter, is my daughter's best friend. They are inseparable. Teenagers. The young girl has come back from a school trip to find her father dead. Her grandfather has asked me to help find out what happened to his son. I've told him that the police are best placed to do that. All I am doing is providing support to the family, nothing more, okay?"

Quick looked Cannon in the eye. "OK, just support?"

"Yes."

"And so being here now, is for what reason?"

"To sit in on the interview with Rachel Crabb."

"You can't do that Mike!"

"Of course I can Andy. I'm only going to be there as a witness, not as a bloody lawyer. Besides, as I understand it, she is coming in today to provide a statement about her whereabouts over the past couple of days. She's not charged with anything, you are basically just starting your inquiries right?"

Quick understood where Cannon was coming from.

Even as they spoke, the establishment of an incident room, the allocation of limited resources from the area to the 'Crabb' case, was only now underway. Skinner was barrelling his way through the 'higher ups' to get what he needed. Resources always seemed to be the number one challenge at times like this.

Quick conceded to himself that they could do with all the support they could get, but he wasn't going to let his thoughts become public knowledge.

While the interviews with the clubhouse staff were underway, and those of the guests who had attended the club at the time of the murder still pending, he knew that there was a long road ahead. Added complications like Cannon's involvement, would make Skinner even more of an *'arsehole'* than he already was.

As Quick was about to respond, the door of the 'station' opened, and Rachel Crabb eased her way into the reception area.

She noticed Cannon immediately, and almost glided across the few yards between them.

"Hello Mr. Cannon," she said, "thank you for coming. Have you been here long?"

Cannon noticed as he replied, that her eyes were no longer as bright as they were yesterday. She had been crying and there was a puffiness and redness about them, which was more evident today than when they had first met. She had tried to hide the signs through the subtle use of her makeup.

She wore jeans and runners this time, along with a white polo neck sweater under a black trench coat. Around her throat, she wore a lightweight pale blue scarf.

"Not very long at all, no," Cannon responded, "and please call me Mike."

Rachel gave a slight nod.

"Thank you for coming Mrs. Crabb," interjected Quick.

He held out his hand. "I'm DC Andrew Quick. Mr. Cannon and I are old colleagues. We were just discussing his *potential* involvement in the matter of your husband's death."

"You don't mean...?" she replied.

"No, no," Quick interrupted her, "I meant his possible support to you and the rest of your family."

Rachel smiled in response.

"Ok, well let's get on with the interview," continued Quick, "I'll lead the way shall I?"

The taking down, re-reading, and signing of the statement took a couple of hours. Cannon just sat in the interview room and listened.

By the end of the session, he was intrigued. There was nothing surprising said, nothing unexpected at all. Rachel Crabb had been away in Edinburgh at a conference, which was to last 3 days and 2 nights.

She had phoned her husband as she always did every night and when she did call, she had not been able to get in contact with him.

Given his job, she hadn't worried about it too much, as he often stayed late at the club with guests or other golfers who wanted to share their golfing 'stories' or buy him a drink.

When she had been unable to get hold of him, *'was it only 36 hours ago?'* she had called her father-in-law to express her concern. Knowing Wendy would be home the next day, that now being yesterday, she was particularly worried.

It was when she had listened to her father-in-laws' messages on the phone the next morning, and she had subsequently called him back, that she had found out what had happened. Consequently, she left straight away and drove almost non-stop, nearly seven hours to get home.

She said she had not been aware of the police trying to contact her.

She said her mobile phone battery had died during the conference and so she had charged it overnight. Eventually, she saw the message from her in-laws and called them straight away. Other than that there was nothing she was able to add.

When requested by the police, she had supplied details of the conference and the hotel. They had asked her if she knew whether her husband had had any enemies, anyone he owed money to, anyone she thought may hurt him, or the family. She had responded in the negative.

She told the police of the circle of friends they had both separately and collectively, none of which she said, were the types to hurt "anyone."

They had also questioned her about their personal relationship and she had answered as expected.

Yes, they had rows, yes they had had *"ups and downs"* at times, *"but hadn't everyone?"*

And, *"no"* she hadn't killed him.

They sat in a small village tearoom.

The tiny establishment could only take 10 customers at any one time. The two of them sat at the only occupied table. Business was slow immediately after lunch.

Both had ordered coffees, Cannon had added a toasted sandwich to the order as well.

Rachel had considered food for a second but ultimately decided against eating. As they waited for their drinks she had asked, "So what happens now?"

"Well," reflected Cannon. "First things first, the coroner will have requested a post mortem to determine the time and cause of your husband's death and...." He stopped for a second, noticing how uncomfortable she had become at the prospect of an autopsy on her husband, whose body she still had not yet seen.

"I'm sorry," he said, "I'm sure this is not pleasant for you."

His natural compassion for a victim's relatives, honed over years of knocking on doors and relaying bad news, was evident in his voice. "I'll stop if this is uncomfortable?" he said, leaving the question hanging.

"No, no, go on ... please," she replied, "I just want to know when I may be able to see him, his body...," her voice trailed off and her eyes moistened again.

"Well, given your father-in-law has already identified the body, the pathologist may well already have begun his examination. From a pure police investigation point of view," he went on, "they will gather all the statements of those that they are aware of that were at the club that day or during the evening, and that includes the staff in the restaurant, gardeners, anyone really that they can trace or become aware of. Then they will trawl through other records they have access to, for example, tee-off time bookings, visitors books, staff records, CCTV that sort of thing. They will review all that, along with the DNA evidence that they have been able to gather so far, look at all phone records, look at every possible angle they can, to see if they can find any connection between your husband and his killer or killers" he said.

Looking into her face, he continued saying, "It's pretty painstaking work, and it's done through checking as much detail as possible. Cross checking with other information or data they have on file about the people they talk to, and then hopefully, finally, draw some conclusions. All leads or pieces of information they have or come across will be followed up. It just takes time and manpower."

She had watched his face light up as he went through the checklist of things that he seemed to be able to recall so easily, almost without thinking.

"Sounds very much like the work I do, but not as boring," she said with a sad smile on her face. "In my job, I am looking at details within contracts and multiple pieces of correspondence, emails, minutes, that type of thing, to substantiate a position or seek redress. Certainly not as complicated as trying to solve a murder."

Cannon sat stony-faced, the memories of the past that he had dragged out of himself so easily, were things he had tried to forget.

"Don't you miss that type of work Mr. Cannon?" she continued.

Before he could reply, noting the formality in her question, the coffees and sandwich arrived.

He watched her sip her coffee as he took a bite of his food. She drank it black.

He indicated that he would reply to her question once he had swallowed his mouthful. In the interim, while he chewed, he considered her question.

Finally, he said, "No, not at all. The Force is a great institution, but I've served my time. Getting out when I did was the best thing I have ever done. Any longer and I would have needed far more support than I require now."

She put her hand on his arm. Her face showing a concern that made him feel like he had opened himself up much further than he had intended.

"Oh, I'm sorry," she said, "I didn't know Mr. Cannon, err, Mike. I hope you realize I wasn't prying," she said.

"Of course," he answered, "I understand."

He moved to pick up his sandwich again, and she lifted her hand from his arm.

After another bite, he continued. "You see a lot of things in the police. A lot of things…"

He let the visions he was witnessing in his mind's eye run through his memory and then disperse from his thoughts. Gone forever he hoped. However, no matter how much he tried to hide them, dispel them, he knew they would return at some point. The visions and memories that made him stay awake as he tried desperately to fall asleep, or that woke him during the night. The visions that came alive in his dreams.

"It's not fair to share them with you, Mrs. Crabb, sorry….," he corrected himself, "….Rachel. But let me say this. There are many people on this earth that are sick, perverted, and neglectful of those who they, themselves, bring into this world. That list includes people in positions of authority that prey on others and those that act worse than animals. For that reason alone I am so glad that I am out of that environment, that world," he confessed.

For a few seconds, his eyes glazed over, his mind contemplating what he had just said.

"I could go on about the past, but I won't," he continued, "though I'm sure you have seen many, many, items on the news, in the press, on social media, or whatever, of man's inhumanity to man. How he can degrade, torture, and maim his fellow citizens, kill his community members, brothers and sisters. Well, reading and hearing about it is bad enough, but seeing it, living with it every day for years, affects your humanity and for me, that just took its toll. With a wife and daughter to look after it, all became too much."

"So why are you willing to help find who killed my husband?" she asked.

"I'm not! That's the police's job," he said. "I have agreed to help gather whatever information I can. Then I will pass it on to them and it's up to them to catch whoever is responsible and get the conviction. I'm not a policeman anymore, I'm just an ordinary citizen now."

Chapter 6

The phone call he took, was more a demand than a request.

He walked into the *Kings Head* pub on Park Lane, which was the regular drinking hole for Skinner, normally quiet, as it was tucked away in a side street just a short walk from the centre of the village.

The roaring fire in the dining area cast flickering shadows on the far wall opposite to where Skinner and Quick sat. At two o'clock in the afternoon, the low cloud outside made the pub seem darker than it was. The dark wood panelling inside contrasted with the pure white exterior of the building. The bar area was almost empty, the restaurant had a few people still enjoying their lunch, but the majority of the lunchtime customers had departed.

It was clear to Cannon that they had been there a while, given the four empty pint glasses on the table in front of them, and the half-empty third that each was holding as he sat down.

"Drink?" said Skinner, almost offhandedly.

"If you are buying Jim, I'll have a pint of *Brakspears* please."

Skinner curled up his lip slightly and with a shrug of his shoulder, urged Quick to get up and make himself useful. With a sigh, Quick climbed over Skinner's legs that were stretched out in front of him and went off to the bar.

"By the way," continued Cannon, "It's a bit cloak and dagger isn't it sitting in the semi-dark?" He indicated the surroundings. "Why here?"

"So I can bollock you without too many onlookers," came the sardonic reply. "I was considering your feelings…," The sarcasm in the words dripped from Skinner's mouth like slime from a cracked u-bend.

"I see you haven't changed over the past 3 years Jim," replied Cannon "You're still a miserable old bastard."

As Skinner started to reply, Quick came back with Cannon's pint and placed it on the low table between them. Cannon immediately took a swig before Quick had even sat down. There was history between himself and Skinner, and it was obvious to him that Skinner was still living with the past.

Skinner laughed, a deep rumble sound within his chest.

Without warning, Skinner began to cough violently, as if the laugh had somehow tried to choke him. He reached for his drink and took a deep slug. When he put the glass down it was almost empty. Foam spilled down the inside of the glass and only a quarter-inch of the amber liquid remained.

Cannon waited for Skinner to wipe his mouth with the back of his hand. He knew what was coming.

"What I want to know," Skinner sneered, "is what the fuck are you doing sniffing around the Crabb murder investigation? Or is it something else you are sniffing around?" he said, slyly.

The implication and innuendo were not lost on Cannon and Quick. Cannon let the jibe go over his head, now was not the time to address the past between Skinner and himself. That would come later. He looked at Quick who had sat slightly deeper into his chair, somewhat embarrassed by Skinner's assertion of his former colleague.

"I'm not sniffing around anything, as you call it Skinner," he answered. "I have a new life now, and one that I thoroughly enjoy. I do not need that shit anymore. And it's clear to me from what I've heard, that the job is getting a bit too much for you as well nowadays. That the reputation you have is getting even bigger than ever."

"And what reputation is that?"

"That you've become even lazier than you ever were," he said, provoking Skinner. "In fact, as I recall it, you had been cruising towards retirement for years even before I left the Force. So what is it now then? Waiting for your forty-year medal is it?"

Cannon could see Skinner was beginning to get agitated, but he carried on, saying, "I hear that your office is this place now," he gestured to the room with his arm, "and that you spend most of your days here. Basically issuing instructions to others while you wait for your pension to grow bigger than it already is."

Skinners face began to show the rage he was feeling inside. In the darkness, it was difficult to see its colour, but the hardening of his normally sagging jaw gave away the emotions stirring throughout his body. He tried to get up from his chair but the combination of age, alcohol, and the low seat, meant that he just toppled over.

"You little shit!" he shrieked, his arms flailing as he tried to cushion the fall, the pint glasses dancing on the low table in a small jig from the vibration of Skinner's shoulder hitting the floor.

Cannon looked on as Quick reached for the arm of his boss to pull him back up off the floor, and back onto the seat that they had been sitting on.

Skinner once seated again, reached for his glass and downed the rest of his drink, seemingly needing it, and giving himself a few seconds with which to regain his composure.

In what seemed like an hour of silence between them but was only half a minute or so, Cannon realized that if he was going to help find out what had happened to Simon Crabb and why then he was unlikely to find much help from Skinner. Not that he had expected any, but it was now clear that today, old scars were being re-opened. Issues from the past still remained, and they churned themselves up, inside the belly of Skinner.

"Thanks for the drink," said Cannon, as he stood up to leave and nodded towards the almost full glass. He had not touched the drink again after his initial sip.

As Cannon tried to slip past the two men and make his exit Skinner grabbed his arm. Cannon stopped dead and looked into Skinners' face.

"Stay the fuck away from my investigation, or I'll have you!" Skinner spat.

"Let go of my arm, now!" responded Cannon, "or I'll break yours," he said, pointing at the senior detective with his free hand. "And don't you ever, touch me again!"

Quick tried to intervene by turning to Skinner saying, "Boss! Boss! Let him go, leave it alone. There's no need for all this."

Skinner hesitated for a second as the red mist in his brain slowly settled. Then turning to acknowledge Quick and his comments, he let go of Cannon's arm.

"Get the fuck out of here!" he shouted, nodding towards the door that led to the bar and the exit.

Cannon smiled, rubbing a hand over the sleeve that Skinner had held.

"See you around," he said, leaving the implication in his voice that he was not going to be scared off by Skinner or anyone else that easily.

He strode from the room, ignoring Skinner who was calling after him, shouting a warning as he walked away.

"Stay away from this case Cannon," he screamed, "just stay away. You had better do as I say because I'll be watching you, you bastard, I'll be watching!"

Cannon sat in his car with the engine idling and with the heater on, as he contemplated what had happened just a few minutes prior. He had known that Skinner and he were likely to clash given their history, but he hadn't expected the vitriol to be as deep.

It had been years since he had last seen Skinner, yet just being in the same room as him had brought it all back. He knew he needed to be careful not to let Skinner get to him, to get under his skin. And he knew he must not give Skinner any excuse, any at all, to use the police powers that would stop him from investigating Crabb's murder. Cannon's colleagues of the past, but now friends of today, had kept him abreast over the past three years of what was going on in local police circles.

He had not tried to keep the links alive, as he had just wanted to move on and concentrate on his new career. But, it was difficult not to run into people at various times with whom he had previously worked. He came across them on occasion when he was in town, at his local pub, or even at the races.

He had been well-liked by most of the people he worked with including his superiors, and despite not wanting to have anything to do with the police anymore, their updates when he saw them, and his recurring dreams, seemed to ensure that the policeman within him, was never really too far away from surfacing again.

He had been successful as a D.I., and he was now making a success of his new life.

He did not want the former to impact the latter, but it seemed like the protestations within himself about not getting in too deep were roused by the warnings of Skinner. His own drive, his own stubbornness to help, and solve this case, were beginning to get the better of him.

He took a deep breath, then putting his car into gear, he drove out of the car park and headed towards the Kirtlington golf course.

There was no sign of any police presence anymore.

The blue tape, which had been used to cordon off the crime scene had been removed. All signs of the SOCO's tent likewise, had gone. What was surprising though to Cannon when he arrived, was the lack of cars in the clubs' parking area. There were a few cars there, but not as many as he had expected. Perhaps the word had not gotten around yet that the course had now re-opened?

On the drive up to the club, he had called Michelle from his car and told her that he would be home by the early evening. He explained what had happened in his meeting with Skinner, and where he was going.

"Take care darling," she had said, "and be careful."

The wind was light but there was rain in the air now. Clouds had moved in during his drive, making the sky a kind of smug grey. He walked from his car, and into the clubhouse.

There was nobody visible as he walked into the building. He noticed to his right there was movement near the bar area. A man stood with his back to the counter drying various drinking glasses, pint glasses, and wine glasses that he was taking from a dishwasher that was out of sight, below the countertop.

The man was whistling away to himself. He did not notice Cannon standing there. Cannon waited for a few seconds listening, then tried to attract the man's attention.

"Excuse me...excuse me," he repeated

The man turned around and smiled.

"G'day," he responded, his accent instantly recognizable. "How can I help you? Drink?"

"Australian?" enquired Cannon, happy to exchange a pleasantry about the man's heritage. "Where are you from?" he asked.

"Adelaide," came the reply. "Yes, an Aussie and proud of it mate," said the man. "Sam Painter's my name." He put down the glass he was drying and offered his hand.

Cannon extended his own and they shook.

The man was just under six feet tall, broad-shouldered, clean-shaven, with blue eyes, and had a world-weary gait that seemed to be a compulsory element for a barman. He was in his mid to late forties. His greying hair showed signs of thinning, but he still wore it down to his shoulders at the back. Across his crown and forehead, there were still some small dark patches that indicated how much hair across his entire head there used to be at one time. He had a broad smile and was not particularly unattractive.

In all probability, he was someone with who any woman who sat at the bar may indulge in an extended conversation, during an evening.

He wore the regulatory black slacks, a long-sleeved black shirt, and what appeared to be new black runners. Given barmen were on their feet most of the time, it was of no surprise to Cannon that he wore good quality shoes.

Cannon looked around at the empty room, on his face a sardonic smile.

"Not many customers today then?" he said.

"No," replied the man, "not after the incident we had here the other night," his voice trailed off in resignation. "I suppose you heard about it?"

"Actually, that's why I'm here."

"Oh?"

"Yes, I was trying to find out a bit more about Simon Crabb, the man who…."

"Was killed the other night?" interrupted Painter. "Yes, I know who he is, sorry was…..He spent most of his time down at the pro-shop," he nodded to his left. "I'm sure those in the shop can tell you more about him. He didn't really drink too much in the clubhouse that I saw. Though he was in here almost every night. It wasn't that he was a teetotaller, but he just seemed to know his limits, not like some."

Painter stopped for a second then queried, "Are you police then? You haven't shown any ID as yet."

"No, I'm not the police…anymore," replied Cannon.

"So what's the interest then mate? Can't the police handle it?"

"I'm sure they can Mr. Painter. I'm just doing the family a favour," Cannon touched his nose and gave a quick wink.

"Ok, no worries. I was interested, as I gave the police a statement the night it happened."

"You were here?" said Cannon.

"I was on shift yes. The place was buzzing actually. Always is on quiz night."

"Did you notice anything unusual during the evening?"

Painter laughed. "Had no time to bloody scratch myself all night," he said, the sing-song lilt in his voice more pronounced, "let alone see what was going on outside!"

Looking past Painter, Cannon said, "Anyone else here?"

"Yeah, a couple of the kitchen staff just tidying up after lunch and preparing for dinner. Though based on this afternoon's debacle, I don't expect them to be very busy tonight. Also, you just missed a couple of the waiting staff, they left about five minutes before you got here."

"Were they here the other night?"

"Not sure to be honest mate. The police have a list I believe of all those who were, but you'll have the ask them. I don't know."

Cannon gave an involuntary shudder. Given the earlier 'chat' with Skinner, he wasn't keen to cross paths with him again, just yet.

"Ok," he said, "thanks a lot for your time. I appreciate it. Oh, and by the way, next time maybe I will have a drink?"

Smiling to himself, Cannon left the building and headed towards the Pro-shop.

As he walked along a narrow pathway beside the clubhouse, he noticed the sky had darkened a little more, with the odd spot of rain starting to fall. In the distance, he heard the sound of a club hitting a ball, followed by a cry of *'four'* Clearly, there were still a few people out on the course, the sound though suggesting the players were near to the final hole.

A couple of elderly men, who Cannon considered to be beyond retirement age, walked towards him, each pulling a trolley with golf bags stuffed with clubs. They chatted and laughed as they passed him, their shoes 'clacking' on the paving as they walked. He nodded a 'hello' and they acknowledged him briefly. A drink at the nineteenth hole, and a chat about their just finished round, was the main thought on their minds.

The Pro-shop was inside a small building just next to a putting green, which in turn was about fifty metres from the eighteenth hole.

It was modern, well stocked with racks of clubs lining the walls.

Clothes in various loud colours and types, polo shirts, slacks, jumpers all vied for attention as they sat on hangers on various stands in the middle of the shop floor. Posters showing various players in different poses, indicating the particular subject's preference for a specific club manufacturer, ball types, watches, and clothing ranges adorned the walls.

In addition, various baskets near a counter contained many different '*sale*' items, including single gloves, caps, sweatbands, club covers, tees, divot repairers, ball markers, and a multitude of other items.

There were various notices and flyers about tee-off times and club competitions on the countertop, behind which, two men stood in colour coordinated fashion of white polo shirts and blue chino trousers. The younger of the two was about five feet seven, around eighteen or nineteen years old, and the other, a much older man. Cannon estimated the older man to be in his fifties.

"Sorry Sir," said the younger man, "but if you want to book a tee-off time, we do that all online now," he pointed to one of the flyers on the counter. "We started it about three weeks ago if you weren't aware," he said, continuing to offer his advice.

"Thank you err…Phil," replied Cannon, pointing at a name badge on the man's shirt, "but I'm not here for that."

"Oh, I thought I hadn't seen you here before, Sir," continued Phil. "How can we help you then?"

Before Cannon could answer, an inquiry was made of himself.

"Are you looking to join the club as a member or just visiting, Sir?" jumped in the older man. "As you can see around you, we do stock everything you need to improve your game," he smiled. "But just to let you know, which I expect you already do, in addition to the normal annual membership fees, plus fees per round played and applicable green fees, to be able to join the club you'll need a sponsor and a seconder to sign your application form," he said. "In addition, I think it's only fair to tell you that there is quite a waiting list currently. I believe it's over a year before you can become a full club member now."

"Must be a good course and have a good bar," said Cannon with a smile on his face.

He had always found golf clubs unnecessarily stuffy, and many of its members extremely pompous.

It wasn't a place he enjoyed attending. He had played rounds in the past at various courses in the vicinity, but more for the fresh air and the camaraderie with his fellow officers, than for the sport itself.

Also, he reminded himself, *"I'm not very good at it either....."*

"No, I'm not here to join the club," he said, "I am here to ask about Simon Crabb, and anything you can tell me about him would be most helpful."

There was hesitation between the two men until the older one challenged him asking, "Are you with the police? We told them all we know when we gave our statements yesterday," he said, looking towards the younger man.

"No," responded Cannon, "I'm ex-police," emphasizing the *'ex'*.

"So what do you want to know about Simon for then?"

"I've been asked by the family to conduct a more private investigation. The family knows that the police are stretched for resources, so they have asked me to help where I can."

Cannon didn't want to go into any more detail, so quickly moved the conversation on. "So you are…?" He left the question hanging, knowing most people would naturally fill in the gaps to the question when asked.

"Tony Book," said the older man, "and this is Phil Pierce," nodding towards the younger. "I'm the manager of this shop and Phil here has been with us just less than a year. He helps me to run the place, whether it is the hiring out of equipment, sales, stock control, that type of thing."

"So you don't play yourself?" enquired Cannon of the younger man.

"Yes I do, at times," responded Pierce, "but it's more a hobby for me. It's not a career choice. I'm just taking a year off before I start university. I'm off to study engineering next summer," he said proudly.

Cannon smiled noting the gleam of anticipation and excitement in the young man's eyes.

He quashed the thought that was rising in his mind about youthful expectations versus the real world. He decided that showing any cynicism would not be appropriate. His own experiences of being in the police, and how his past still raised its ugly head at times within his dreams, were things peculiar to his own life. He had no right to project them onto others.

"Well best of luck," said Cannon.

"Thanks."

"So Mr…" hesitated Tony, waiting for a formal reply.

"Cannon," came the response.

"OK, Mr… Cannon. How can we help you?" asked Book.

"I was wondering if you could tell me anything about Simon Crabb, that had seemed unusual or out of place in recent days or weeks. I assume with him being the golf pro, it would have meant that if he wasn't teaching on the course, then he would have spent a lot of his time here, in the shop, right? "

"Yes, that's right," replied Book. "Any lessons wanted were recorded here on our system." He pointed to the computer terminal on a desk just behind the counter. "People could book online or here in the shop or also over the phone. So during each day, if not teaching, Simon would be either here or on the practice tees or the putting green."

"Every day?" enquired Cannon.

"More or less," said Book. "Being a golf pro doesn't leave much time for anything else. Especially at such a busy club like this one. It's almost a seven-day-a-week job."

"Did he ever have time for himself or his family do you think?"

"I'm sure he did," answered Book, "but I can't tell you much about that. You would have to ask his wife I guess."

Cannon considered this for a second, remembering the comments of Joseph Crabb about the arguments between Simon and Rachel.

"Thanks, I will," he replied. "Any friends?" he continued. "Surely he would have plenty of those?"

"Oh yes," said Book, emphasizing the reply, "he certainly did have friends, lots of them if you know what I mean?"

The innuendo in the comment was obvious, even to a blind man.

Cannon considered this for a second, finally asking. "So do I understand you to mean that he *played around* when he should have been playing *a* round?"

The joke was not lost on either of the two men.

Pierce sniggered, while Book laughed out loud.

Cannon didn't think his comment was particularly amusing but allowed them to get over their juvenile responses before he carried on.

"Tell me about his friends if you can."

"Well, he played a regular three ball here almost every Wednesday afternoon unless the weather was bad. He played with a couple of local businessmen. Seemed to have been doing so since before I started working here. Looked like they were very good friends. I do not know about anyone else though, as I hardly ever saw Simon outside of the club and he never talked about other people. If he did, I can't recall."

"Do you know their names?" enquired Cannon, "of those in the three-ball?"

"Yes I do," said Book, "we have them on our system."

"They are all members," interrupted Pierce.

Cannon knew that an investigation had to start somewhere, and getting names like this of those close to the victim, outside of the immediate family was good information.

He needed to sort out the links to Crabb, of these other people, and then see where it led.

The fact that Crabb appeared to have a reputation with some members of the club as someone who 'played away,' meant that there were potentially any number of suspects if what he had been told was true. Jealous husbands, boyfriends, other women even. The possibilities were endless.

Where to start was the biggest challenge. His experience told him that it was all about putting the pieces together, however, he was no longer part of a team with huge resources. He was one man and he had a new focus. He was beginning to regret getting involved.

'Was it too late to back out now?' he thought to himself.

Book was speaking, as Cannon's thoughts returned to his immediate surroundings.

"Sorry, I missed that," said Cannon apologetically, "could you repeat it?"

"I said, do you have a pen?" repeated Book.

"Ah, yes I do, thank you." Cannon reached into his internal jacket pocket and pulled out a small notebook, which he used for taking notes, up on the gallops. From a side pocket, he extracted a soft click ballpoint. "Carry on..." he said.

Looking at the screen, Book read out the first name. "Graham Jefferson", then continued, saying, "and Alex Wilson. Did you get that Mr. Cannon?" he inquired.

Cannon quickly finished writing down the names.

"And do you have any addresses for these men?" he asked.

"I'm afraid Mr. Cannon we can't do that. As you know in terms of the Privacy Act we would be disclosing more than we are allowed to if we did so. Especially given the fact that your inquiries are not through any official channels. Am I right?"

Cannon nodded, realizing that police warrants and search orders opened more than just doors, but also people's minds to be cooperative. When you no longer had access to that kind of backup, your options could at times be limited.

"Of course Mr. Book, you are correct," said Cannon feeling slightly sheepish, "and I don't want you to compromise yourself in any way but if you could indulge me just a minute longer, that would be appreciated."

Waiting a few seconds to ensure he had both men's attention before carrying on, he continued, saying, "Until the crime is solved I suspect the police will be crawling all over this place at various times, making it quite difficult for some of the members to just relax whilst they are here. The entire place, who comes and goes, and what they do will be watched. From my experience, many members will likely stay away for a while until this has all blown over. That could be weeks or even months which could impact your bookings AND your sales from the shop here."

Stopping for a few seconds, to let what he had said sink in, he continued, "And I suspect you both get paid commission based on your shop turnover, yes?"

Leaving the question hanging, he then said, "So it's in everyone's interest to try and wrap this mess up as quickly as possible before the club begins to lose customers. You can already see from attendance for lunch today that the dining area and the bar are already being affected, which in turn will potentially impact your own pockets as well I'd guess. Not something I'm sure either of you would want. Am I right...?"

Silence stretched between the three men, with the younger man looking towards Book for guidance.

Eventually, Book relented saying, "Ok Mr. Cannon, but you didn't get this from us."

In an almost furtive manner, Book leaned over the counter and said, "Mr. Wilson is a businessman and is the owner of a company called 'INet Solutions' in the Bicester office park, about seven miles from here. Mr. Jefferson, in turn, owns a dry cleaning business in Brackley, up towards Banbury." Book considered what he had just done then commented, "Now that is far more than I should have divulged and I will completely deny any knowledge of this conversation," he said, "what I have given you is all I am prepared to say."

Cannon feeling contented, silently acknowledged the information he had received by winking back at Pierce and shaking the hand of Book. He mouthed a '*thank you*' then turned and left the shop.

Heading straight to his car, he felt a surge of adrenaline flowing through his veins.

He had not wanted this, but now his body tingled with anticipation. He felt as he did when one of his horses won a race that he had specifically targeted them for. That *high*, that feeling of deep satisfaction he had, when his horse was a winner of a race, a maiden plate, a novice chase, or even a listed or Group race that he had picked out specifically for that specific animal and which resulted from a well planned and executed campaign. That feeling of excitement, of achievement, of being alive.

Chapter 7

When he arrived home, he parked his car, then strode straight to the stables to check with Rich Telside, to check on how things were going. It was dark now and the stables were lit in a soft glow from the lights in the house and the tack room where Rich was busy supervising the last duties of the day.

The horses were settling for the night having been fed, watered, and rubbed down. Some were bandaged, to protect their legs from any knocks that they could accidentally inflict upon themselves during the night. Blood samples had also been taken by the vet from those horses that appeared not to be up to their normal level of work.

It appeared that most of the horses were well though.

The yard was also clear of any infections, viral or bacterial.

Biosecurity was a significant issue. Everyone in the industry knew of the decimation that could occur if equine influenza, or equine anemia, African horse sickness, or even 'foot and mouth' were to break out. There were strict guidelines around Biocontainment issued to all trainers, and if there was any sign of an outbreak, horses would not be allowed to move around the country, effectively limiting them to their stable block, turning them from primed equine athletes into very expensive pets. Something owners would not be too happy with.

Cannon was conscious that getting so deeply involved with the Crabb murder, albeit in an unofficial capacity, was taking him away from where he really should have been spending his time. He was torn between the commitment he had given Joseph Crabb and the joy that his life as a trainer brought him. He had worked hard since he had left the Force and had no desire for his previous occupation to take over his new one.

His priority was clear. He had family, staff in his employ, owners who paid their bills, and more importantly, the horses themselves that were under his care, and that was where his focus should be.

Cannon waited outside the tack room until the last of the lads had finished with Rich and had said their goodbyes to him before they made their way home for the evening. He could hear a couple of them outside calling out to each other to meet in one of the local pubs for a quick drink before they went their separate ways.

"Hi Rich, how are you?" he said

"Guv'nor," responded Rich as he hung up a highly polished saddle onto a rack next to a string of bridles and mouth bits. The reflected light from the open bulb on the tack room ceiling danced on the metal of the polished stainless steel.

"Everything okay? Any issues I need to be aware of?"

"Only the one," stated Telside, "Red Flag had a bit of soreness in the knees this morning after gallops, so we got the vet in who suggested a scan. It does not look too bad and he doesn't think it needs scoping just yet, but he's found a bit of swelling. He's suggested a treatment to take out the heat from the legs using corticosteroids and compression bandaging and to keep her in her box for now. If it gets worse we may need to look at alternates, but let's see how it goes."

"Ok thanks. And how is *Mr. Scarecrow*?"

"Oh, he's fine," came the reply with a chuckle, "he's jumping out of his skin. I think he's got a great chance next time. He fairly flew over the fences today. He's eaten up and seems very relaxed."

"The owners will be pleased. I'm really looking forward to Cheltenham."

"Me too Guv."

Cannon stayed silent for a moment, the only sound between the two men the odd grunt and sneeze coming from the stable boxes. Eventually, he said, "Rich, I need your help, and I'll understand if you say no, but what I'm going to be asking of you is a really big favour."

Telside looked at his boss. "Mike," he said, the informality of the response pleasing Cannon, "we have been friends for a long time now. We know each other pretty well, don't we?" he continued. "We have a good working relationship and you wouldn't ask me for help if you didn't think it was in the best interest of the horses or the staff. You're a good man Mike, so whatever it is must be important to you. And if it's important to you, it's important to me. So who am I to say no to it, whatever it is?"

Cannon relaxed a little.

"Thanks, Rich" he stated, his voice indicating to Telside, how much he appreciated the offer of support.

Continuing he said, "Look, I've been dragged somewhat *kicking and screaming* into the murder investigation of Cassie's friend's father…," he quickly held up his hand to stop Telside interrupting his flow, and letting him know that he had more to say. "And as you know, I used to be a cop years ago in this area. So while my involvement is in some way *"unofficial"* I will need to spend a bit of time away from the stable during the day over the next few weeks. I know it goes against my grain to get involved in this case after all the shit I've seen in my prior life, but given how it's impacted Cassie and even Michelle, reluctantly I feel I have had no choice."

"And you want me to …?" enquired Telside.

"I want you to run the stable for me for the next couple of weeks. Everything. From the training, nominations, arranging transport to and from the tracks, arranging feed ….everything."

"Including giving myself and the rest of the lads a pay rise?" answered Telside jokingly.

"Except that," countered Cannon, with a broad smile across his face. "I think we should be able to catch up every night just after lockdown if that's ok? Just to see how things are going. But if you are still on the road after racing at that time, we can catch up on the phone. I can ring you or if that's a problem we can see each other face to face the next day. Does that work for you?" he asked.

Realizing what it meant to be giving up direct control of his stables for the period he was investigating Crabb's murder, made Cannon feel uncomfortable. He knew that it was a necessity in order to investigate the crime, but he still wasn't sure it would be worth it. The payoff seemed *good*, given the promise of more horses, but at what cost to his family?

Finally as if noticing for the first time that Rich was waiting, he asked, "So what do you say?"

The smile across his old friend's face told him all he needed to know.

"I'd be delighted," he said, holding out his hand for Cannon to shake.

"Thanks, Rich," Cannon replied, grasping Telside's hand "It's a big ask but I wouldn't have asked anybody else, and if you had said no then I would have understood," he said. "I thought you'd be happy to accept, but it was important to me to ask you outright. I really do appreciate it."

"No need to thank me Guv', I just hope you can find the bastard ...."

They sat together on the couch in the living room.

The TV was on but without volume. A BBC documentary on yet another NHS failure was being aired. It was warm inside the house but the feeling between them was much cooler.

Dinner had been eaten with hardly any small talk punctuating the twenty minutes or so that it took them to complete their meal. Each had wrestled internally with their thoughts, their own demons.

Contrary to the normal routine they had developed since Michelle had moved in, they had left the dishes, cups, glasses, and cutlery on the table. It was unusual, but given the events of the past few days and the conflict both of them had within themselves, nothing seemed normal anymore.

Cannon had thought when he had entered the kitchen that things were falling into place after his conversation with Rich, so he couldn't quite understand the ambivalent response he got from Michelle when he kissed her on the neck as she was cooking dinner. He realized immediately that something was wrong, and he knew the best way to address it, was to give Michelle space. She would open up when she was ready.

The challenge with Cassie, the murder of Crabb, and how it was dragging him back into his old world, plus the impact the murder had on the school children Michelle taught, Cannon knew, was not something Michelle nor he needed right now. Especially when he considered that investigating the murder would likely exacerbate his dreams and in doing so, bring to the fore the nightmares of the past.

Would it also bring back thoughts of Sally?

He could never tell if his dreams and how they made him feel inside, ever really showed on his face or affected his behaviour towards other people. However, to the extent they did, he was hopeful that others just saw it as a reaction by him to a dream or a nightmare, not anything else.

At times he had felt guilty about how they impacted him and the problems they had created with those he loved. He especially hoped that whatever happened didn't make things worse for Michelle. He loved her very much and didn't want to lose her, but he knew relationships could be fragile. He needed to be mindful of that.

"I spoke with Cassie this afternoon," she said quietly, breaking the silence between them.

"Thanks," he responded. "I should have called her myself but I just got so tied up with this…..this….."

"I know," she said softly, interrupting him, "I know."

She leant over and put a finger to his lips as if to say to him that it was her turn to speak, and she just needed him to listen. He nodded slightly, accepting the invitation to be still, and waited for her to carry on. She placed a hand on his thigh, gently stroking it with her thumb as a sign of reassurance and he relaxed a little. He didn't know what to expect, but in his mind, he still feared the worst.

"She seemed okay," Michelle continued, "and it looks like she and Wendy are being spoilt a little. I spoke with the Grandmother, Irene, and she said that both girls were a little quiet, but that they appreciated Cassie staying over for the next few days."

"I should give Cassie a call myself tomorrow," interrupted Cannon.

Michelle sighed. "I'm sure Cassie will be fine, but it probably would be good to let her know that everything's going to be alright."

"And you…?" he asked, leaving his question unfinished but with enough uncertainty that called for a response.

She looked absently towards the television, watching the pictures but not seeing them. Cannon felt his stomach churn. He looked at her face in profile and tried to guess what she was thinking. She was silent for only a few seconds but to Cannon, it felt like an eternity. He didn't want or need his world to start coming undone now.

"It was only a few days ago that my main worry was Cassie coming home, and all I wanted was to try and find a way to get closer to her. To make her realize that while I'm not her mother, I want to be as close to her as Sally was."
The use of his former wife's Christian name made Cannon gasp slightly, involuntarily. He hoped Michelle hadn't noticed, but it was the first time in a long time that the ghost of the past had been spoken of, and coming from Michelle made it all the more painful. He sat silently but placed his hand over that of Michelle which still rested on his leg.

Continuing, Michelle said, "Now I'm not sure I can do that at all now. Her best friend has just learnt her father has been murdered. You're now getting involved in something akin to your former life, and who knows how she sees that? And finally, the only person she can talk to is her teacher and someone who has, in her eyes, taken her mother's place in her home, in your heart, and in your bed. I'm sure she sees me as some form of interloper who has taken away all she holds dear."

"Don't be silly," he tried to say, "it's……."

"Not true?" she questioned.

It was clear that this was a pivotal moment in their relationship. He reached out and put his arms around her shoulders. Initially, she tried to pull away but he held her firmly. Reluctantly at first, but eventually, she put her head onto his shoulder, the sides of their heads touching. He knew he needed to say something.

"Cassie is a teenager. You know how teenage girls are. You know that *any* problem is bigger than Everest to them, but you also know that it is just a phase," he said. "Yes it can be difficult, and I am sure we will have our challenges, but we need to keep perspective."

He turned his face towards her and gently kissed her on the top of the head. "Cassie herself is not affected by this murder, only her friend is. Cassie has a loving home, and yes Sally isn't here anymore, but…" he stopped for a second, thinking what he wanted to say, "But YOU are, and that's the way *I* want it! I love you so very much Michelle. You are my life now!"

In that instant, it appeared that all her concerns melted away.

She turned her face up to meet his, and soft tears ran down her cheeks. He brought his other hand around to caress her face with his fingers but before he could, she said, "Happy tears, these are happy tears," indicating the single drops that rolled from her eyes. "Thank you," she said.

Cannon smiled at her, his eyes likewise felt moist. He touched her face again slightly, brushing away the remnants of her sadness. Then he gently cupped her chin and drew her closer and kissed her mouth. Their tears mingled as their mouths sought each other. They moved closer, hugging each other in a deep embrace. Their tongues slid together in and out as their breath became more excited, more ragged. In seconds they had slipped from the couch onto the carpet and they reached for each other's clothing. Lifting, tearing, unbuttoning, yet all the while trying to keep their lips together like two flying insects locked as one as they mate on the wing. Like two newlyweds, excitement and fear drove them. Touching, squeezing, tasting. Their bodies eventually moving as one. Their lovemaking was aggressive at times, passion dominating. They both knew it was a release they needed. The act was the physical outcome of their feelings for each other and it was clear that their commitment to each other was paramount. Neither of them could act so animalistic if there wasn't that counterbalance of mutual respect and love.

Finally, sated, they lay together on the carpet. Their breathing slowly returning to normal. Michelle slowly turned her back to him and he held her tightly in his arms.

"Thank you," he said, kissing her neck.

She sighed in response.

He lay there for a few minutes, before eventually getting up to collect a blanket from the bedroom.

When he returned, he noticed that she was fast asleep.

He covered her with the blanket, collected pillows for her head, and once he had turned off the TV and all the lights, he lay down beside her, and again held her close before he too fell into a dreamless sleep.

Chapter 8

"So what have we got!" grunted Skinner in exasperation.

Three days in, and he had nothing to show for it.

He was in the 'incident' room, as much as it was, for the 10 am briefing. It was a small room capable of holding eight people at a maximum, around an oblong wooden table that had seen much better days. Probably much better *years* if everyone was honest. Stain marks and teacup base outlines had imbued themselves into the wood. No amount of polishing alone would bring the table back to life. It seemed like the wood it was made from, not only died when it was first made but had died a thousand deaths since. The original grain now having turned so dark, that the table was the colour resembling a Victorian-era school desk that one could only find in an old photograph from years ago – black!

Around the edge of the room, stood a few old metal beige filing cabinets. These were primarily used now to lean against, should there be more people than chairs.

It was hot. The tiny windows sitting two-thirds of the way up the wall and that backed onto the car park, struggled to let fresh air in, fighting with the heat generated from the large radiators along two of the other walls.

Before anyone could answer Skinner's question, Quick entered the room.

"Sorry I'm a bit late, Sir," he said as he went to shut the door, "just following up some information for this morning." He indicated the file in his hand.

"Leave it open," indicated Skinner, "it's bloody boiling in here." And then to no one in particular he moaned. "And who the hell do we need to kick up the arse to get this heating turned down…? It's a bloody disgrace. We'll all be falling asleep soon."

The team he had around him, already knew he was in a bad mood. It was pretty obvious that by the end of the briefing it could be much worse. All of them in their own way would rather be working on other cases, than working with Skinner. The outburst about the heating just being the start of what could be a very unpleasant hour.

The three others sitting at the table, in addition to Skinner and Quick, were all the direct resources Skinner was given to work with on the Crabb case. A young Constable, a geeky IT specialist carrying a laptop computer, and a female liaison officer.

Others who would play peripheral parts in the investigation, including doing the grunt work such as statement cross-checking, follow-up phone calls, report production, etcetera, stood around the edges of the room.

"Carpenter!" Skinner barked, addressing the Constable, "have we now got all the statements from those at the club on the night in question?"

"More or less, Sir," responded the young Constable. In his mid-twenties, he found working with Skinner intimidating. He was trying to do everything right in order to develop his career further and keep his nose clean but found himself feeling inadequate at times when he had to deal with the Inspector. He knew he wasn't alone feeling as he did, but when faced with Skinner's black mood, he struggled to maintain his composure.

"What do mean, *more or less*. Do we have them or not?" came the angry reply.

"There are three outstanding," he replied, looking at the notes that he had placed on the table in front of him. "Seems like the three men concerned, are all in the same place in Valencia on a golfing trip for a week. We checked with HK Customs and Immigration, and they left the day after the murder. We've followed up with the wives and partners, and it seems the booking was made some eight months ago. We are confirming that now Sir with the applicable travel agency, but according to the wives, it's been an annual event for the past seven or eight years."

"Bloody convenient," was Skinner's response. "Anything else?"

"No Sir. Just highlighting though that we have checked all the statements, from the guests, visitors, and staff and they all seem to check out. No one appears to have seen anything unusual. No one really spent any time with the victim that evening, and no one was aware of any threats having been made either."

Skinner sighed. He knew this case would be difficult, and it wasn't one that he needed. He wanted easy cases. He wanted to be cruising. Let the 'newbies' work their arses off for thirty years, and see if they could stick it out as he had. He doubted they would. The younger generation was soft and wanted everything done for them.

He failed to see the irony of his thinking concerning his career. Skinner felt he knew the answer in his *waters*, in his gut instinct, and that one of the guests was the murderer. He felt a name on the list of attendees who would have given a statement, was the likely killer.

"Well I think someone," he waved a finger in Carpenter's direction, "is lying!" he spat. "We need to get onto our Spanish colleagues as soon as we have finished here, and get statements from those three sunning themselves on the 'cost-a-bomb' asap. And if something doesn't smell right, bring them back immediately!" he emphasized. "Also check those statements again. Someone must have seen something – bloody hell!" He threw his hands up in the air in exasperation.

"Yes Sir," responded the Constable, feeling as if he had just been through three rounds inside a boxing ring.

"Quick!" called out the Inspector, "what have you got for us that made you late?"

As Quick opened his mouth to speak, Skinner interjected by turning to the Liaison Officer, and without being aware or caring about sensitivities said, "sorry Anne love, could you get me a coffee please, I'm bloody parched in this room." He held a hand across his throat for a second, then said, "And maybe a chocolate biscuit as well?" He smiled, cocking his head slightly to one side. All in the room could see the lack of sincerity in his demeanour.

Anne Flowers stood up, considered protesting, and then looked towards the others as if to ask whether anyone else wanted something.

"Well, what are you waiting for love?" enquired Skinner, "get on with it, we haven't got all day!"

Flowers left the room with a disgusted look on her face and deliberately closed the door behind her. The others, not surprised that Skinner had not asked them if they had wanted anything, just looked around in different directions. Some at the table, some at the ceiling, and others just stared towards the wall. Each of them with their own thoughts, but all desperate to get out of the room.

Turning back to Quick, Skinner gave a subtle nod, like Caesar acknowledging a champion gladiator before the slaves entered the collseum to fight for their lives.

Quick opened the file that he had brought with him.

Clearing his throat and addressing the wider team, rather than just Skinner, he said, "I have a couple of things here that came in overnight that are of interest, but I've only had a chance to take a brief look at them." He stopped for a second to make sure he had everyone's attention, then continued. "We have the toxicology report from the lab, and some initial findings from the forensics boys that includes a report on the content of the phone found at the scene, plus some information about the financial position of the family."

"Ok, that's a good start," said Skinner, "so go on, share…," he nodded towards the rest of the room. "I'm sure everyone here, is waiting with bated breath."

The sarcasm in Skinner's voice was not lost on Quick. He knew Skinner had been through it all before, and that after all these years Skinner was bored with the process, but that he had to go through it anyway. Skinner would have preferred to pull people in off the street that he felt were the key suspects, and 'pressurize' them until he got an outcome.

Policing wasn't like that anymore. Too many smart lawyers. So things needed to be done properly, by the book, in order to get a result.

"Forensics have been unable to turn up anything useful so far. It seems the golf club used to attack Crabb with, was one of his own," he said. "He had left the bag in a corner of the clubhouse near the bar when he went in for a drink, and that's where we eventually found it. From what we can conclude from the 'prints' taken, it seems that whoever used it to strike him down, was wearing gloves." he continued.

The room stayed silent as Quick carried on. "As we know it's not unusual to see people holding a golf club while wearing gloves, so someone carrying his club wouldn't easily have stood out." He looked at Skinner who did not seem to be listening at all. "In addition," he went on, "even the footprints around the area have not yet provided us anything useful to follow up on. With the rain that day, it didn't help at all." He paused to clear his throat that was becoming scratchy in the stifling heat of the room. "Finally, toxicology wise, analysis has shown that the deceased was being treated for arthritis using prednisolone, a steroid. This is not uncommon in sportsmen like golfers, especially as they often suffer muscle or bone degeneration in the back, knee's and hands over time. However, he had no other drugs in his system, not even for cholesterol or blood pressure, which means that one can conclude that he was pretty much a picture of health."

"Any alcohol Sir?" called out Carpenter.

"He had consumed a little alcohol, but certainly not enough to be drunk or be unaware of what was going on around him. From what we can gather it seems he was generally pretty responsible and took his position as the club golf-pro pretty seriously, so being inebriated in public was a big 'no-no' in his and the clubs' eyes."

"So," Skinner said, "a clean-living man it seems. So why would anyone want to kill him hey?"

"Well here is where it gets interesting Sir," responded Quick, "the boys from forensics have found a couple of items on the phone that are worth pursuing."

This piqued the interest of the room. It always caused a murmur of excitement when anything that the team could get their teeth into, and which would move the case along, was revealed.

"Ok, ok," said Skinner, silencing the room with a raised hand, just as the Liaison officer entered the room with his coffee. She placed the polystyrene cup in front of him and sat down with folded arms and a very unattractive pout of her lips. Skinner ignored her body language and nodded a cursory *'thank you'* in her general direction as he took his first sip.

"It seems," continued Quick, "that apart from regular calls to and from his wife, the club, and some other numbers that are being followed up on as we speak, he was receiving calls from an unknown number or a series of unknown numbers that appear to have started about three or four months ago and ..."

"Girlfriend?" called out someone.

The room burst into an explosion of laughter and brief chatter. Most of those present had heard this story about unknown numbers, on phones before.

"Quiet!" shouted Skinner, silencing the room.

Waiting a few seconds before continuing, Quick said. "Maybe. But the analytics team, of which Scott here," he pointed at the IT specialist sitting next to Anne Flowers, "is a member of, are of the view that it's highly unlikely."

"Why?" Constable Carpenter queried.

"Maybe I should let Scott answer that."

The focus of attention in the room turned to the man whose entire being personified the classic IT nerd. Scott Mason was a short man, no taller than five foot six. He had a mop of dark unruly hair that had probably last seen a comb when he had been forced to use one in high school. He was almost as round, as he was tall. While others found the room extremely warm, he sat at the table with a brown cardigan on buttoned to the neck, under which he wore a cotton red and black checked shirt He wore dark beige chino trousers and black loafers. From a distance, he could have been mistaken for a camel, the way his back bent over. In his early thirties, he seemed to be in a state of constantly peering over a keyboard and staring at a screen, even when there was neither in front of him.

"We've done some analysis on the data that we have been able to extract from the phone records of Mr. Crabb," he proudly announced, "and there are three strings of information that we have been able to establish so far. I must point out though that the data we have analyzed, is just from the last twelve months." He stopped for a second for effect. It wasn't often he was *'given the stage'* so he wanted to extract all he could from it.

"Get on with it lad," implored Skinner, showing his displeasure at all the theatrics.

"Sorry Sir, yes, well…." he stammered. "Firstly, the majority of calls made and received were to and from family members. There are regular patterns of calls to his wife and his parent's home, and his place of work. These include early morning and late evening calls, weekends as well. But these latter calls were quite limited in number. This would make sense given his job. Secondly, there is a regular series of calls every Thursday and Sunday to a group of phone numbers that we have been able to establish were friends of the deceased. In recent weeks though these calls seemed to have been more than once a day. At times they seem to have been as many as ten times a day. These all range from a few minutes to the longest one being around forty minutes."

"And is that long one also a recent call?" enquired Skinner.

"Yes, it was just the night before the murder," said Quick.

"And do we know who to?"

"Yes, one of his golfing friends. A Mr. Alex Wilson, businessman," relayed Mason.

"Ok," noted Skinner.

Turning to Quick, Skinner commented, "I think we need to pay Mr. Wilson a visit don't you?" The question being rhetorical, not needing an answer. "I'm sure he can explain what a forty-minute conversation was about? A bit coincidental though that it occurred so soon before the murder and as you know," he faced the room and through gritted teeth said, "you all understand how I feel about coincidence."

The room nodded as one in acknowledgment.

"Anything else?" he continued, as he finished his coffee.

"Sir," answered Mason, "probably the most important part of our analysis. Remember I said there were three strings?"

Issuing a sigh, followed by an expletive under his breath, Skinner indicated that Mason could continue.

"The third set of calls seems just to have been one way. *Incoming*," relayed Mason. The excitement in his voice becoming more obvious.

"So what does that mean?" Skinner responded. "It could have been crank calls, cold callers, scammers, anyone. If I got calls from those bastards, I'd just ignore them as well, and I certainly wouldn't call them back!"

"Well the interesting thing here Sir, is how often these calls were received by the deceased. Mostly cold callers or nuisance calls are irregular, sometimes every few days, or a couple of weeks apart, but certainly not at the same time every day as these were. Plus one can normally trace the number through the carrier provided detail if it was from a landline, but these calls weren't."

"Go on," Skinner said, finding the information more and more intriguing as Mason spoke. "I'm not sure what are you telling me."

"It seems the calls were from pre-paid mobiles, so we don't know who they belonged to, but what we do know, is where the calls were made from."

"And where was that?"

"South Africa!"

"What!" came the bellowed response, "Are you trying to tell me that calls from ten thousand kilometers away, were from someone who could have been involved in the murder we are investigating here?" shouted Skinner.

"Yes Sir."

"And when did the last one take place then?" It was clear to the room that Skinner had almost had enough of Mason's comments and opinion.

"The night of the murder, about nine pm."

Skinner let out a roar, the room responded with each attendee remaining frozen in their chairs or where they stood.

"What the fuck is this Mason? Are you trying to tell me that someone calls Crabb at 9 pm, all the way from South Africa, and then in less than a few hours is involved in bludgeoning him to death with a golf club? What makes you think that?"

"I don't Sir. I'm just pointing out the data from the pattern of calls on the mobile phone."

"My God," said Skinner in frustration.

"However Sir," went on Mason, "there is something else related to these calls that we were able to tie up, and hence why I wanted to highlight this to you, no matter how implausible it may seem."

"And what is that?" came the reply from Skinner, rolling his eyes heavenwards.

"We have been able to extract a recording from the phone's voicemail that ties in with the time that the calls from South Africa were received."

Skinner pondered this for a second.

"You mean to tell me, that the caller left a message on Crabb's phone?"

"Yes Sir."

"And you are 100% certain, that the recording was made at the time the phone records show there was an incoming call from South Africa?"

"Absolutely."

Skinner looked stunned. Maybe this was the breakthrough he needed?

"And is this recording the only one?" he continued.

"No, there are several. All left on voicemail, but they are all the same."

One of the group standing near the filing cabinets raised a hand and asked a question that had been on the mind of most of the people in the room. "Do the recordings imply any threats? A reason why the caller was contacting the deceased?"

"No," said Mason, "nothing at all like that."

"Well then, what use are they?" implored Skinner.

Quick jumped into the conversation to save Mason from further punishment, just like a referee would do, as one boxer was being pummeled by another and was unable to defend himself.

"Sir, I think we should listen to the recordings first, and then based on that, perhaps we need to meet with Mrs. Crabb, to see if she can shed any light on these calls. See if her husband had mentioned anything to her. What do you think?"

"As good a place to start as any," mumbled Skinner. Turning to Mason he said, "right lad let's hear it."

Mason opened his laptop. Hit a few keys and waited, conscious of those around him anticipating what he was about to share. Once the machine had come out of sleep mode, he clicked on a file marked *'Recordings'* within a *music folder* and turned the volume up on the machine.

Without any introduction, music came out of the laptop speakers. The sound was quite tinny, like something played from a distance. It played for 12 seconds, and then suddenly stopped with the sound of a phone being disconnected.

Everyone in the room looked towards Skinner for his reaction. His face remained passive, yet slight bemusement played at the corners of his mouth. Eventually, he said, "Play it again."

The room remained silent as the music played a second time. Twelve seconds in, it stopped with the phone being put down. It was clear that it was a pop/rock song of sorts. It seemed like the opening bars or the introduction to a song but as there were no vocals, no words, unless one knew the song itself it was almost impossible to know the tune's name.

"And this is from Crabb's phone yes?" Skinner enquired.

"Yes."

"Are there any more, recordings I mean?"

Quick answered on behalf of Mason. "Well we have three recordings from the phone, and they are all the same."

"Exactly the same?"

"Well there are slight differences, in that one is eleven and a half seconds long, the other just shy of thirteen. And then of course there is this first one we have just heard, which was exactly twelve seconds long," responded Quick.

"And it's the same tune, same piece?"

"Yes," replied Mason.

"Any idea what it is?"

Mason smiled, a glint of excitement in his eye. He looked around at the room. He hadn't had a chance to share his findings until now as he only had access to the recording for a few hours after the forensics team had passed it on overnight. "One of the advantages of modern-day technology Sir is that even if we don't know what the music is called, we can always find out."

Skinner's eyes again rolled in his head. "Spare me," he mumbled to himself, "pray tell," he said.

"Well, there are several pieces of software available today that can be used. But I used the most common one to identify the piece we just heard. Shazam!"

"So what's it called?" asked Skinner eagerly.

"It's a song called, *'Took you away'* by a band called *'Everyman'*. Seems they were quite popular in the UK for a few years and this was one of their *hits*," said Mason. "I've never heard of it myself before. A bit before my time Sir, unfortunately," he smiled wanly. "It seems they broke up about fifteen years ago having had little success in their final few years together." He looked around the room noticing no one seemed to be aware of the song or the band either.

Skinner turned to Quick and said sarcastically, "You had me going there for a minute, Constable. I thought this was going to be of interest. I'm struggling a bit here. Help me out."

"Well, when Mason here played this to me earlier just after I got in, I did some digging. It seems from what I've picked up from the internet and Facebook that there were five members of the band. They were originally from Newcastle, and it seems that most of them live in the area still, but one of them moved to London for a while and another went to South Africa."

The room suddenly exploded with excitement and a smile spread across Skinners' face. Now we are getting somewhere he thought.

"And what's more," continued Quick, attempting to calm everyone down, "it seems like they are getting together again and reforming. According to their Facebook page, they have been following what's been happening in the music industry, and it appears that there is a liking to hear the music of bands from their era. In fact, the *'nostalgia circuit'* as it's called, seems to want to see bands again from the 1960s onwards."

Skinner considered what he had heard, then said, "Good work Mason. Maybe we have our first real lead in this case, but we also have a number of other things to follow up on as well. So far what we have here," he pointed at the laptop, "is nothing but a start. Let's hope it's not a false one. Get hold of our Geordie colleagues and get them to track down those band members and pull them in for a little chat."

Turning to Quick he said, "Anything else?"

"Just that on the face of it, the family had no financial problems that we can see. We are looking into who benefits from Crabb's death, insurance policies that type of thing so work to be done there. Finally, we have the CCTV footage now and the lab is doing some analysis of that as well. We'll know a bit more later."

Skinner nodded. Too early for a drink but he was starting to feel positive about the case.

Addressing the team, he said, "Right, this is what we need to be doing today, and over the next forty-eight hours…here's my plan…."

Chapter 9

Graham Jefferson was not a well man.

Cannon sat across from him in a small coffee shop, on the opposite side of the road from the Dry Cleaners, Jefferson had owned and ran on Market Square for the past thirteen years. There were a dozen tables available, of which only three including their own, were occupied. Two groups of four women each, sat at separate tables, leaving the two men space to talk without the women hearing what they discussed.

Between them on the table, were the remnants of a small salad that Jefferson had ordered and a large lasagne that Cannon had easily consumed, along with the tea both had shared.

For Cannon, it had been an interesting morning, for although he had effectively handed over control to Rich, he had been unable to let go completely. He had slept in an hour longer than normal and had enjoyed the experience of waking up at the same time as Michelle. She had been allowed the next week off from school duties and was planning to visit Cassie and Wendy later in the day, as well as meet with Rachel and her parents to discuss how long Cassie could stay with them. After breakfast together, he had gone on to the gallops to watch a couple of strings work, and he was particularly interested in how *Mr. Scarecrow* was going, the Cheltenham meeting being just a few days away.

On balance, the horses were all working well, and it seemed that Rich had already started to make his mark. Cannon knew that soon he would have to formalize the arrangements. *'Rich would make a great assistant trainer, in fact, he was good enough to take on my job now,'* he had thought. *Mr. Scarecrow* was in good order, and his training was being tapered back just a little to keep him fresh for the upcoming meeting. Likewise, *Belle o' the Ball* due to run at Southwell in just over a week was beginning to have her work reduced slowly.

"Nice little town, Brackley," Cannon commented to Jefferson. "Though not a place I've been to very often in recent years."

"Gone down a little, to be honest," replied Jefferson, "certainly when you compare it to when I first got here and took on the business. Such a pity really, but I know the council and local chamber of commerce have plans to get more businesses into the wider area through the development of office parks. A pity it won't be in my lifetime though, as everything today seems to take forever to get done."

Cannon had managed to track down Jefferson by calling Jack Winton the events manager at the club, telling him that he was with the police, and asking him if he knew the first names and addresses of both Jefferson and Wilson. While Cannon knew it was a risk calling the club unofficially, he did not use his real name when he spoke to Winton, just indicated he was a DC involved in the case. Winton was happy to oblige, given the impact the murder was having on turnover and bookings, over the past few days, as well as the club's good name more broadly, in local golfing circles. He had willingly provided the information. After all, he knew both men well. In the past having joined up on several occasions with both of them or sometimes just the one of them as required. Sometimes it was to help make up a four-ball in a club competition or sometimes when they were just short a player over a weekend.

So, he had no reason not to provide the details the *'police',* were looking for.

With the information to hand, Cannon had been able to find Jefferson easily, and he had called ahead to say that he would pay him a visit later that day. Again, he had not mentioned he was with the police but did imply it was relevant to an investigation that he was working on. He had stated that he had some questions to ask that needed to be done face to face and he was happy to come to Jefferson rather than have him come to the police station. The implication in the call was strong enough for most people to assume it was an official police request to help them with their inquiries. Jefferson had expressed thanks on the phone that Cannon had agreed to come to him.

After finding parking for his car and walking to Jefferson's shop, it was almost twelve-thirty. Jefferson had been waiting, sitting in a small office at the back of the shop premises, and was called by one of the ladies manning the counter when Cannon arrived.

There had been no other customers when Cannon had walked in, and while he had stood waiting at the counter, he had studied the various racks of clothes standing in lines. Each piece was covered in clear plastic and hanging on wire hangers waiting to be collected. Rows and rows of them. He had counted at least six rows. Cannon was always fascinated with there being so many items passing through the cleaning process, that there were not more mix-ups of items belonging to one person ending up with another than there appeared to be. *'However, whatever system they do use, it does seem to work'* he had mused.

There was another person in the shop that he had seen, besides the woman at the counter. She had been unpacking a machine that stood silent with its great door open, like a giant mouth regurgitating its meal. Three other machines whirled around at various speeds, throwing the clothes within their bellies in an anticlockwise direction, occasionally the items within hitting against the glass doors. Towards the back of the shop, Cannon had heard a radio playing and the regular hiss of an ironing press that someone was using to take out the creases from whatever clothes had been entrusted to the establishment, before they also were covered in plastic, and added to the already bulging rows.

It was obvious to Cannon why Jefferson was happy that he had come to the shop. He was a tall man, around six feet, but he had a belt around his waist drawn in extremely tightly. So much so, that it appeared to be cutting him in half. He wore a dark leather jacket over a red pullover and he was wearing black boots and jeans. He appeared to be in his sixties and his hair was just a thin wisp across his scalp. The skin at his neck was loose like a chicken, and the colour reminded Cannon of brie cheese. His face was sunken in, like someone whose bones had continued to grow while the skin had not. His eyes sat deep within their sockets, and dark lines accentuated them, almost as a cave mouth frames what lies deeper inside the hole.

"How long?" enquired Cannon.

"You mean, how long do I have to live?"

Cannon nodded. Jefferson considered his answer for a few seconds.

"You can tell, can't you? Most can't," he said, almost with a hint of surprise in his voice.

Cannon nodded slightly.

Jefferson waited for a few seconds before he answered Cannon's question. "I guess that really depends on the treatment," he said, "though I'm sure that's not why you came to see me, is it?"

Cannon had seen many people with a terminal illness during his time with the police. He had been trained on how people could react to authority when a family member was ill, injured, or killed, even though the authorities were just trying to help or provide support.

He also knew that on occasion, receivers of bad news, a consequence of an accident, bad luck, or through a terminal illness diagnosis reacted so badly to it, that in some severe cases, they had taken their own lives out of sheer desperation, almost without thinking or rationalizing what it really meant to them or others.

Sometimes people had become so angry that they fought with loved ones, strangers in the street and had completely lost all sense of right and wrong. Others thinking their life was over and that nothing could harm them anymore had gone from law-abiding citizens to petty criminals. Others had gone much further and got into porn or drugs. Some went from teetotallers to raging alcoholics. Effectively they had just given up on life, even to the extent of foregoing treatment. It was something Cannon struggled to understand, but he knew it happened. Human nature was difficult to predict at the best of times.

"No, it's not why I came to see you. As I mentioned on the phone, I wanted to talk to you about a case I am investigating. I wanted to ask you a couple of questions about someone you know, but before I do, is it cancer?" he inquired.

"Yes," came the reply, "from Perchloroethylene poisoning," responded Jefferson sadly.

"Cancer, from a poison, in a Dry Cleaning shop?"

"Yes, cancer of the liver, an indirect consequence of the business. Can you believe it!" More a statement than a question.

Cannon looked somewhat confused.

Jefferson continued. "Dry cleaners use chemicals to clean the clothes. That is why it's called *'dry cleaning'*, no water used. When I first started in this business, I was a novice. I had no experience. I bought the business from a guy who had set up the shop but wanted out within weeks of opening. Seems he didn't like the hours," he chuckled. The laughter in Jefferson's throat suddenly turned to a racking cough.

Cannon stood up and quickly rushed over to a water cooler sitting on a counter near the till. He grabbed a glass, half-filled it with water, and then rushed back over to his table offering it to Jefferson to sip from. For a few seconds, the women's conversation stopped as they looked towards where the men were sitting. Cannon waved them away, and suggested they carry on with their conversation, advising them that everything was, "alright, nothing to see here."

Once Jefferson had relaxed, and his coughing fit was over, he carried on with his story. "Health and safety was always one of those things that I thought applied more to large construction sites, big projects, and such like," he said. "You see, I've lived in this area all my life, so I have never really worked in large businesses. Sure over time I got to realize that as a business owner I needed to be careful about things. Simple things like water on the floor, hot machinery, loose-fitting clothing near presses, and all that sort of thing, but by the time I realized that the chemicals we use could cause cancer, the damage had already been done."

"You mean you were diagnosed *before* you stopped using the chemicals?"

"No," said Jefferson, "I became aware of the dangers when a new rep from the supplier who sold me the chemicals, told me about a training course he had been on and that it was important to handle the product safely."

"And when was that?"

"About seven years ago. Since then I have adopted much better practices in chemical use, storage, and disposal, as well as clothes handling. The problem was….," he said, stopping suddenly. Cannon waited for him to continue, but could see in Jefferson's eyes that he was thinking of past times, then just as suddenly he carried on speaking. "For the six years preceding the warning, while I knew I was dealing with chemicals I didn't realize that spills on my skin, splashes on my face, or even the fumes I was breathing were having any impact."

"So when did you first fall ill?"

"It was just over two years ago," replied the dry-cleaner. "An x-ray found a lesion on my liver and while I still felt ok, it was the start of the end of my life. Look at me now," he said. "When I was first told I had the disease I was thirty-seven years old. I'm nearly forty, but I don't think I'll make it to fifty."

Cannon stayed quiet for a few seconds. He realized that given the way the conversation had gone so far, he hadn't even had the chance to discuss the real reason he wanted to meet with Jefferson.

"I'm so sorry," he said "what's the prognosis?" he inquired.

"I have been on a list for a liver transplant for a year now, but so far have not been able to find a donor with a perfect match. In the interim, I am having treatment but that's almost as bad as the cancer itself," he said. "So while there is no definitive answer to your question, I have in the past four of five months lost lots of weight as you can see. Pretty much skin and bone now," he said pointing at his midriff, "and I have begun to become more and more tired recently. To be honest, no matter what the doctors say, I don't think I have much longer than twelve months, the cancer has spread way too far. He stared at Cannon, his eyes huge, like a rabbit in a spotlight, almost pleading.

Cannon felt sympathy for him knowing how hard it must be for the man's family. He said, "I lost my wife a few years ago, breast cancer. Miss her every day."

"I'm not married, divorced actually," responded Jefferson. "Two kids, but they don't come and see me anymore. It has been three years since I set eyes on any of them. She remarried, moved up to Scotland," a note of disdain in his voice. "Just have a few friends now. Don't go out often anymore either. I do go up to the golf club, Kirtlington," he said, "just go for a drink and conversation nowadays. I used to play up until August but I can't do it now, so I just try to run the business as best I can. It is all I have to be honest. Though I don't think my life is of much interest to the police now is it?"

Cannon noted the change in the topic of conversation and took his opportunity.

"Yes, I'm sorry Mr. Jefferson. I do apologize. I hope you didn't mind my asking about your illness?" he said contritely. "It's just that I noticed that you appeared unwell and I didn't want to just dive into my questions. We do have some compassion you know, though many in the general public may argue otherwise."

Cannon smiled, trying not to let his discomfort at pretending to be in the police force, show in his body language.

"What I wanted to ask you," he continued, "was whether you were aware of the recent death of a Mr. Simon Crabb?"

"Simon?" responded Jefferson. "Dead? When? How?" He reached for the glass of water and finished it in a single swallow. Genuine shock registering on his drawn face.

"I'm not at liberty to go into all the details, but suffice to say we think foul play is involved," Cannon responded. He always found it strange the language they were required to use in the Force but it was deemed necessary to ensure no loophole could be exploited by clever defence lawyers about *'leading witnesses'* or of *'having undue influence'* or *'drawing conclusions without the facts'*.

"My God."

"Are you okay Mr. Jefferson, can I get you some more water?"

"Thank you, that would be good."

Cannon stood up from the table and walked over to the counter to fill the glass again. As he did so, he noticed the dry cleaner shudder as if a ripple of fear had run along the man's spine.

Taking the refilled glass from Cannon, Jefferson drank quickly. Cannon noticed the trembling hands as the glass met the man's lips. A slight dribble of the liquid splashing onto his chin. After wiping it away with the back of his hand, Jefferson said, "Do you think this has anything to do with the strange phone calls Simon was getting?"

"Calls?" enquired Cannon.

"Yes," returned Jefferson, "have you not found Simon's phone yet? He said he was keeping the recordings so that if they continued, he would take them to the police."

On the back foot but trying to imply more than he knew, Cannon responded, "The phone is still being analyzed by the technical team, so we haven't got any information as yet, but it would be useful if you could shed any light on these calls."

Hoping he had gotten away with the bluff, he waited for a response. Jefferson duly obliged.

"Simon was getting calls from someone, but they never said anything on them. Just played the same piece of music down the phone. Alex and I…"

"Alex…?" interjected Cannon.

"Wilson, Alex Wilson. He is a very successful businessman, involved in IT and Website design, stuff like that. He has offices in the Bicester office park on Lakeview Drive, about ten miles away from here, just off the A41. The three of us, Simon, Alex, and I played golf for years together. We've known each other since school days," a smile crossed the man's face, for an instant showing that life had been good to him at one point.

Cannon feigned ignorance of Wilson, but at least he now had concrete confirmation of the linkage between the men.

"So did Mr. Crabb have any idea who may have been making the calls to him?"

"No, it seems the number was blocked or something."

"So he had no idea at all?"

"No, but we did speculate." A twinkle appeared in Jefferson's eye. He continued saying, "Simon wasn't exactly the perfect husband shall we say," the forthright comment seemingly contrary to the view Cannon had formed through his conversations with Rachel Crabb. Though, as he thought about that first meeting in the car park, something still bothered him.

The inference in what Cannon heard from Jefferson made him dig a little deeper. "You mean he messed around?"

"Big-time," came the reply.

"Do you think his wife knew?"

"Not sure, but I'd be surprised if she didn't. She is a very smart woman. A Lawyer."

"Yes I know," replied Cannon.

"You have met her?"

"Within twenty-four hours of the investigation starting," he said. Another lie to maintain the illusion of his official capacity in the case. "She has been most cooperative so far."

Jefferson remained quiet for a few seconds, then said, "We, Alex and I, told Simon that he had better be careful. That whoever he was screwing may have an extremely jealous husband or partner and maybe he was trying to warn him off?"

"What did he say?"

"He just laughed it off. It was not the first time he had been threatened you know. Simon had been messing around for years. Said he would just ignore it, dump the woman concerned and move on to the next."

Cannon considered this. If Rachel Crabb was aware of her husband's ongoing adultery, she certainly hid it well. "And what of this music you said was left on the phone? Did he let you hear it?"

"Yes, both of us had a listen. Didn't mean anything to us though," he shrugged.

Cannon noticed the man opposite him had stopped trembling. He got the impression that with the *'police'* now involved in the investigation, Jefferson felt more at ease. As if the secret threats that someone had made to Crabb, that both he and Wilson were aware of, were no longer something he needed to keep hidden within himself.

"Well thank you Mr. Jefferson for your assistance in this matter. We may need to speak to you again at some point, but for now, I think the information you have provided has been very useful."

"Thank you, officer," came the reply.

The men stood up, Cannon holding out a hand to assist Jefferson. After paying the bill he watched Jefferson slowly cross the road and go back into his shop, as he did so Cannon noticed him put a mobile phone to his ear and begin talking.

Cannon strode off towards his car. A few yards from the vehicle, his own mobile phone rang.

"Hello," he said, not bothering to check who was calling.

"Hi, boss," Rich Telside's worried voice came down the line. "Can you get back home as soon as you can, we've got a problem…"

Chapter 10

The offices of *INet Solutions* were salubrious when compared to the '*hole*' that Skinner and his team were required to work in.

It was places like this, in Skinner's mind, that justified him spending more time out of the office, and in the King's Head. He took the view that given his standing and experience he deserved better than he was getting. The cuts in budgets over recent years had not only impacted the number of staff in the Force but had also impacted the capital spend available for new facilities and equipment. This environment was more to his liking. While he didn't like the colour scheme, he liked the feeling of power. There was money here.

He sat next to Quick, on a three-seater bright green leather couch in the reception area. It was late afternoon and was already dark outside. Lights from passing cars could be seen through the gloom as one looked out from the glass-fronted building. The rain had held off, but it was still cold. Winter was still a month away, but she was sending out early warnings.

Despite this, the receptionist still looked like she had just walked into the building only five minutes before. She had greeted them with a huge smile, and when told that they were there to see *Mr. Wilson,* she had asked them cordially to "please take a seat," and had pointed them in the direction of the couch. She had then sat down at a white single bench desk and began to tap away on a keyboard while observing something on a flat-screen monitor.

Skinner observed her as they waited. She had almost perfect white teeth. He noticed she was tall and incredibly slim. She had on black high heel shoes that must have given her an extra three inches in height and wore a red pencil skirt which sat around narrow hips, topped by a white blouse open to the third button. Around her throat sat a pink cotton scarf. Under her almost white-blond hair that looked like it was cut with razor blades and extremely short, her make-up and lipstick were still perfect, something that Skinner struggled to understand how, given the lateness of the day.

"Mr. Wilson won't be long," she said, indicating the earpiece and tiny microphone that sat in her left ear. While Skinner didn't notice, Quick realized that her headset was wireless, allowing her to move around the reception area freely, while still talking to visitors and communicating with others on the phone or via her computer. "Could I offer you, gentlemen, some tea, coffee, a soft drink, or water in the meantime?"

Both of the policemen shook their heads simultaneously. The receptionist just smiled.

"What do you think?" said Skinner through half-closed lips, indicating the surroundings with his eyes. Apart from the reception desk and the couch they were sitting on, there was a small alcove to their left containing a small bar fridge packed with soft drinks, expensive branded water, and various types of milk in half litre bottles. A silver coffee and tea-making machine stood atop a counter directly above the fridge, and along one side of the counter stood rows of glass containers with various types of biscuits, health bars, and nuts within them. Also below the countertop, there were cupboard doors to the left of the fridge that Skinner speculated may have held a cutlery draw and a dustbin.

Quick had another look around and then said, "Not sure boss, but this place doesn't come cheap. Must be doing pretty well."

Suddenly, a door opened just behind the right shoulder of the receptionist. The door was flush to the wall and had the same patterned patina as the wall in which it stood. If one didn't know it was there, it would have been impossible to have guessed that it was there at all.

A middle-aged man walked through the door, he was carrying a computer bag on one shoulder, clearly heading home. He walked straight towards the receptionist from behind, touched her briefly on the arm, and then continued walking towards the entrance to the building that just a short while earlier, Skinner and Quick had entered through.

"Bye Cheryl," he said, "have a good evening dear. Don't stay out too late."

"Bye Greg," she answered, "see you tomorrow."

"No you won't *dear*," he responded, "I have a few days off. Phil and I are off to Devon for a long weekend. Can't wait," he said, clearly excited. "See you later, Ciao."

Cheryl just smiled.

Skinner and Quick had observed the interaction but said nothing. It was an open society now, not that Skinner was happy with it, but he had to live with it. He would be glad when he had retired and could move away to a place with fewer people. People he hoped, would be more normal and more private about themselves. It seemed everyone today was way too happy to share information about themselves that others didn't need, or want, to know.

"Nice man," she said, nodding in the direction of the departed colleague.

"I'll bet," replied Skinner, his mood having changed, reflecting the bile he felt inside given what he had just seen and heard. "Look," he continued, "Miss...err,"

"Mossman," she said, her smile still intact, "and it's Mrs. actually." She waved her left hand for Skinner to see her ring finger.

"Well Mrs. Mossman, can you hurry Mr. Wilson along, please? We haven't got all day!" his voice rising, mirroring his temper.

Quick tried to engage Skinner in conversation, but Skinner ignored him and stood up, walking menacingly towards the reception desk. Just as he reached it, the same door that '*Greg*' had come out from opened up, and Alex Wilson walked into the reception area.

"Gentleman, so sorry to have kept you," he said sounding genuinely sincere. "Please accept my apologies, I was just on a conference call with the US, and it ran overtime."

Skinner, though not impressed with Wilson's excuse, introduced himself and Quick, both men showing their official police badges.

Nodding in acknowledgement, he continued, saying, "Please follow me," then indicated that they should use the door that he had come through, that was still partially ajar.

They walked down a passage with offices on their left and a large open plan section on their right. The latter filled with banks of computer monitors on top of desks, and at which sat numerous people, mostly in their mid to early twenties, with their heads down and their fingers flying across keyboards.

"I hope Cheryl looked after you while you were waiting?" he said, peering behind him as he led the way.

"Yes, she did Sir," responded Quick. "Thank you."

"No problem," came the reply, "Ah, here we are. I hope you don't mind, but I thought we could use the boardroom if that's ok?"

The three men stopped as Wilson placed a keycard against a reader on the wall, to the right of the door. The door then clicked, and he invited them to go in ahead of him. As they crossed the threshold, the lights in the room came on.

"Motion-activated. Saves money, much more efficient," said Wilson. "Please sit down," he gestured.

Once Skinner and Quick had removed their coats and settled themselves in their chairs, Wilson said, "Well gentlemen, how can I help? Your call to my PA earlier, from what she told me, suggested you wanted to talk to me about Simon Crabb. Is that correct officers? What's he been up to now?" he said smiling.

Skinner studied the man. He was clearly very successful as could be seen by his surroundings, and he had an aura about him that gave the impression of self-confidence and success.

He was wearing a blue checked shirt, unbuttoned at the throat, expensive-looking cufflinks in the shape of crossed golf clubs at the wrists. There was an air of contradiction and a sense of informality about him, given his designer jeans and black brogue shoes. He had removed his jacket when he asked them to sit down at the table, throwing it casually onto the chair next to him. He placed his mobile phone on the table, turning it face down.

Wilson was a big man. Attractive features. A handsome face, under a thick head of dark, almost black hair. Clean-shaven, a small scar down the left-hand side of his face just above the jaw. His nose was short, but his eyes were deep and dark, almost impossible to judge the colour. He also had an unusually large head and neck with powerful biceps. His chest and thighs indicated that he worked out, or at least used to. *'It seems almost incongruous that he is in I.T.'* thought Skinner. *'I.T. is a world full of geeks'*.

"Unfortunately Sir," said Quick, "Mr. Crabb is dead. Murdered."

"What?" the big man sat up in his chair, almost getting to his feet. His response, combined with his bulk would have intimidated many. The two policemen had interviewed many individuals over the years and many did the unexpected when faced with similar revelations. They remained passive.

Wilson put his hand over his mouth as if by doing so he would be able to control his emotions. "Oh. My. God," he said, each syllable spoken slowly from behind his hand. "What a bloody mess."

Leaning forward slowly, Skinner spoke, "You don't seem surprised Mr. Wilson, or am I misinterpreting?"

Wilson put his hand down, bringing both together and resting them on the table in front of him.

"I'm, I'm so shocked. I can't believe it," he stammered, "I only saw Simon a couple of weeks ago when we last played a round together," he pointed at his cufflinks. "You see I only got back from LA yesterday, hence why I was on the call earlier. So this...this, well it's just mind-numbing. How did it happen?" he went on.

"We are not at liberty to say," responded Skinner. "Not at this stage of the investigation anyway. However, what I can say, is that he was attacked and killed at the Kirtlington Golf Club. What we are trying to find out are the last known movements of Mr. Crabb, and more importantly, trying to understand why someone would want to kill him."

"And you think I can help?"

"Well we know you are, sorry were, very good friends with Mr. Crabb. From our inquiries to date, we understand that you played golf with him regularly and we hope that you may be able to provide us with some information, no matter how trivial. Perhaps you could tell us about Mr. Crabb's mindset when you last saw him?"

Skinner paused letting Wilson take in what he had said. Wilson just looked back at him.

Quick noted, "We have been able to establish that Mr. Crabb had been receiving some strange phone calls of late, did he ever mention that to you at all?"

"Yes he did," replied Wilson, "he told all of us at the same time when we were in the bar at the club. I think it was about a month ago."

"All of us?" questioned Skinner. "Could you be more precise?"

"Sure. As I said, about a month ago after we had finished our normal Saturday round at the club."

"That club being Kirtlington?" interjected Quick, "I just want to be clear Sir."

"Yes, Kirtlington," repeated Wilson. "Simon told us about these phone calls he was receiving. Apparently, no messages left, just music. Short pieces of music."

"Did he play you the recording?"

"Yes he did, but none of us recognized it. Didn't seem to make any sense."

"And the others were......?" encouraged Skinner, giving a sideways glance to Quick.

"Sorry, yes, umm, well it was me. Graham Jefferson, a friend of ours for years, owns and runs a Dry-Cleaner's in Bicester, though unfortunately not very well at the moment. Greg Carr, he works for me here, you may have seen him leave a few minutes ago and the other person with us was…was…," he hesitated for a few seconds appearing to struggle to remember the offending name. Eventually he said, "ahh yes, I remember now. The other person was Jack Winton."

"The events manager at the club?" said Quick.

"Yes, that's right. Have you met him?"

"Indeed we have."

"So what did Mr. Crabb say he was going to do about these phone calls?" interrupted Skinner, trying to bring the conversation back to where it needed to be.

"To be honest Inspector, I think we all just laughed it off. Simon wasn't taking it seriously, and none of us thought he should do either."

"Well clearly perhaps he should have?" retorted Skinner.

"Hindsight is a fine thing Inspector. But we all know that the police are so stretched at times, that even if he did report it, he would likely have gotten the reply that as no crime had been committed, there was nothing the police could do. Am I right?" Wilson commented, knowingly.

Skinner noticed Wilson's eyes began to grow darker, colder, contemptuous, his body language changing instantly from friendliness, to being distant and closed. It was clear that Wilson had little time for the police. Skinner's hackles started to rise. Self-made men often pissed him off because of their superior attitude. Their success often achieved by stepping on others. He got the impression that Wilson was one of those people. He did not like the man.

"I suspect Mr. Wilson that the reaction received, would depend on the facts as presented. If Mr. Crabb feared for his life or property then I am sure the applicable Superintendent would have done his best, based on the assessed risk, to provide all the necessary resources he could, to ensure Mr. Crabb or his family, were not put in any danger."

Wilson gave out a snort.

Skinner ignored the outburst. "Was there anything else bothering Mr. Crabb that you were aware of Mr. Wilson. Anything at all that he may have mentioned in passing, or you could gather from his behaviour?"

"No, nothing Inspector."

"Are you sure?" asked Skinner, pushing a little harder.

"Yes, absolutely. Look, Inspector, Simon Crabb was not perfect, but he certainly did not deserve to be murdered. He was well respected as a golf professional at the club, and he was well-liked by the members there."

"But..." Skinner let the statement hang in mid-air.

"But what?"

"If he wasn't perfect, what were his weaknesses then?" Skinner smiled, hiding how he really felt about Wilson. "Did he gamble, drink? We all have them, Mr. Wilson."

"Inspector, I am not one to throw stones. Simon was a good friend of mine, and I am extremely upset to hear about his death. I hope you understand that?" Continuing he said, "I can assure you I am not aware of any reason, or of anyone, who would want to harm him."

"Do you think the strange calls he was receiving could be relevant now, Mr. Wilson?"

Wilson sighed. "Perhaps Inspector, but maybe that is *your* job to find out," he said emphasizing where he believed the focus should be. "Rather than *you* asking *me* to speculate."

Skinner took the hint and decided for now that he had gotten about as much as he could from Wilson.

"Well, thank you, Sir, for your time," he stood up, extending a hand.

Quick and Wilson rose from the table simultaneously. Wilson shook Skinner's and Quick's hands in succession.

"I'm sorry I can't be of much more help, Inspector," he said.

"We understand," Skinner replied, "if we need to, we'll get back in touch."

They walked down the passageway, and to the door through which they had originally come. Wilson shook their hands again and they said their goodbyes. He let them walk into the reception area that was now empty, but he did not follow. He closed the door quickly behind them.

As they walked out into the darkness of early evening, Skinner turned to Quick saying, "He's lying. He knows more than he's telling. Something is going on that he's not sharing. I can just feel it in my bones."

Quick just nodded.

As they walked to their car, silhouetted against the orange glow of the street lamps in the car park, soft specks of sleet began to fall.

As they climbed into their seats, Skinner said, "Let's go for a drink, there are a couple of things we need to have a chat about."

Chapter 11

"What happened?" asked Cannon, to Rich Telside.

They were standing in front of *Katmandu's* locked stall. Outside, the sleet had turned to steady rain, the sound of water gushing down the drainpipes at each end of the stables.

The attending vet had gone off to make a phone call, to arrange transport for the horse who was standing quietly inside his stall, despite being highly distressed.

A head collar had been put on, effectively immobilizing the horse. This was in the animals' best interest by restricting his movement. The vet had used painkillers to settle the horse down, but his racing days were over.

"He was doing extremely well," responded Rich. "Sean was taking him over his fences and he was going beautifully. Then between two fences, Sean felt the horse suddenly stumble and favour his near-side. He got off straight away as he knew the horse was in trouble."

"What did the vet say?"

"Well, once we had managed to get the horse back into his box, he was here very quickly. He had a look and knew straight away. Confirmed my own view. The poor horse has shattered a fetlock joint in his off-side hind leg."

"Shit!" exclaimed Cannon.

"I've been in touch with the owners already. Told them the news," he said. "Also, I've let them know that the horse will need to be put down."

"I'll give them a call later myself," said Cannon "did they say anything else?"

"Not really. They said that they understood that things like this happen in racing, but they are disappointed because they thought they would have some fun with him, and that's all over now."

"And Sean?"

"Well to be fair, I think he is devastated too. I told him that none of this was his fault, but you may recall he had been working with him for quite a while. Schooling him, teaching him the ropes, and I think they had a good bond."

"Where is he now?" asked Cannon.

"He's gone home. A while ago. I told him not to worry too much. I'm sure he'll be fine."

As they concluded their conversation, the vet walked towards them from where he had been making arrangements to have *Katmandu* collected.

"Hello David," said Cannon to the vet, "not much hope I understand."

"None," replied David Bright. "He's cut tendons, nerves, and severed blood vessels on the ragged pieces of bone in that leg. Don't even need to feel it, you can see how much damage there is," he continued nodding at the horse. "Poor fella" he concluded.

Cannon sighed. The offer by Joe Crabb to put a number of horses with him once his son's murder had been solved, was now essential for the stable to grow.

"We were just talking about how the owners had taken the news. I know them well as they have been patrons of mine almost from day one. I feel sorry for them as I think he could have done quite well. I know he's insured, but that will be of little comfort."

"I understand," replied Bright, "but in this game, you have to expect the unexpected. Anyway, let me crack on and get this over with," he said, nodding towards *Katmandu*.

Euthanizing a horse, or any animal, was something vets had to become used to. It was part of the job but was never really something vets enjoyed doing.

As Bright went into the stall, Cannon turned to Rich. "I'll sort out the paperwork for Weatherby's tomorrow, and send *Katmandu*'s passport back as well. With it being Friday tomorrow, I suspect they will get it by Monday or Tuesday next week, so that's well within their thirty-day time limit. I'd like to get it done quickly so I don't forget, so if you could get it for me asap Rich, that would be great."

"No problem Mike," he said.

"Any good news *at all* for me?" enquired Cannon.

"Only to tell you that I think *Mr. Scarecrow* is ready for Cheltenham on Saturday and will run a great race. In fact, I think the lads are planning a bit of a plunge on him, to be honest. *Belle o' the Ball* is also coming along really well for Southwell next week. The rest are at various stages, but I think we'll be seeing a few winners shortly."

"I hope so Rich," said Cannon. "It would be good to add to our eighteen winners so far this season. Between now and the end of the season I'm hoping to get to about forty, forty-five. If we do that, it will be our best season to date," he smiled.

"That *would* be good," responded Telside.

"And hopefully a few more owners, or a few more horses," Cannon said, thinking of the commitment he had from Joseph Crabb.

Once back inside the house, Cannon's mood started to improve slowly. While he was upset about losing *Katmandu*, he knew he had to be philosophical about it. He had seen it happen before when he worked for Charlie Barnes, and he had seen the impact that a disappointed owner could have on a trainer's livelihood or reputation if they tried to blame the trainer for the loss of their animal.

As he reviewed the day, he realized he was very lucky. The owners concerned had accepted the loss as part of the game, and for that, he was grateful.

He also considered that he had made reasonable progress with Graham Jefferson, and he had an idea about the next steps he wanted to take in the investigation.

Sitting at the dining room table, he and Michelle discussed what had happened with *Katmandu*. Michelle was saddened to hear that the horse had to be destroyed, and he mentioned to her that after dinner he would call the owners, and give his apologies. Then he told her what he had found out from Jefferson.

"So do you think Crabb was killed by a jealous husband or boyfriend?" she inquired.

"I guess it looks that way," he responded, "but what surprises me, is that it appears as though Crabb was known to be playing around, yet Rachel didn't say anything about it to the police nor me. Either when we had coffee, or during the taking of her statement."

"Well it is very personal," said Michelle. "Would you want all our dirty laundry aired in public?" she smiled.

He took her hand in his, saying, "No I wouldn't, but I think this is different. Her husband was murdered and it seems to me that it has something to do with their relationship. When I met her the other day at the school, something about the whole meeting didn't make sense to me and I still can't put my finger on it."

"Talking of that," she replied, "I went to see Cassie today. I took her some clothes and she said she was happy to spend the rest of the weekend there, but she wants to come home soon. Ideally on Monday night. I'm not sure if I told you," she went on, "but because it's half term she doesn't want to be at Wendy's the whole time, so she asked if Wendy could come here for a few days."

"Oh, that's great" Cannon responded.

"Yes, probably just as well, as I understand from Rachel that the funeral for her husband, is scheduled for next Thursday."

"Oh, so the coroner and the police have given the authority to release the body?"

"I guess so."

"Okay, thanks." He reflected on this for a few seconds.

"In addition," she went on, "Cassie told me that Wendy appears to be over the shock of losing her father and seems to be accepting it now. With her Grandparent's love, and the support that they have been providing, both Wendy and her mother appear to be slowly getting their lives back on track."

"Cassie can be very perceptive," he said.

"That's true," she agreed, "but I still think her perceptions about you and I are not right."

"How do you mean?"

"Well, as we discussed the other night, I still think she hopes our relationship is not permanent."

Cannon sighed, trying not to sound too impatient. "Darling, as I told you then and I'll repeat it again. *We are a couple*. No matter what, Cassie will *not* come between us. So please put that out of your mind," he implored. "When she gets back here after the weekend, I'll have a chat with her and make it clear where everybody stands. Is that ok?"

Michelle shrugged her shoulders. "Ok" she responded. A few seconds later she smiled, saying, "You win." Cannon reached over, hugging her to himself.

"Good. Let me quickly make that call to the owners of *Katmandu,* and let them know how sorry I am about the poor horse. I'm sure they are not exactly over the moon right now," he suggested, "and then, what do you say we leave the dishes until the morning and have an early night?"

"That will be a great idea."

"Good," he said, his mood returning to a more positive state. "I'll see you up there shortly."

Chapter 12

After another late breakfast, Cannon had gone up to the gallops to watch his second and third-string work.

The events of the previous day, and the loss of *Katmandu* still played on his mind. However, once the lifeless body of the animal had been removed and the stall cleaned out, he and his staff moved on to the activities of the day. This was racing, and sometimes death, was, unfortunately, part of it. It was a cliché, but life *did* go on, no matter what trials and tribulations each person had, even in their own lives.

Despite his best intentions to let Rich do most of the work while he investigated the murder of Crabb, once back in his office, Cannon went online to confirm the actions needed, and the associated paperwork required, surrounding *Katmandu*'s death.

He then completed the necessary correspondence with all the details from vet David Bright's report, took the horse's passport that Rich had brought in for him, and put them all in an envelope to post off to Weatherby's, the official body managing registrations of all thoroughbred horses in Britain and Ireland.

He then called Rachel Crabb, who was still at her in-law's home and agreed to meet with her at her own house around three in the afternoon. They decided that it was best for Cannon not to go to her in-law's house where Wendy and Cassie were but rather meet elsewhere. The obvious place suggested by Rachel was her own place, as she needed to collect a few personal things anyway, and she had some work in her study that she needed to follow up on. She gave Cannon the address.

Finally, he made a call to Alex Wilson's office.

He was put through to Wilson's *assistant,* and he asked for an appointment to see him. The PA advised him that she had been away from work the whole of the week given Mr. Wilson had been travelling, and she was just back in the office that day. So she was still checking his diary to determine what spare time he may have. Cannon made his request to meet Wilson sound official, and was able to convince the PA that he was available to meet with Wilson at lunchtime for an hour at *INet Solutions* premises if that would help?

Upon confirmation by the PA of the time, he realized that he needed to get a move on if he wanted to get there by one o'clock.

Sitting in Wilson's office was an uncomfortable experience for Cannon. He tried to hide his discomfort as best he could.

From the outset, Cannon realized that Wilson had worked out that he wasn't a policeman anymore. Either that or someone had tipped the businessman off.

"I'm surprised to have another visit from the police already, given I told the Inspector and his colleague everything I knew about Simon, yesterday," he said.

Cannon realized immediately that Wilson was stringing him along. He hadn't even asked to see any ID, and Cannon realized Wilson was street smart enough to know it was the first thing to ask for. In addition, a smug smile on Wilson's face was a dead giveaway.

"I understand that, Sir," he said, "but we just have a few more questions."

Wilson folded his arms and sat back in his chair, his body language clear. Cannon realized that Wilson was going to play along with the charade and that he, Wilson, had his tongue figuratively, but firmly, planted in his cheek. It was obvious to Cannon that Wilson was enjoying this.

"Go ahead, I'm all ears."

"I understand from your PA that you have been in the US for the past few days?" he said.

"That's right."

"When did you get back Sir?"

"The day before yesterday. I told the Inspector that, last night."

"And when did you leave for the US?"

"Just over a week ago actually," came the reply. "In fact a week ago last Wednesday. I went to Frankfurt first, and then flew straight to the US from there."

"Can anybody vouch for your movements, in Germany, and in the 'States?"

"Yes, of course," came the reply, "would you like me to provide you the details?"

Cannon didn't want to have to chase people across the globe and potentially expose himself to others as he needed to keep a low profile, but he played along. "Yes, Sir that would be useful," he responded.

"No problem. I'll arrange for my PA to get that detail for you now." He stood up and walked to the door of his office. "Janet," he said, hiding his irritation with Cannon from his voice. "Could you get me all the details, email addresses, phone numbers etcetera of all the people I had meetings with last week, and bring them through as soon as you can please?"

The PA responded positively and said she would bring it through in the next ten minutes. She also reminded him of his next meeting, scheduled for 2 pm.

"Thank you," he said, acknowledging her efficiency.

Sitting down again, he resumed his pose.

Cannon realized that he needed to find out what he could, and then leave Wilson's office as soon as possible. He guessed Wilson would be on the phone to the police as soon as he left the building if he hadn't already done so even before Cannon had arrived.

Based on his discussion with Jefferson, Cannon decided to take a risk, and stir up a bit of mud, which he hoped would somehow stick. Somewhere.

"We interviewed a Mr. Graham Jefferson yesterday, and he told me that you and he, along with Mr. Crabb were good friends and had been for years. He also told us that Mr. Crabb had been receiving strange calls recently…"

Wilson sighed, interrupting Cannon, his voice rising in annoyance. "Look as I told the Inspector last night. *Yes*, Simon had received calls. *Yes*, he had shared them with me and Graham, but *No* we didn't have a clue what it was all about. In fact…." Stopping in mid-sentence, Wilson suddenly changed tack. "Sorry…. Should have done this earlier. I didn't ask to see your ID….Mr.….?"

Cannon responded quickly. "Cannon, Detective Inspector…" he said, hoping the bluff would work, and ignoring any attempt to show Wilson anything related to an ID.

"Well *Inspector*," came the reply, with a hint of subtle menace, "all I can tell you is that a good friend of mine is dead. I don't know why, but I do *expect* the police to find out. I can also assure you that if I ever get my hands on the person who did this, there wouldn't be much left when I had finished with them. I can assure you of that!"

Cannon nodded silently. It was clear that Wilson's threats could easily translate into action if he really wanted to.

Changing the direction of the conversation somewhat, Cannon asked, "Tell me, Mr. Wilson, what exactly do you do here? From what I can see, it appears to be a very successful operation."

"We do software development."

Cannon's frown spurred Wilson to be more revealing.

"We write programs. Primarily concerning company websites. We are unique in that we do bespoke applications for small and medium businesses."

Cannon pretended not to understand, though he knew a lot more than he was given credit for. When he had originally set up his own training business, he realized at the time that he needed to market himself, to communicate with the wider industry. He worked with a similar entity to that of Wilson, but on a much smaller scale, and built up his skills allowing him to enhance his own website to include a database of the horses under his care. The food they ate, the times they had run in training, their illnesses, results from their blood tests, the dates and places of good and bad runs at the track.

In addition, working with his IT provider he built up knowledge around purchasing and payment systems, the invoicing and accounting systems available. Eventually realizing that his site was his window to the world. In time, his own website developed into his primary method of engaging with his owners, notwithstanding at times the need to revert to the telephone, as he had done yesterday with those of poor *Katmandu*.

"Our offering," went on Wilson, "includes everything from Web-design, web-development, managing the site, making any changes, that type of thing," he said waving a nonchalant arm, "but we also provide add-ons as well."

"Add-ons?"

"Yes. We have a finance arrangement with a bank that allows us to do work for a customer, and once done, we invoice the bank directly for that work. We get paid by the bank, and the customer can pay off the bank over an agreed period of time."

"Ok, a bit like a mortgage or a loan?"

"Yes effectively. In addition," he continued, "we provide consulting work, we do maintenance of the websites and we have a hosting service as well. This means the client doesn't need to have equipment in a data centre of their own, we host the site in a secure environment or in the *cloud*."

This was getting too technical even for Cannon, so he asked, "Did Mr. Crabb ever come here?"

"To this office you mean?"

"Yes."

Wilson thought about it for a second and then said, "Maybe once or twice over several years. Certainly not much more than that. Why do you ask?"

Cannon noticed the interest from Wilson in the question.

"I just wondered that's all...no reason."

He noticed a slight twitch in Wilson's posture. There was something in the movement that made Cannon realize that he had struck a nerve somehow. Pretending he hadn't noticed he made a mental note, deciding he would follow up with Rachel Crabb when he met with her in the next hour or so.

"How well do you know Mrs. Crabb?" asked Cannon.

"Very well," came the reply.

For a second there was silence between the two men. Cannon looked directly into Wilson's eyes.

Over the years in the Force, he became more and more aware that the eyes could never really keep the spoken lie hidden. The eyes often resulted in the liar looking away in a different direction to the person they were addressing. At times there would be signs of excessive blinking, or on occasion, the eyes actually wept. Not tears per se, but a sort of internal excitement that somehow had to escape, often manifesting itself in the eyes glistening.

Continuing, though it was clear that he was starting to get annoyed, Wilson said, "Look, *Inspector*," raising his voice to emphasize the point that he wasn't enamoured with the game being played and his patience was wearing thin, "I've known Rachel for many, many, years. Simon and I grew up together. I was his best man. So of course I know her well!"

As Cannon was about to reply, there was a knock on the door to the office. Without waiting for a response, the PA opened the door and poked her head around it saying, "I have those details for you, Alex." She walked into the room with several pieces of paper in her hand.

Wilson nodded towards Cannon, and she placed them on the desk in front of him.

"Thank you," he said smiling.

"You're welcome," she said. As she went to leave the room, she turned to Wilson saying, "Oh, and by the way I've ordered you a chicken sandwich for lunch, and remember your next meeting is in ten minutes."

Wilson nodded.

Cannon realized that he had overstayed his welcome, such as it was and decided to make a move.

"Well thank you for your time, Mr. Wilson, it has been useful." He stood up and held out his hand. "If we have any more questions we'll come back to you. In the meantime, thank you for this information," indicating the papers he had picked up from the desk, "we will follow this up in due course."

Wilson got up from his chair. "No problem," he said. "If I can be of any further assistance please let me know."

The smile on his face was in contrast to his body language. He took Cannon's hand in his own. As they shook, Cannon could feel the pressure being placed on his fingers and his palm. He could feel Wilson clamping tight. The grip becoming firmer, like a vice steadily trying to crush what it held. Cannon realized it was Wilson's way of telling him that he knew he was a fake, that he could see through him.

Outside the building, Cannon took a few deep breaths. His heart hammered in his chest. The cool air was bracing. The early afternoon sky was still a deep grey. The light was already starting to fade. The sun had started its wintery descent towards the western horizon. It would be dark in a couple of hours.

He walked towards his car and as he did so, he pulled out his mobile phone. Tapping the pre-set number, he called Michelle. She answered within a couple of rings.

"How are you?" he said jumping into his car.

"I'm fine," she responded, "where are you?"

"Just leaving Alex Wilson's place now. I'm off to see Rachel next at her house. I need to check a few things with her. I should be home just after four."

"Good," came the reply. "Just doing a bit of shopping for Cassie and us. She wanted a few toiletries, and we needed a few things, so see you later. Bye."

"Bye," he said, disconnecting and inserting the phone into the hands-free holder.

As he did so, he suddenly became aware of a presence to his right, and also at the passenger side door. Without warning his door was pulled open, and he was dragged unceremoniously out of the car. As he did so, his legs thrashed and he kicked the mobile from its holder, landing just below the seat edge on the passenger side floor.

"What the fu…" he tried to say. The expletive being lost in his throat as his head hit the roof of the car, as he was pushed against it. Hands gripped his arms and they were pulled back behind him. He tried to turn his head to see who held him, but then he heard the voice from the other side of the car. He looked over to where the sound was coming from, as his wrists felt the cold steel of the handcuffs being locked around them.

Skinner smiled back at him. Quick stood next to Skinner.

It was clear that Skinner was enjoying himself.

Cannon tried to speak, but Skinner ignored him, putting a finger up to his own lips to silence him then said, "Michael Cannon, I am arresting you on suspicion of murder. You do not have to say anything. But it may harm your defence if you do not mention when questioned, something which you later rely on in court. Anything you do say may be given in evidence."

After a short pause, he turned to the junior officer pressing Cannon against the car, and with gusto said, "Constable, take this bastard away."

Chapter 13

The interview room at the Woodstock police station was similar to many he had been in before.

The starkness of the floors and ceilings, and the plain furniture, brought back to him the many times he had endured sitting through hours and hours of questioning of suspects, during his own policing career. Even the water jugs and cups, no longer glass but plastic, were the same shape and design as those in hundreds of *stations* across the country.

He had made his one phone call. It had been to Michelle. He had asked her to arrange for his phone to be collected from his car and to drop it off at the 'station' for him. He had hoped to have her pick up the vehicle and take it back to the stables. Skinner however had told him that it was likely to be impounded so that the forensics team could examine it for evidence.

"For what?" Cannon had said.

Skinner had ignored the question but had replied that he was to be interviewed in the next few hours. Given he had been cautioned, Cannon knew that time was on Skinner's side, but Cannon wanted out as soon as possible. It was now just before 6 pm. He needed to get to Cheltenham, for *Mr. Scarecrow's* race tomorrow.

Cannon sat at the table with a duty solicitor next to him, Skinner and Quick sitting on the opposite side. A Constable stood outside the room. Skinner went through all the formalities correctly so that the recording of the interview would show that everything up to that point, was done by the book.

"Mr. Cannon... Mike," Skinner said sardonically, "for the record could you please say your full name?"

Cannon played the game. Skinner was aware of who he was, yet persisted in being dogmatic. "Michael George Cannon," he said.

"Thank you, and your occupation?"

Cannon looked at Quick, who flinched a little. It was clear that as much as Skinner was enjoying the process, Quick wasn't.

"Racehorse trainer."

"And your former occupation before that?"

"Look Inspector," jumped in the solicitor, "that's hardly relevant to what my client is being accused of, so please can we move on?"

The Inspector looked at the solicitor with an *'if looks could kill'* expression on his face.

"Oh, and by the way, Inspector," said the lawyer, "just a heads up. I have already started the process of a bail application. I expect my client to be released by tomorrow morning at the latest." It was clear the contempt the lawyer felt towards Skinner.

Cannon smiled inwardly. The young solicitor, who looked in his mid-twenties, wore his tie askew and his straight mousy coloured hair, worn long. He may have looked a little dishevelled, but it was clear that his brain was sharp.

"We'll see about that Mr. Sherman," came the retort.

"Yes, we will *Inspector*. Now can we get on please?"

Quick took the mantle, and it was clear to all who was playing good cop and who was the bad cop throughout the interview. Cannon knew how it all worked, the techniques. He also knew that Quick didn't really have time for Skinner. That was evident from the earlier altercation in the pub. He quietly sympathized that he had been allocated to work with Skinner.

"Could you tell us where you were, between the hours of 9 pm last night and 7 am this morning?"

"I was at home," replied Cannon.

"And can anyone vouch for that…. Mike?" Using his Christian name, it was clear that Quick wanted to make this easier for both of them.

"Yes, of course. My head-lad, my vet, and my partner, Michelle," he replied. "I suggest you give them a call, they'll be able to confirm what I've just told you." Quick stood up from the table and left the room. He was gone for just a minute or so before returning.

"Look, what is this all about?" said Cannon. "You have arrested me for something you believe I have done, yet told me nothing as to what. Other than a ridiculous accusation concerning someone having been murdered."

"Your brief here has all the details," interrupted Skinner, pointing at Sherman "didn't he tell you?"

Sherman took umbrage at the inference, "Inspector," he said, "it is Friday night. You arrested my client but a few hours ago. I received the paperwork just a short while before I was due to leave my office for the weekend. Up until a few minutes ago, Mr. Cannon and I had not met and I have not yet had time to brief him properly! Given my earlier comment that we will be seeking bail immediately, as I don't think you have any evidence to present, I only had time to advise him that given the nature of the charges that he leave it to me to do the talking."

"And is he aware of the charges?" said Skinner.

"Other than you have accused me of murder, No!" said Cannon.

"Well then, let me a bit more specific," said Skinner.

Cannon sat back in his chair, exasperated at Skinners' approach. Sherman touched him on the arm, and with the slightest of shakes of the head, indicated to Cannon that he should just be patient. Sherman's eyes showed that in his view, Skinner had no case that Cannon needed to answer to.

"Early this morning around 10 am, we found the body of a Mr. Graham Jefferson at his home."

Cannon sat up in his chair. *This is unbelievable* he thought.

"And you think I had something to do with it?" he exclaimed.

"We know from his staff, that you went to see him yesterday at his business premises, in Bicester. We also know from the people at the shop, that after your meeting he seemed highly agitated as if he had been threatened by someone. We think that threat was from you."

Cannon was almost apoplectic at the inference. Though knowing Skinner was trying to bait him into saying something that he could latch on to, Cannon tried to remain calm.

Before he was able to answer, Sherman jumped in saying, "What evidence do you have to link my client to this so-called threat Inspector, or indeed to the murder of Mr. Jefferson? What motive would my client have?"

"Look, Mr. Sherman. I don't believe in coincidences, and I still need to work out a motive, but just yesterday, your client," he said, pointing at Cannon, "went to see Mr. Jefferson, who we also wanted to talk to in connection with the recent murder of a Mr. Simon Crabb." Skinner let the lawyer consider this for a few seconds, before continuing. "Mr. Crabb and Mr. Jefferson were long-standing friends and they had shared information about a series of strange phone calls that Mr. Crabb had been receiving recently. Mr. Crabb," he emphasized, "was found with his head smashed in just a few days ago and before we were able to interview Mr. Jefferson about these same phone calls, he was found dead this morning!"

Raising his voice still further, Skinner continued on the attack. "Today, we find *your client* visiting another friend of Mr. Crabb, a Mr. Alex Wilson, who we interviewed yesterday, and we want to know why!"

Sherman looked at Cannon, and as he did so, Skinner went for the jugular. "A few days ago I told your client to stay away from the Crabb investigation and let the police handle it. Your client being a former police Inspector knows what that means, yet he chose to ignore it. Accordingly, we are looking at the...." The door to the room opened, interrupting Skinner in full flow, and a young female Constable walked in, passing Quick a note. Skinner remained silent, waiting. Quick leaned over to Skinner and whispered into an ear.

"Well Mr. Cannon," Skinner said through gritted teeth, "seems like you are in luck. It appears we have been able to get hold of the people you referred to earlier, and they have corroborated your story about where you were last night between the hours of nine last night, and seven this morning, which is when we believe the murder of Mr. Jefferson was committed."

"And that is the basis upon which you arrested my client?" joked Sherman.

"Not at all, Mr. Sherman. Mr. Jefferson was asphyxiated. Effectively he was strangled to death, and it appears he was murdered while he slept. Someone broke into the house during the night. We found signs of forced entry on one of the downstairs windows. I am not going to reveal all the details, but I will highlight one specific item that we found which does affect your client."

Skinner dragged out the seconds as he stared at Cannon, before revealing his rationale behind Cannon's arrest.

"Mr. Jefferson was strangled using a bridle. A very distinctive bridle. Etched into the leather were the initials *MC,* and on the side of this bridle was a small metal plate with the name and address of the farm belonging to your client."

Cannon gave out a laugh. This really pissed off Skinner, who began to rise from his chair at the outburst.

"And on that basis, you pulled me in?" said Cannon. "Notwithstanding the fact that, even if what you said is true, it is purely circumstantial, and clearly had been planted to set me up! Do you think I would be so stupid as to leave a bridle with my name and address on it, at a crime scene?" he continued. "I said a few days ago you were lazy Skinner, but I think I undersold you. Actually, you're a joke!"

Skinner's anger got the better of him, and he lunged across the table. Cannon and Sherman reacted quickly and were on their feet backing away, as Skinner hit the table hard with his midriff. As he did so, Quick moved to pull him back by the shoulder but only succeeded in knocking him off balance, and they both crashed to the floor.

In the seconds that followed, Sherman hit the call button in the room that was used for when suspects got out of control. As Skinner dragged himself up off the floor, swearing as he did so, the door opened and the Constable from outside rushed in. Seeing the commotion, his first reaction was to move towards Cannon.

"Stop!" roared Skinner, breathing heavily, cleared winded. The *uniform* took a step back, waiting.

"Inspector," responded Sherman, "I must protest in the strongest possible terms at what is going on here. It looks to me that my client is being victimized and is the subject of a personal vendetta. I am appalled at your behaviour, and I will be raising the issue with local command at the earliest opportunity!"

Skinner looked at the solicitor, at Cannon, then at Quick, in succession. Hate and anger showed on his face.

Turning back to Sherman he said, "Get your client out of my sight. Get him out of here!" he shouted, his jaw quivering with rage. "But be aware, something is going on here which your client is involved in, and I *will* find out what it is. When I do, I will throw everything I can at him. The book, the kitchen sink everything...!"

Cannon smiled inwardly. He knew where this was coming from. He turned to Sherman who gathered up his papers, including a few that had fallen onto the floor after Skinner's attempt to intimidate them both. They left the room together in silence.

Having been allowed to leave so quickly, he had been able to call Michelle from the police station to let her know that he would get a taxi back to his car, which was still in the parking lot at INet Solutions, and that he would drive home himself. He was pleased that it had not yet been removed by the police, but such was the focus on Cannon himself, that he wasn't surprised by Skinners' lack of organization or process compliance.

As he drove home, he called Rachel Crabb.

"I just want to apologize for not being able to get to you this afternoon, but something came up," he said, not wanting to tell her about his arrest and release.

"No problem, I understand."

"How are things with you?"

"I am beginning to get back to normal, though it's very quiet here at home, just myself," she sighed. Continuing, she asked, "I am not sure if you are aware but I got a call from the police this morning to tell me that Simon's body was to be released," her voice cracking as she said it. He could sense her pain. "So with Joseph and Irene's blessing, I have arranged for the funeral to be held this coming week. The undertaker is still to come back to me tomorrow as to whether it will be Wednesday or Thursday," she said. "Anyway I have taken the week off work, the office has been very good on that score, offering a lot of support if I need it."

Cannon considered this for a second, his mind half on the road and half on what he wanted to ask her. Given what he had recently heard about her husband.

"How is Wendy taking all this?"

There was silence on the line for a few seconds before she answered. Cannon found her tone when she did speak, just a little odd as if something was bothering her.

"We had a long talk about it last night. A mother to daughter bonding session if you like. She has been remarkably grown-up about it, but I still think she hasn't quite come to terms with things as yet. I think Cassie staying with her has made a huge difference though, and I wanted to thank you for allowing her to stay."

"No problem," he responded, "I understand she's coming home on Monday. The mid-term break is perfect timing. Once they have gone back to school after the break, it will all about looking forward to Christmas."

For a few seconds, neither party spoke, Cannon realizing that his words may be adding more stress on Rachel, given it would be the first Christmas without her husband. He continued driving waiting for her to say something else. She didn't.

Eventually, as he turned into the stable yard, he said, "I'm home now, but just before I go, I wanted to ask you something."

"Fire away," she said.

"Graham Jefferson, did you know him?"

"Yes, he's been a friend of Simon's for years. Not very well at the moment, I believe," she replied.

"Not very well at all," he stated, "He's dead! Murdered."

He heard the phone drop and Rachel cry out, "Oh my God...!"

It was almost time for last drinks. The patrons at the *King's Head* had slowly drifted away. Only the hardened drinkers, or those that had no one to go home to, were still in attendance.

The fire in the hearth around which Skinner and Quick sat, reflected off the beer glasses on the table in front of them. It had been a slow night really, especially for Quick who wanted to go home. Skinner on the other hand was pushing through his fifth pint. They had been in the pub for just less than two hours.

After the debacle with Cannon, they had driven, rather than walked, the short distance to their drinking hole, so that they could keep out of the rain that had begun to hammer down. It was a miserable night, the cold seeping into anyone's bones who happened to be outside for too long.

The wind chill had brought the temperature down to 2 degrees. Fortunately, with all the cloud cover it wasn't likely to go any lower, but it meant with all the rain, everything would remain damp.

Quick didn't want to drag this out any longer than he needed to. He found the discussions in the pub, especially with Skinner in the mood he was in, to be very hard work. He wanted to go to bed. It had been a long, shitty day and the episode in the interview room was the cherry on the top, crowning it all. He had felt embarrassed and annoyed at Skinners' behaviour. Having tried in the past to get to the bottom and failed, as to why Skinner hated Cannon so much, he knew the only way to find out was to ask Cannon himself.

"What did the CCTV footage show, the night Crabb was killed?" slurred Skinner, "did we get anything?"

"Actually it showed nothing at all, Sir," replied Quick. "When I went to have a look at the setup at the time, something bothered me, but I couldn't work out what it was."

"Go on."

"Well, when I looked at the film this morning, I realized what it was."

"What? Spit it out," encouraged Skinner, as he downed the last of his drink.

"Well Sir, it's the cameras themselves. They were pointing away from the walls of the clubhouse. There was one above the main entrance door facing the pathway leading towards the building. There was one at the backdoor filming the rear exterior, and another was facing the putting green, plus several others in the car park."

"And? And...?" Skinner said, his impatience becoming more intense, his arms flailing away.

"And...well, it means that the pictures one gets from the cameras are of people coming towards or leaving the building who are in *full view*. That is to say, that they are walking *on* the pathway. But if you walk *against* the building itself, and are off the pathway, the camera won't pick you up at all. The line of sight is limited and so if the perpetrator stayed in the shadows, remember it was a dark night as well, with heavy clouds and rain around, the camera wouldn't be able to see him or her."

"Fuck!" retorted Skinner. The people in the pub were used to bad language, especially the regulars who knew of Skinner. They ignored the outburst. "So we have nothing at all then?"

"The only thing we know is that someone left the kitchen around the time of the murder, as we can see the kitchen door open on the TV footage. But we have no idea who that was. Plus the place was so busy, no one seems to have seen anyone slip out of the building either."

"So it must have been someone at the Club, on the night?" Skinner replied.

"Maybe, but maybe not. Someone could have been waiting for Crabb for ages outside, just awaiting the right moment to strike. We don't know if the kitchen door opening on the CCTV footage is even relevant. It's just something we need to consider."

"Umm."

"One other thing Sir, and then after this I must be off. I need to get home to see Megan. It's Friday night and if I don't get home before 11, I doubt I'll have a wife for much longer."

"OK," said Skinner, a drunken smile on his face. "I'll have your *one for the road* then shall I? Go on, what's the other thing....?"

"The CD player that the SOCO's found in Jefferson's bedroom where his body was."

"What about it?" Skinner asked.

"It was playing when they found it, but the sound had been turned down very low. It was on repeat play. On just one song. That song was *'Took you away'* by *'Everyman'!*

Chapter 14

The past twenty-four hours had been an absolute nightmare for him.

Cannon welcomed the fact that since he had been able to leave the police station, his main focus had been getting his horses to the track. He was not sure why he had thought that he could easily revert back to being a detective, and he had questioned himself many times as he had driven home.

Once home, he spoke with Rich Telside, to find out if any of the tack was missing. The answer had been an emphatic, '*No*'. All the gear in the yard was accounted for and there had been nothing mentioned by any of the staff about missing equipment. This puzzled Cannon. He decided not to mention anything about the bridle.

He had then called Joseph Crabb and advised him of what had happened. The murder of Jefferson, his discussion with Alex Wilson, and the '*meeting*' at the police station with Skinner.

Crabb had been sympathetic, and at one point suggested that if Cannon wished, he could stop his investigation. Crabb did not want any further deaths on his conscience. He had wanted to find out who had killed his son and why, but he now felt that a second murder meant that there was much more to it than he had first imagined. It appeared to Crabb that his son's death was not a random act and perhaps the investigation into it would benefit by letting the police, who had greater capacity and capability, try and solve the case themselves without interference. This, despite his reservations and desire for family privacy and anonymity.

Cannon had told the older man that there were a few things that he had discovered already which bothered him and did not seem right. That he would follow them through as long as he could. When he got to a point that he felt has was no longer making progress, he would be the first to call it out and stop wasting his own and everyone else's time.

During the night as he lay with Michelle beside him, the clock ticking down to a 6 am start, Cannon tossed and turned as the events of recent days played on his mind, ultimately tricking his brain to revive thoughts and events of the past. Bodies, some with eyes open, flitted across his mind. Blood, death, screams, pain, cries for help from people trapped in burning buildings, crashed cars, knives, rapes........he had woken with a cry of despair, sweat seeping from every pore, heart racing.........

Thank God for Michelle. She had held him tight as his consciousness combined with his surroundings, taking away his confusion and bringing him back from the darkness towards reality. The dreams, the nightmares he thought were fading, were still coming back, clearer and stronger than ever, to haunt him. Afterward, as he lay back on his pillow, still hours of darkness left until his alarm would advise him that the day was to start, he replayed the anomalies he had witnessed during the past few days, over and over in his head.

The Cheltenham meeting was therefore a welcome distraction. *Mr. Scarecrow* had travelled well. His two-and-a-half-mile chase was the main race of the day. A Grade 3 event, to be run just after 3 O'clock. Cannon had also entered two other horses in earlier competitions, one a juvenile hurdle race over 2 miles and the other a class 4 chase, run over the same distance. While Cannon had limited expectations of success in those races, the owners hoped for a different outcome.

The weather was cold, but the sun shone. The forecast was for it to remain that way. The earlier low-pressure system had moved off northeasterly, and a crisp blue sky was expected to greet the punters the whole day. This was always good for race meetings. Large crowds were expected when the elements were favourable.

The famous stands were immaculately clean, and the tents and other hospitality areas were ready for the coming day. The hills in the distance that created the valley, stood majestically overlooking the course.

The track looked a picture, the grass thick and rich. The wind from the west had dried it out and the going was declared to be *'good'* by the time racing commenced just before 1 pm.

This was the case across the entire course with one slight exception, which was at the base of the famous hill. Just at the beginning of the final straight, there was a slight area of about 50 yards of softer, and therefore heavier going, where the rainwater had not quite drained away completely.

The jockeys and trainers who walked the course made mental notes to keep their mounts away from that section, especially the second time around when their mounts would be tiring and the pressure to quicken up the hill towards those last few fences, in a final primeval charge to the line, was at its most intense.

"What do you think?" asked Cannon of Rich. "Will you be okay on your own?"

"Sure boss, I'll be fine. I'll see you just before the second race when *Seat Pocket* runs in the novice plate," he said. "You go and look after your guests."

"Thanks," he replied, feeling relieved that he had someone like Rich to take care of his runners. "I'm meeting the other owners in the Owners and Trainers bar in about 20 minutes, so I'd better be off. I see the crowd is beginning to build already," he said, as he walked away to catch up with the owners of the horses he had racing throughout the day.

The trip to Newcastle had taken far longer than Skinner would have wanted.

With Sunderland, Middlesbrough, and Newcastle all playing at home on the same day, the drive had been ridiculously long. The roads had been so busy at times, that it seemed like they would never get to their destination, which was the headquarters of the Northumbria police, Central command. On occasion they barely moved, it seemed to both of them that the journey was taking forever.

Quick had driven the whole way. Skinner at times nodding off, sleeping with his mouth open, snoring. When he did so, Quick was able to listen to his own music on the mp4 player, increasing the volume when the snorts from Skinner became too loud.

When Skinner finally did surface from his sleep, he was not in the best of moods.

"I hope these bloody *Geordies* have got their act together," he said. "I don't want to have spent all my Saturday driving up here to find out that they have screwed things up!" he lamented, looking out through the side window at the darkening sky. The clouds from the west were blowing in, and a wicked wind brought with it a touch of ice and snow in the air. They had been on the road for nearly 5 hours and it was nearly two pm when they finally arrived at their destination.

"I'm sure they're fine, Sir. Inspector Samuels has a good reputation up here," Quick went on. "When I spoke with him earlier this morning, he said he had managed to track down all the band members and that they were willing to be interviewed this afternoon."

"Good to hear," muttered Skinner, "at least we get to stay overnight this time, as there is no bloody way we are driving back tonight," he said. "A few pints of the local brew afterward will go down well!"

Quick raised his eyebrows, thinking the sooner he got away from Skinner the better. *'The man is a real piece of work'* he thought.

As they drove into the car park of the headquarters, Skinner gave out a whoop, "Thank God," he shouted, "here at bloody last!"

The bar was full. The noise meant that everyone in the place had to shout to be heard, which in turn meant everybody else shouted even louder! The only time the place quietened down a little, was when the following race was being run. The owners of *Seat Pocket* were delighted to buy the drinks. A third place, winning a purse of £3000, in addition to their own each-way winnings, had made the trip worth it.

The horse had done well. Running on extremely strongly at the end, catching those ahead of him. Being beaten by just over 4 lengths by the winner and just a short head behind the 2nd place horse was an outstanding result.

Unfortunately, *Switchback Rider,* his second runner of the day, had lived up to his name and had fallen at the 9th fence of 12 when he was contesting the lead. Fortunately, both horse and jockey were okay. The jockey was a little shaken up, which was natural and part of the job, the horse however appeared to have no ill effects at all.

While the owners of *Switchback Rider* had left after their race extremely disappointed, those of *Seat Pocket* relived their horses' run over and over again, with whoever was prepared to listen.

"Next time," said one of the five syndicate members who each had a 20 percent stake in the horse, "next time...he'll win."

"You're damn right Anthony," said another.

Anthony, who was the spokesman for the group, turned to Cannon and speaking through the mist created by the whisky running around his veins said, "That jockey of yours gave him a good ride Mike, let's put him up again next time if he's available."

For the third time in a matter of fifteen minutes, Cannon answered the same comment asked of him. "If young Finch is free, Anthony, of course, we'll put him up. He's a good lad," he said. After the race, Tim Finch had been able to give Cannon a clear, concise summary of the run. How *Seat Pocket* had felt beneath him during the event, the fluidity over the jumps, how strong he was at the end of the race, and how he would win *very soon*.

As the fourth race got closer to starting time, the bar volume eased slightly as those enjoying its atmosphere started to take notice of the TV sets, placed at various intervals along the walls. The horses were beginning to get into position. Cannon took the opportunity to say his goodbyes to his very happy owners, who he expected would still be drinking long after the last race, and excused himself so that he could go down to the stables to see *Mr. Scarecrow* being saddled up for the 5th race.

When he arrived at the racecourse stable boxes, just to the right of the parade ring, the fourth race had just been completed. Won by an outsider, at twenty-five to one.

"Some win that," said Rich nodding in the direction of the track.

"Too right."

"Let's hope we don't have some rank outsider in our race do that to us," Rich commented.

"I hope not. Looking at the 10 horse field there are only two of them ahead of us in the betting, so the bookies must know something we don't," he laughed. "I would have thought we would be about 8 or 10 to one, not a 7-to-2 third favourite."

"Shows you that the connections of some of the other runners may not be too happy with their chances, and have decided not to risk as much money as we might have thought," said Rich.

After saddling *Mr. Scarecrow*, Cannon stood in front of the horse, who looked a picture of health with his bay coat gleaming and his hindquarters brushed into a chessboard pattern. He picked up the horses' front foreleg, pulling it upwards and forward towards himself to stretch the muscles and tendons. This helped to get the blood flowing more easily throughout the valuable but sensitive and strangely delicate legs. It was necessary to do this, to protect these equine athletes that were about to give their all on the track. It was the beginning of the warming up process, something not every trainer did but it worked for Cannon. He then did the same with the other front leg, and once completed, gave the horse's mouth a quick rinse with water, limiting any drinking of it. A horse with too much liquid in its stomach, taken just before a race, could hardly be expected to run well.

With a pat on the neck, he moved aside, and Rich took the horse from the stable towards the parade ring.

The *'Geordies'* had indeed got their act together.

Barry Samuels had managed to track down four of the five members of *'Everyman'*. Samuels agreed not to be part of the meeting with the band members as he didn't have anything to add, but he did say he would watch proceedings on CCTV to ensure nothing was said or implied that he was uncomfortable with. This after all was his *manor*, and he didn't want outsiders causing unnecessary problems within it. If things got out of hand, he would stop the meeting immediately. His reputation on the street, for being firm but fair, was something he leveraged every day when investigating incidents of robbery and murder in the area. He needed his contacts, his underground network to trust him at all times. His word was his bond, and he needed to protect that.

They were in an interview room. The band members having waited for over an hour while Quick and Skinner had battled the last of the traffic. They were not pleased.

After the formalities were completed, Skinner advised the band members that they were not suspects in any crime, which was a lie on his part, and told them that the discussion they were about to have, was in order to help him with his inquiries into a murder in the *South*.

He began by saying. "I understand you are getting back together as a *band* again, is that right?" He looked across at the four men sitting in a series of wooden upright chairs set in a semi-circle in front of him. It was clear Skinner didn't consider anything from the 1970s onwards to be music at all, and certainly looking at the men in front of him, he doubted how they could produce anything that sounded reasonable.

"That's right," said one of the band, a ginger-haired man in his mid-fifties.

"And you are?" enquired Skinner.

"Darren Hall," said the man, "lead singer, guitarist."

Skinner and Quick both noticed immediately that the man's accent was not a very pronounced regional Geordie sound, but was much softer sounding.

"And you still live around here?" questioned Skinner.

"No, I moved to London over twenty years ago. I've been back up here a couple of weeks to rehearse with the boys here," he indicated the other three men sitting with him. "We are going out on the road in February next year. Touring the UK mainly, so we need to get some practice in, hey boys?" he laughed.

The other three men laughed with Darren, with one of the others adding, "And we need to write a couple of new songs, just to show people that we are not dead yet!" the others laughed again.

Skinner looked at Quick, almost bewildered at how the four overweight, balding men, all in their fifties could ever appeal to anyone.

"So let me understand something," Quick interrupted, "there were five of you in the group right?"

"Yes, that's right," said Darren.

"So do I assume the fifth member who isn't here today, is the one that went to South Africa?"

"Right again. Rod Senden was his name. He went to live in Cape Town we think. It was just after we broke up. During the early eighties, late seventies, somewhere around there."

"I see," said Skinner, "and is he part of the reunion then? When is he coming back to join you?"

The band members all looked at each other, somewhat confused.

"None of us has spoken to Rodney for years," said Hall.

"Why is that then?" enquired Skinner, knowing that the mysterious calls to Crabb were emanating from South Africa somewhere. The absent band member was likely to be the prime suspect.

"Because Rodney was killed in a car high-jacking a few years after he got there. He's been dead now for over fifteen years!"

Mr. Scarecrow ran the race of his life.

Over the fifteen chase fences, he hardly put a foot wrong.

His jockey stayed out of trouble for the first mile and a half, just sitting mid-race biding his time. His silks of lime green, pink sleeves, and a pink cap were easily identifiable as the field made its way around the course.

Cannon watched through his binoculars, from the trainer's section high up on the main stand.

As the leading horses turned for home and up the hill towards the finish, only four were in contention. The others having dropped back, strung along in a single file like fish hooked onto a long piece of line.

Two horses had been pulled up, and there was just the one faller so far.

Fortunately, the fallen horse having hit the very first fence hard and had come crashing down, was up on its feet. It had been caught on the track, then led away to a visit with the on-course vet. The jockey however was rendered unconscious for a few seconds but was now recovering from his concussion in the onsite medical rooms.

As the horses turned into the straight to face the final three fences, *Mr. Scarecrow's* jockey took the horse a little wider around the bend in order to miss the softer patch of ground where the hill climb began. It was a winning move. The other three horses hugged the rail, the men on the backs of each animal driving their mounts to reach deeper inside themselves, for that extra bit of courage and stamina.

At the 3rd last fence, *Mr Scarecrow* was second to the favourite, *Itsnevertoolate*, by a half-length, with the two others another length behind him. All the horses cleared the fence and the crowd erupted as the chase up the hill started in earnest. The roar as the quartet reached the penultimate obstacle grew louder. *Mr. Scarecrow* on the outside nearest the stands, the other three almost abreast across the track.

As they jumped the obstacle, *Itsnevertoolate* screwed awkwardly over it, almost hitting his nose on the grass as it slipped on the landing side of the fence. The jockey pulled hard on the reins to bring the horse's head up but as he did so, the legs beneath the animal buckled with the momentum and the favourite fell, disgorging his jockey.

A groan, then a cheer ripped throughout the stands as those in attendance realized the race was still on, despite the loss of the favourite.

Cannon's heart hammered in his chest as *Mr. Scarecrow* came to the last fence. He was being chased by the other two horses, their jockeys urging their mounts on, whips cracking as the crowd's roar grew to a crescendo. He just had to clear the fence, then give it all he could up that last energy-sapping furlong and a half, to the line.

Cannon focused on his horse and watched as almost in slow motion he rose above the birch, clearing the top easily, and landed safely. A huge cry went up from the crowd, Cannon punched the air, his face turning from a deep frown to a huge grin in an instant as he cheered the horse home, eventually winning by seven lengths.

In that moment, all that had happened in the last few days seemed inconsequential. He knew what he wanted in life. He knew this was his world. He would finish what he had started for Joe Crabb, but it would be the last time.

Chapter 15

Normality.

After he had returned home from Cheltenham late on Saturday, he and Michelle had gone to bed almost immediately, and he slept soundly through the night for the first time in months. No dreams or nightmares broke his sleep and he awoke refreshed.

After breakfast he had a very brief look around the stables, checking on how his runners from Saturday had pulled up. He noticed that all had eaten up well. He asked Rich about *Belle o' the Ball*, who was due to run later in the week at Southwell, and Rich's positive comments made him feel that life was starting to return to normal. Inside his mind, however, he knew that normality would only re-occur once the two murders had been solved, but in that instant Cannon decided that given all that had happened over the last week or two, for the next 48 hours it would be family time only.

He needed to be with Michelle, and he needed to be with Cassie. He decided not to wait until the next day when Cassie was due home. He wanted to be with her now. He called Joe Crabb and told him that he wanted to bring Cassie home a day early.

"That's okay," said Joe. "I think Wendy has settled down now. It's the funeral on Thursday, and then after that, we will see where we go from there."

"Thanks for your understanding, Joe. It's been a tough time for all of us."

"That's okay.....Mike," said Crabb, remarkably tenderly. The use of his Christian name took Cannon slightly by surprise, given his perceptions of Joe Crabb. He had been solely business-like to date, now he was showing a sense of humanity that Cannon had not seen previously.

"I just want to thank you for allowing Cassie to spend time with us," Crabb continued, "she's been absolutely marvellous." The smile and thanks expressed in his voice and that resonated down the phone line, was very evident.

They said their goodbyes, and Crabb had then passed the phone to Cassie. Cannon explained that he wanted her to come home early and that both of them and Michelle, would go off for the day, together. Cassie was thrilled.

As they drove over to collect Cassie, Cannon decided he would follow up with Rachel Crabb on Tuesday. The fact that he hadn't been able to talk to her since they had spoken briefly post his arrest and release, didn't worry him at all. He wanted to get back to some semblance of order in his own life, and he was sure others would want to do the same. Even though he was no closer to finding out who had killed Simon, the fact that Jefferson had been killed using what appeared to be one of Cannon's bridles, was particularly worrying to him.

Someone clearly had an agenda. Someone who knew he was investigating Simon Crabb's murder was behind this, but try as he might, he couldn't put the pieces together as yet.

Perhaps a couple of days not focusing on the murders directly would free up his subconscious, allowing him to clear any confusion in his mind? He didn't believe he or his family were at risk, despite a poor attempt at implicating him in the Jefferson murder. He believed that it was an attempt to send the police down a rabbit hole, and in a completely wrong direction within their investigation.

Combining his immediate personal needs, and knowing that the funeral of Simon Crabb was to be held the following Thursday, he considered it would be best to leave Rachel alone for a few days. He would speak with her again on Tuesday, by when he expected all the arrangements for the funeral were likely to be in place.

Cannon and Michelle had agreed that everything they would do on Sunday and Monday could be chosen by Cassie.

Taking time out with the family would go some way to trying to bring some semblance of order back to his life. Even the weather was expected to play its part. At least it was not expected to rain. It was still cold, a mild frost having greeted Cannon when he had gone across to the stables to speak with Rich, but by late morning the sun was shining. Thick clouds were anticipated to roll in overnight, but no rain was forecast for the Monday either, so the days were to be taken up enjoying lunches and shopping in the malls and retail parks of Oxford and surrounds.

Cannon acted as the mule, carrying parcels and packages, while Cassie and Michelle started to bond. He noticed at times that they were like sisters, and at other times they were like best friends. He was pleased that they were beginning to build a relationship but saddened that the impetus for it, came from a death.

By Monday evening, straight after dinner, Cassie had gone to her room. She was desperate to share what she had done and bought, with her friends. Like all teenagers, Facebook, Twitter, and other forms of social media were used to share her thoughts, to get back comments on her postings, and to generally bring the *world* up to speed with what she had been doing over the previous 36 hours.

Cannon and Michelle sat on the couch looking at the TV but neither really watching what was on. It was getting late, almost ten pm when suddenly, the phone rang.

"Leave it," smiled Michelle, as he stood up and walked across to the receiver. Instinctively, even though he had not intended to pick up the phone, he answered it anyway.

"Hello?" he said, not revealing his name or number. It was a good idea nowadays to keep that detail private if possible, given there was now a complete industry *out there,* of people defrauding others. Phone numbers, names, bank account details, pin numbers, etcetera could all be easily scammed and much of it was done over the phone.

"Is there anybody there?" asked Cannon, looking across the room at Michelle and shrugging his shoulders as he did so. "Look I can hear you breathing," he said into the mouthpiece, "either get on with it or I am going to put this phone down!"

His words seemed to energize the person on the other end of the line.

"Can you hear me?" came a voice through the speaker. It was muffled, almost weak as if a person was talking through a handkerchief placed over the mouthpiece of the phone at the other end.

"Yes I can," responded Cannon.

"Mr. Cannon?" A question. "Mr. Mike Cannon?"

"Ye.e.e.s," was the reply, somewhat cautiously. Cannon still wondering what this was all about.

"You don't know me, but I believe you met with Mr. Alex Wilson last week, is that correct?"

"Yes it is, what about it? And who is this anyway?

The voice ignored the question. "Well, maybe I can help you regarding the issue you and Mr. Wilson talked about?"

"And how would you know what I talked to Mr. Wilson about?" replied Cannon.

"Let me put it this way, Mr. Cannon. I have information that I think may be useful to you."

"And why would you be willing to share this information with me so readily? Mr….ummm," he said, trying to pull a name out from the mysterious caller.

"My name is irrelevant at this stage," said the voice. "But in regards to your question, let me say, I have my reasons….." His voice trailed off.

"Okay," responded Cannon, still not sure where this call was going. He put it down later to his own cynicism. "And?" he inquired.

"And…Mr. Cannon, let's meet tomorrow afternoon around 1 pm and I will fill you in," said the disembodied voice. "There is a small restaurant on Sheep Street called Amici, in Bicester. Can we meet there? I have already made a booking in *your* name."

"Sure, but I ……what?" replied Cannon, his voice a little wary at the surprising call and even more so when he realized that his name was being used without his knowledge. His instinct told him that this was someone trying to set him up again. To lure him into a trap. After all, only a few days ago he was a murder suspect due to someone having tried to do exactly that. Was this caller the person responsible?

"Look, whoever you are. I'm a bit uncomfortable with all this. Why should I meet you anyway?"

"As I said," came the reply. "It is in *your* interest."

Cannon sighed again, but let his natural curiosity get the better of him. "Ok," he went on, "but how will I recognize you?"

"Don't worry about that," the voice replied, "I'll find you!" And with that, the phone immediately disconnected.

Cannon held the silent phone in his hand for a few seconds, while he considered what he had just heard.

The lovely extended weekend break he had been enjoying was now well and truly over. "What next?" he said to himself.

"Well that was a day I'll never get back again," said Skinner, his irritation obvious

He was sitting in the passenger seat as Quick drove them back to Woodstock. They had checked out from their hotel after an early breakfast and had hoped to be back just after lunchtime.

"All this bloody way, and what did we find?" he continued. "That the local brew is shit and that the main line of inquiry here turned out to be dead. Literally!" Raising his voice at Quick to emphasize the point, he said, "Does nobody do any proper checking nowadays? When we get back I am going to kick Mason's arse for wasting my time."

Quick ignored the outburst from Skinner. His boss was starting to piss him off. Never a good word to say about anyone, and not a lot of guidance had come from him either. To Quick, Skinner was nothing more than a sponge. He absorbed what people told him, but didn't provide much thought leadership back to his team. But when he wanted to, he took all the credit for the work his team had done for him.

"I'm sure Mason will have done a lot more digging by the time we get back home," Quick said, "but I doubt anyone officially would have known about Rod Senden's status, especially if nobody ever informed the proper Home Office department of his death. All that would have been recorded in their database, was that he had emigrated to South Africa."

Skinner pondered this for a while as they drove along on the A1 heading South. "So how did Mason know that this band was reforming then?"

"I believe he looked at their Facebook page, once he was able to determine that they were the correct band and that the song on Crabb's phone was indeed one of theirs. He then *liked* their page and started to *follow* them.

Skinner looked at Quick as if he was speaking a language other than English. To him all social media was anathema. A newspaper, a phone, and face-to-face contact with suspects and witnesses was all he knew, and anything outside of that he didn't understand, nor care to.

Quick carried on. "From that point on, Mason was able to determine from the band's posts that they were planning to play publically again and that they were reforming."

"So how come he didn't know about Rodney Senden then?" Skinner complained.

"Well, I can only guess they never said anything about it. If it happened 15 years ago, maybe to them it didn't matter. I understand he was the drummer. I guess we can ask Mason if he searched online for all the band member's names and what their status was. But again if it wasn't reported anywhere, then it's possible that none of the search engines we use would have found anything about him."

For the rest of the trip back, Skinner stayed relatively quiet. Just about 20 minutes from their arrival back at the station, Skinner told Quick to pull into a non-descript pub called the *Wagon and Horses* that had seen better days and was likely to go the way of many pubs across the country, in the next year or two. The establishment was what one would call, a *drinkers* pub. The car park itself had cracks in the tarmac with weeds poking through at different heights and thicknesses like tentacles of a giant octopus that slithered in all directions. The parking bays stood to one side of the building, the lines of the bays barely distinguishable due to age. The pub itself was a two storey Edwardian-style building that had originally been painted white, but now had flakes of paint and plaster peeling off both inside and outside of the building.

It was clear that no one intended to invest in the place, and that the owner had either decided to put their money into something else or alternately, and this was more likely, given the number of people frequenting the place, the owner had no money at all.

As they towards the entry to the building, Quick asked, "So why are we stopping here Sir, when we need to get the team together asap? They are all waiting for us back at the station," he continued.

"Because I need something," Skinner replied.

"I could have stopped at the Services just a few miles back if you had said, Sir."

"Look, Quick," replied Skinner, anger in his eyes. "I don't need the facilities. What I need," he bemoaned, "is a drink!"

The expression on Quick's face at this statement irritated Skinner even more than the original question.

"You may disapprove Quick," retorted Skinner, "but you took me all the way to Newcastle, for bugger all. In addition, we still don't know why Cannon was snooping around the Crabb case, or whether he knows anything about the Jefferson murder. But what we do know, is that two people are dead, and our main lead, up in Newcastle, turned out to be a real waste of time. So basically we are back to square one. I'm not sure if the Superintendent is going to be happy with the situation and lack of progress to date, or not, but if *I* get a bollocking, so will you!" he said. "But yours will be from me! So to answer your question, I need a bloody drink, and I need it now!"

They walked into the pub, the bar area only had two people sitting at it. They were locals, whose patronage kept the whole place going somehow. These were the people who would sit for hours, every day, drinking a half-pint every half an hour or so and talking rubbish to each other.

The rest of the place was empty.

Skinner walked up to the barman who was busy with an old dirty cloth drying the glasses from a red crate standing at the back of the bar.

"Sorry mate," he said in his *friendly* voice, "can we organize a couple of pints and something to eat?"

"We don't do food no more," he said, "but we can do the beer. Anything specific?"

"No, just two pints of bitter."

Once the drinks had been poured, Skinner nodded at Quick to pay the man and then walked off, taking both glasses to the furthest corner of the pub away from the bar.

The carpet underfoot was damp and sticky, a mixed spilt residue of beer and wine. The smell emanating from the wall against which they sat, was like an old ashtray that had been filled to bursting point and beyond with half-smoked cigarettes, and then left to rot inside a closed room.

As Quick sat down, he saw the glass in front of Skinner was already a third less than it was just a few seconds before.

"I'm not happy with where things are at," bemoaned Skinner. "Since we left Newcastle, I have been trying to understand the relevance of this music left on Crabb's phone and that in Jefferson's CD player. And I still don't get it."

"Me neither," replied Quick, almost gagging from the odour filtering around them "but it must mean something."

"Does it?" said Skinner, taking another gulp of his beer. "Or is it just a red herring to send us down the wrong path? Plus where does Wilson fit into all this? He knew both dead men very well. Yet, he doesn't seem the slightest bit worried about his own safety. There must be a link somehow, but what?"

"Well he certainly couldn't be a suspect, nor have been involved in the murders, as we have checked his alibi. The fact that he was overseas in Germany and the US during the time of the murders was confirmed when I called the people last night that were on the list we got from his PA."

"Then we need to do more checking and double-checking," said Skinner.

More work for others to do thought Quick. He was beginning to realize how Skinner operated. He would criticize everyone for what they did, however, he would never dirty his own hands by *actually* doing anything himself.

"So when we get back to Woodstock, arrange a meeting with the team for 4 o'clock today, and let's share what we've learnt," Skinner said.

"What bothers me, after all, this time," stated Quick, "is the fact that we still have very little information to go on with right now. There is no evidence of any kind we have of linking anyone we know to these murders. We have no DNA, no CCTV, and no obvious suspect. Fucking great" he said.

"That's why Constable," smirked Skinner, "in order to stir things up a bit, we are going to the funeral of Simon Crabb on Thursday."

The room was keen to hear feedback from the visit to Newcastle, as well as being ready to share what the team themselves had learnt over the past 24 hours.

Skinner's mood had progressively gotten worse over the past couple of hours and as he entered the room where everyone was waiting, the attendees could see it in his eyes.

Earlier, after he had finished his second pint, he had begun to ruminate about the job, the old days, and the lack of attention by today's *newbies*. He also regaled against the Command at the highest level and their focus on being politically correct, rather than supporting the membership. The removal of *important* resources, thinking more of budgets and the introduction of unnecessary paperwork preventing the signing off of expenses like it used to be in the *old days*. Expenses that Skinner had always seen as justified, even if it was just for drinks in the pub after hours, in hotel bars, or even snitch money. In the past that was part of police culture, he had said, and as far as he was concerned, it was still part of the job today.

To some extent, Quick had concurred with Skinner on some of the issues, however when Skinner said he had wanted to stay and have a third drink, Quick called time on it. Skinner was pissed off at the lack of respect shown to him by his own team member but he underestimated Quick's reaction, who by now was getting sick of hearing the same old shit from Skinner every single day.

"I'm your Guv'nor," Skinner said, his eyes showing contempt. "You do what I tell you too! If I want to stay for another drink, then we stay!"

"Fuck off," responded Quick, his expletive and tone taking Skinner by surprise. "I'm assigned to you on this case, but you don't own me," he continued. "I'm taking us back to the station right now. I've driven for hours yesterday and again today, and for most of the time all I've heard is you carping on about everything and everyone," he stated. "Frankly I'm sick of it, and I'm sick of you! I'm bloody exhausted and I want to get home to see the family. But I can't do that yet as *you've* called the team together for the debrief meeting, and I want to get going so that we can get it over with."

The short drive back to the station was made in total silence. Both men ignoring each other, each in their own world. The outburst from Quick, confirming to Skinner that today's lower ranks were *soft*. To Quick, Skinner had proven he was *out of touch* with the modern world and modern policing.

The briefing was eventually set for 4:30 pm. The rumour around the traps was that Skinner wasn't in a good frame of mind, so everyone was seated and ready for when Skinner and Quick came into the room. It was clear to all that something had occurred as the atmosphere between the men was cold. Neither man looked at the other. The body language was awkward. Despite sitting together, there was no warmth between them, even when they had to talk to one another.

"Okay," commenced Skinner, looking at the group sitting around the table in the makeshift incident room. "Let me start by saying that the last 2 days have been a complete waste of *MY* time." Noticeably to the rest in the room, he didn't acknowledge that Quick and he had been a pair that had taken the trip up to Newcastle.

"Frankly," he continued, "it was a wild goose chase. And I'm not happy about it!"

Looking at Mason he said, "Genius boy here, our so-called technical whiz, forgot to check that the member of the band we went to see in Newcastle and that had moved to South Africa, is now dead! And what's more, he's been dead for about 15 years."

At these comments, Quick raised his eyes upwards and sighed his breath. *What a prick Skinner is,* he thought, *to be blaming Mason for data he had not been able to find. If the data didn't exist, there is no way Mason could have found it. It was no way for Skinner to endear himself to anyone, let alone Mason.*

"So what have we learnt?" the Inspector said rhetorically. "Well, for one thing, I want to know how a person can make a phone call after he's dead!" It was supposed to be a joke, but it fell flat with the team in the room.

"Secondly, we know that Graham Jefferson and Simon Crabb's murders are somehow linked to this particular band, but how?" he asked.

"Sir," said one of the Constables. "What if the linkage is not with the group, but with the song itself?" he said.

"What do you mean?" asked Skinner.

"I'm not sure Sir, but I was trying to see if there was another angle that we may need to pursue? I mean, does the song itself have any meaning?"

Quick jumped in before Skinner could comment. "You may well be right Constable, perhaps the words of the song or even the title itself?" he said. "But we need to find out to whom, and for what reason? Everyone we have spoken to so far seems not to have any inkling of the song's meaning. Do we know the year it was released?"

It was clear they were clutching at straws. The proverbial needle in a haystack. The inability to track a call from a pay-as-you-go mobile, the lack of any useable vision on the CCTV footage from the golf club, and no obvious witnesses, was not helping the mood.

"In the meantime," Quick went on, "what have we got from the scene at Jefferson's home. DNA? Fingerprints? Anything as yet?"

He turned to Dale Carpenter, the young Constable on the team, who had the responsibility to coordinate all the various strands of the investigation while Skinner and Quick had been up to Newcastle. He shook his head. At this point, there was no good news. "Sir," he said quietly, remembering the previous meeting when he had been thoroughly castigated by Skinner. "So far, what we have been able to establish is that the bridle used to strangle Jefferson was a fake. We checked with the stable and they had no equipment or tack missing…"

"Well, they would say that," interrupted Skinner, "wouldn't they?"

Carpenter looked at Quick as if to say '*why should I bother*?' but Quick encouraged him to carry on by giving him a wink.

"Perhaps Sir," Carpenter continued, "but we have had it analyzed nonetheless. It seems it's just an ordinary bridle that anyone can buy from any horse or riding supply shop. It is not the type used by Mike Cannon's stable anyway. Plus the metal plate on it is also different to that used by Mr. Cannon."

If looks from Skinner were daggers that could kill, Carpenter would have been skewered several times over.

Skinner was mortified. Yet again, he felt let down by the team. In *his* mind, he felt vindicated in his conclusion about them. To him, the systems now in place and the cuts made throughout the Force resulted in good old-fashioned detective work being put at risk, due to decent coppers being replaced by *'desk jockeys'*.

What he failed to realize was that working on a gut feeling about a suspect, and police dragging people in for questioning off the street just on a whim, was just as bad, and always had been. The world had changed now, and policing had to keep up. Yes, crime was crime, but given the nature of crime today and the sophistication of much of it, it was necessary to bring in skills that matched those of today's criminals. Skinner though, while understanding of the issue, was not one to fully embrace it. Accordingly, his relationship with others, up and down the line suffered for it.

"In addition," continued Carpenter, breaking into Skinner's thoughts, "while we have been able to extract prints from the metal tag, we haven't been able to match them to anyone on our database. Likewise, no luck so far with the DNA that the forensic boys have been able to extract off the bridle."

"So what are you doing about that then?" responded Skinner.

Quick jumped in to the conversation at this point.

"Last night when we were at the hotel, I called Constable Carpenter here and asked him to pull a list together of all the people we know at this stage, that Jefferson would have regularly come into contact with," he said. "We know at his business he had many customers, and the team here are already working through the shop's database. In addition, there are a large number of people from the hospital and at his doctor's surgery who he also saw regularly. Finally, there are those in his social group, for example, those at the golf club and his other friends that we need to investigate further." Looking at Skinner with a contempt that he struggled to hide, he continued, saying, "I believe it's likely to be an extremely large number of people and as you know we have limited resources. Mason here," he nodded towards the IT expert, "will help Carpenter, while at the same time looking into the other leads we have, relative to the band and the song."

"So what does that mean?" said Skinner showing his frustration.

"Well, for one, we are looking at the number of tackle shops that carry the type of horse bridle that we found at Jefferson's home to see if we can trace who may have sold it and to whom."

Before Quick could continue, Mason jumped into the conversation. "Ermm, sorry Sir, but I did some research on that already. There are several places in the area that sell the very one we found, but," he stopped for a second, "and it's a very big *but*, I have also been able to establish that the same bridle is available on Amazon as well."

"Fuck!" exclaimed Skinner. "This is getting worse by the minute."

"Well maybe you are right Sir," went on Mason, "as we will need to get a list from Amazon in the UK, as well as all the shops around here, of everyone who ever bought that type of bridle over the last 12 months or so. Then we will need to correlate the name and addresses with the database that we have already, and see if any of them are on the list that we are compiling concerning Jefferson. But I think it will be a long shot."

"Why?" responded Skinner.

"Because not everyone buys using their own name," said Mason. "Some people use *nom de plumes* or use parts of names. Obviously, some people do use their own names but many do not. We also don't know if the bridle was bought using the UK Amazon site, or say the one in the US, or even elsewhere. Also, Amazon does not readily share information about their customers unless subject to a court order. At this stage, we are a long way from even asking for one, given what we know so far." As if to rub salt into the wound he looked at Skinner saying, "Today, if you want to, you can have complete anonymity on the web, even when you buy something."

"But aren't most purchases made online say with Amazon linked to credit cards?" said Quick.

"Credit cards and PayPal are the main ways of paying yes, but…"

"But…?" asked Quick, noting the inflection in Mason's voice and wanting to understand the caveat that was coming.

"Well, given the amount of credit card fraud around, if the purchase was made with a stolen credit card or a card in someone else's name, it will be extremely difficult to pick it up against our database."

"OK, but I guess we have no option right?"

Mason shrugged his shoulders, "I guess so," he said, "I'll give it a try."

"Good," responded Quick. "If we need additional help from higher up the chain we may need to ask for additional support," he said, turning to Skinner. "Surely if we can track terrorist communication and chatter using the tools we have at our disposal today, then hopefully we can follow a transaction flow?"

Skinner rubbed his eyes with the palms of his hands. The drinks from earlier were catching up with him. He was feeling both tired and very old. "I don't know," he said, "I think we may be clutching at straws at the moment."

Chapter 16

The weather had turned bitterly cold overnight. The relatively good weather of the weekend, and Monday, was now over.

Along with the wind, deep angry rain clouds had moved in, and the rain had started falling during the night. Deep puddles had greeted Cannon, as he had splashed his way across the yard for his now regular early morning chat with Rich.

The conversation was predominantly the same each day. The welfare of the horses, their progress and fitness levels, any upcoming races or meetings that they were thinking of nominating for, and the normal discussion about how the lads were doing. This covered any day-to-day personal issues, disputes, or queries.

Cannon was pleased Cassie was home, and that she and Michelle appeared to be growing closer. If there was ever a silver lining for him in the death of Simon Crabb, it was that the relationships in the house were heading in a positive direction. It was one less thing he needed to worry about.

He wasn't sure if the change in the atmosphere between his daughter and his lover, had helped, but he found that he was sleeping better and that his dreams and nightmares were certainly less evident. Over the past couple of days, he had slept extremely well.

As he drove towards his meeting at the Amici restaurant, the rain hammered on his windscreen. Leaves lay scattered across the road, flying up into the air as oncoming traffic whizzed by him heading in the opposite direction. Where the water had gathered at the roadside kerb, the headlights of the cars and trucks reflected off the surface and onto the windscreen like stars exploding. The roads were slippery, and the traffic slowed to a crawl at different times along the journey.

Cannon used this time to reflect on his investigation.

The funeral of Simon Crabb was to be held the next day. He was going to attend it, as he had a few more questions for Rachel. There were certain anomalies that were bothering him. Things that had been said over the past few days, things that confused him. Things that he had observed, that didn't fit.

He knew from Cassie, that the service for Simon was to be held in a small chapel at the funeral director's premises, and not at the church of St. James's in Stonesfield, where he recalled Joe Crabb and his wife, were parishioners. He could only surmise how that would have gone down within the family, but it was none of his business.

Clutching his coat tightly around him to keep himself warm, he walked across Sheep Street having found parking in Market Square. The rain continued its heavy beat, causing rivulets to run down his face and the back of his neck. He knew he should have brought a hat or umbrella, but had been in such a rush knowing that the traffic would be slow, that he had left the house without either.

When he arrived at the restaurant, he was drenched. His hair lay flat upon his head, his trouser bottoms were dark with moisture. His shoes squelched uncomfortably.

Once inside, he took out a handkerchief and wiped his face and hair to try and bring some semblance of respectability to his looks. The shoes, and other exposed clothing he would just have to live with.

The restaurant itself was small but cosy. The external windows were steamed up with condensation, due to the rain and cold outside colliding with the warmth inside. Clearly, the air-conditioning inside wasn't coping very well.

He noticed that about three-quarters of the tables were occupied with diners. He was already a few minutes late but quickly saw that there was no table with just a single occupant. The person he was due to meet had not arrived yet.

A man walked over to him, as Cannon stood at the front door next to the obligatory sign asking patrons to *'wait to be seated'.*

"Yes Sir, can I help you?" the man asked, in a very practiced manner. Cannon wasn't sure if this was the manager, owner, or a very well-trained waiter, but he had an aura of efficiency about him.

"I was meeting someone here at one o'clock, sorry I am a few minutes late," replied Cannon, "but I can't see him yet."

"Do you have a booking?" said the man.

Cannon always thought this strange, that people ask the same question when there are lots of empty seats or tables in a restaurant. It amused him, but he understood that it was part of the dance customers and restaurateurs always did.

"Yes I do actually," responded Cannon, who then proceeded to tell the man his name.

"Ah yes. I see," he said, having found the page in a diary beside the till. "Table for two."

The man led the way to the back wall of the restaurant as if suspecting Cannon was meeting someone with whom he needed to be as far away from the front door, as possible. Cannon was offered a menu and some water. He noted the irony. The fact when he sat down, he was still dripping wet from the rain hammering down outside.

As he waited, he looked around at the existing clientele. He saw business people, families on early Christmas shopping outings, and a group of elderly ladies who were obviously regulars, given the way they spoke so openly with the waiter who was busy serving them.

The restaurant itself was pleasantly decorated. Pictures of various Italian landmarks adorned the walls. Rome, Venice, Pisa, Naples and Vesuvius. The colour scheme of green, red, and white, dominated the interior. The furniture included green tables, upon which stood red salt and pepper pots atop crisp white tablecloths. The chairs that people sat upon were painted bright red, finishing off the overall effect.

Cannon looked at his watch. He had been asked twice if he wanted to order, but in each case declined, saying he was waiting for his 'guest'.

At 1:20 pm, a man walked into the restaurant, shaking the rain off his bright yellow umbrella and removing his coat for the same waiter who had taken Cannon to his table, to take away and hang up in a small cloakroom.

The man walked straight towards the table that Cannon occupied. He was of medium height, about forty-five, and wore green jeans and a white round-necked tee shirt under a blue aran wool cardigan, that was fully buttoned up. On his feet, he wore green leather boots, around his neck a sky blue neck scarf.

Flamboyant was the word that immediately came to Cannon's mind.

"Mr. Cannon?" the man said, holding out his hand for Cannon to shake.

Cannon grasped the man's hand, which was firm, despite Cannons' expectation that it would be like gripping a wet fish.

"Mr....uumm?" responded Cannon, trying to hide his confusion, but searching for a clue.

"Thank you for coming," said the man. "I'm Greg Carr, sorry I am so late."

Cannon began to feel more at ease, noting that his mysterious guest had offered him a name without provocation, and while it could have been a fake name, Cannon surmised it was genuine.

He had interviewed many people over the years and had developed an instinct for how people were who were lying, reacted, or spoke.

It was not foolproof but it had served him well over many years. Given the forthrightness Cannon had just witnessed, the man was either who he said he was or a damn fine actor. In which case he would be making a fool out of Cannon if his experience failed him. Cannon's gut feeling though, was that he wasn't wrong.

"No problem," said Cannon in response, "though I have to admit I'm a little perplexed, as well as pissed off right now."

Carr looked at Cannon. Cannon stared back and saw in Carr's eyes a window into the man and how he was feeling. *Uncomfortable* was Cannon's first impression. It was clear from Cannon's perspective that the man opposite him was deeply troubled somehow.

Cannon could not retract his comments as they were already out there but tried to soften them a little. Smiling back at Carr he said, "Last night when you phoned, it was the second such call that I received in just over a week. Since that first call, a man has been murdered and I was arrested as being a suspect. You can imagine why my hesitancy to meet with you."

"I totally understand Mr. Cannon," came the reply.

Cannon noticed that Carr's voice was much higher than he had heard over the phone the previous evening. It was strangely effeminate as well. Add to that the clothes and the mannerisms, and it was easy to conclude that he was gay.

Cannon had no hang-ups with gay men, nor with gay women. It was part of life as far as he was concerned. People were people. He had seen all types when he was in the Force. The good, bad, straight, gay, bisexual, fetishists, and many others. If they stayed on the right side of the law, then it had never bothered him. Cross the line though, and he would be down on them like a ton of bricks.

"Call me Mike," he said.

"Thanks, Mike, please call me Greg."

There was a short silence between the two men before Carr asked if Cannon was hungry. They both decided on pasta dishes, with Cannon adding a starter of Bruschetta. Carr ordered water, with a double expresso for after lunch. Cannon ordered a beer.

After the starter had been delivered to their table, Carr changed the subject of conversation from the weather to the real reason for their meeting.

"Oh, and before I start, I need to leave at 3:00 pm to get back to my office," he said, "so I need to keep an eye on the time."

"And where is it you work, err, Greg," said Cannon, finally accepting the ease with which he could address Carr and the use of his Christian name.

"I work for INet Solutions, just up the road here," he replied, nodding in a general direction behind Cannon's right shoulder.

For a second Cannon couldn't quite place what he had heard, then as the mist in his head cleared, he said, "Whoa, wait a minute, you mean you work for Alex Wilson?"

"Well actually," came the reply, "in reality we are partners."

"Partners?"

"In the business, yes," said Carr.

"Wait a minute, I thought INet Solutions was fully owned by Wilson?"

"Well that's the way it's reflected to the outside world, but I am in fact a fifteen percent shareholder."

"And has it always been that way?"

"No," said Carr. "I think I had better explain the relevance of all this and why I wanted to talk with you."

"Okay," said Cannon, intrigued. "Please go ahead."

Before Carr could continue, their pasta dishes arrived. After the first mouthful, he said, "It's a long story and one I am not proud of, but given recent events, it's about time I unburdened myself."

Cannon stayed silent for a minute or two. He took a bite of his meal and chewed thoughtfully.

He had so many questions to ask but now was not the time. He needed Carr to fill him in with whatever he wanted to share. After all, he had said on the phone that what he had to disclose, was in Cannon's interest.

Eventually, Cannon said. "So Greg, why did you ask me to meet you here?"

"It's because I'm scared," came the reply.

"Scared of what?"

"That, I'll be next."

"Next?" said Cannon, confused.

"I think I'd better explain."

Over the next hour or so as the restaurant emptied, Carr told Cannon the story of the rape and murder of the girl that had been picked up at a concert venue in Oxford, now known as the O2, but some twenty years earlier, had been known as the Zodiac club.

The detail relayed to Cannon was harrowing. He felt sick to the stomach. He listened intently to every detail, only realizing as Carr neared the end of his story, that they were the only people left in the restaurant. The waiters and other staff were nowhere to be seen.

"I couldn't do it," Carr said, as silent tears ran down his cheek. He tried desperately to wipe them away with his hand. Eventually using a serviette to wipe his face and blow his nose.

"I tried to stop them. I tried to stop *HIM,* but they all just laughed at me because I failed to perform. They didn't know I was gay. In those days, people were still involved in *queer-bashing* as a popular sport. I was too scared to say anything, so I just hid my shame."

"You said there were five of you?" interjected Cannon, his anger having risen as the story unfolded. Despite how he felt, he had tried to remain calm in order to encourage Carr to carry on with his tale. "Who was the other?" he enquired.

"Yes, there *were* five of us. As I said, it was me, Graham Jefferson, Simon Crabb, Alex Wilson, and Peter Grey."

"And what happened to Grey?" asked Cannon.

"Well I'm not totally sure, but a few years ago I heard he had committed suicide."

"Was it ever confirmed by anyone?"

"Not that I remember," responded Carr. Cannon noticed the area around Carr's eyes becoming bloated and red from his tears.

"Let me ask...." Cannon was cut off mid-sentence by the arrival of the waiter, who asked them if they required anything else from the menu.

Both men shook their heads and Cannon suggested that they carry on the conversation somewhere else.

"What time is it?" enquired Carr.

"It's almost three," answered Cannon.

"Oh shit!" replied Carr, "I'm not sure this was a good idea. I'm going to be missed at the office and Alex is going to be mighty pissed."

The waiter returned with the bill, which Cannon paid on his credit card, and despite initial protestations, it was finally agreed that they would continue to talk for a further half-hour in Cannon's car.

As they walked through the continuing heavy rain towards the parking garage, his almost dry shoes becoming wet again, Cannon's anger grew further.

While he pitied Carr, the very nature of the rape and murder of a young girl so long ago, brought home to him why he had left the Force eventually. What he was seeing every day at that time made his dreams and nightmares real, impacting his life in ways only he could understand. All due to the level of depravity that humanity stooped to, and into which he had been dragged every day. The lies and deceit he had come across over the years had begun to affect him. His very sanity, tested.

Guilty people abusing the system. Lawyers using technicalities to plead a client's innocence, when they knew the person was guilty of the crimes they were charged with. The mess they left behind. Families broken and devastated, questions remaining unanswered. Death, all-pervasive. He felt sick.

Once inside the car, his anger exploded. As Carr sat down in the passenger seat, Cannon reached over and grabbed his necktie, pulling Carr towards him. Carr flinched, his hands rising to protect his face, closing his eyes and turning his head away.

"Don't hit me," he cried, the violence of Cannon's actions making Carr tremble. "Please don't….please..please," he whimpered, his hands useless as a defence if Cannon really wanted to do some damage.

Cannon held the necktie for a few seconds longer, his anger slowly subsiding. He clenched his teeth together, wanting to inflict pain on Carr, but realizing that he needed more information than he had already. He pushed Carr away with contempt.

Carr cowered against the passenger door window, mumbling how sorry he was, tears streaming down his face.

"So you don't know if Grey is alive or not?" asked Cannon eventually.

Carr answered softly, through his veil of fear, "No, I don't."

"So is it possible he could still be alive?"

"I guess so."

Cannon considered this for a second, then asked, "The obvious question is why you didn't go to the police with this information years ago? Why only now?"

Carr wiped his face with a serviette that he had found in his pocket and looked at Cannon for a few moments.

"I couldn't."

"Why?"

"There were two reasons," he paused, trying to rearrange his necktie and shirt and gather himself together. Sitting upright, no longer cowering and with a sense of confidence returning, he went on.

"The first reason is that I was in *love* with Peter. I would never have done anything to hurt him or to expose him. I couldn't. I knew what *they* did was wrong, but I was only seventeen, my whole life ahead of me. I had done nothing wrong myself and Peter was all I ever wanted. I didn't want to harm him or see him go to prison," he said. "I know that I would not have survived being locked up," he went on, "do you understand that Mr. Cannon? Do you *honestly* understand what I'm saying?" Tears again streaming down his face.

"You may not have participated, but you didn't stop them either," Cannon answered. His disgust was apparent in the tone of his voice.

"I tried," said Carr, still weeping, "I tried, but they were all out of control!"

Looking at this pathetic excuse for a human being, Cannon asked, "And the second reason?"

"Wilson!" the name was spat out like poison.

"He was the instigator right?"

"Yes. If any of us would have challenged him, it was likely that he would have killed us that night as well. He was and is a bully. Frankly, a malicious bastard. Always has been."

"But there were four of you."

"And do you think by telling the police, any of us would have been happy to go to jail. To give up what we had, our lives, our futures? If we had said anything to anyone, then all of us would have been convicted, he knew that and he played on it for years."

"So you lived with the secret all this time?"

"I'm not proud of what was done, Mr. Cannon," said Carr, "nor am I proud of living with the knowledge that a young girl was killed, murdered. I often relive that night in my mind. I don't think anyone intended to kill her, but things just got out of hand."

"And you think that there being no intent to kill someone, justifies keeping quiet?" asked Cannon.

"No I don't," answered Carr, "But I, we, was frightened. We panicked. We didn't know what to do. We were just kids…."

"So what happened after that?"

"We buried her!" responded Carr, his eyes showing that he was reliving that night in his mind. "We spent all night moving the body deeper into the woods. We found a spot where the soil was soft, the undergrowth damp with leaves covering the ground. We dug a hole using broken tree branches as shovels, and once it was deep and wide enough, we put her body in it. We listened to Alex, all of us. He was like a madman and we just did his bidding," he went on. "He had told us to strip the girl of all her clothes, each of us was given a piece to get rid of. We wanted to burn them right there, but we were worried about a fire being seen, so we took them away, each of us burning their respective pieces later, where and when they could."

Cannon considered how manipulative Wilson must be to convince four men to do what they did and to keep it secret all these years. Each living in fear of exposure.

Carr went on. "Alex talked about the possibility of predation, so once we had covered the body with soil and leaves, we searched the area for over two hours for stones to cover the site. When we were finished, the mound of stones over the body was at least two feet high. We were exhausted, freezing cold and it was still dark. We had been lucky because there was just enough light for us to see what we were doing. Alex then made us throw leaves over the stones to make it look like the stones had been in place for years. Finally, we took dead branches with long empty limbs on them and scrubbed the forest floor as best we could, to remove our footprints from the area, and then threw more leaves on the site to hide any sign of anyone having been there."

Cannon held his breath while Carr talked, not daring to interrupt his flow.

Once Carr had finished he asked. "You must have been filthy, covered in mud. How did you manage to avoid your families or anyone else asking about that when you got home?" he said.

"For any of our families who asked, we told them we had gotten into a fight."

"And you got away with it?"

"Yes," said Carr, "we did, though God knows how."

Cannon needed more.

"So in all this time, nothing has ever been said about this?"

"Other than between the five of us, no. And over the past 15 years or so, nothing at all."

"So why now? Why do you think that suddenly, out of the blue, two of the group have been killed?" asked Cannon.

"I don't know, and that is why I am so scared." Carr began to tremble again.

"Has anything been said in recent weeks?"

"Not that I can think of."

"Are you sure?" pressed Cannon.

"Yes!" insisted Carr, who just for a second was so sure of himself. Then without warning, he let out a cry, almost a wail of despair. "Oh my God," he said, then repeated, "Oh my God!"

"What?"

"I just remembered. It's the only thing it can be...."

Cannon was becoming quite agitated, urging Carr to reveal what was on his mind.

"About two months ago, we were at the club at Kirtlington having a drink, and Simon happened to mention that the band we saw on the night all *this* took place were reforming. He said he had noticed it on Facebook, and wondered if *we* wanted to go and see them, for old time's sake?"

"Who were the 'we'?" Cannon asked.

"Me, Simon, Alex, Graham, and a few others."

"And you spoke about the incident openly?" asked Cannon.

"Of course not! We had kept the secret for years, why would we bring it up again?" said Carr, "especially in public."

"Can you recall the others with you?"

"No, I can't. But there were about three or four others there, I can remember that."

A thought was forming in Cannon's mind that he wanted to test. He looked at his watch, it was now almost 4 pm. He needed Carr for a few more minutes, so he softened his tone.

"Tell me about Wilson. Why are you working for him still?"

"The simple answer," came the response, "is money."

"You mean you work for a man you despise, purely for the money?"

"Alex has kept all of us close, to make sure that none of us ever opened our mouths about that night. He has been very successful in his business as I assume you know. He had influence at the golf club, getting Simon the golf-pro job. He has been very generous with me too. He even helped set up Graham in his business."

"And Peter Grey?"

"Pete moved away because he couldn't handle the guilt. I think over the years he realized that it was too much for him. It was eating him up inside." Carr stopped for a second, his face giving away how he felt. A sad smile on his lips as he recalled the past.

"We spoke many times, the two of us, about what had happened that night. He knew it was wrong, and he knew he should have gone to the police, but he couldn't. I think it was loyalty to the rest of us. Not to Alex, but to us." he said.

"Did he tell you where he was going?" asked Cannon.

"No. It happened very quickly. He had been in a relationship, no children. His partner was involved in a car accident and was killed. He took that very badly, believed he was being punished for what we had done. Within six weeks after she died, he just left."

"Did you ever tell him how you felt about him?"

"I tried, subtly, but I don't think he ever understood where I was coming from," answered Carr.

"And when you heard that he had died, how did you hear about that?"

"Alex told us," he answered.

Chapter 17

They had spoken for a further half-hour, and it was quarter to five before Greg Carr finally left Cannon's vehicle.

As he walked away, looking battered and bruised, his shoulders slumped as he walked deeper into the darkened streets, Cannon watched him go. Sitting in the driver's seat, Cannon considered the information he had gathered.

Since Carr had not been able to fully verify that Peter Grey was dead or not. Killed by his own hand, someone else's, or not at all, Cannon was willing to keep an open mind.

Carr had also told him that Wilson had made him a partner in INet Solutions, and given him a 15% share of the business. Not only to keep him close but also because Carr was the actual driving force behind the successful operating of the business.

Wilson was the front man, the business development lead. Wilson undertook all the wining and dining of customers, all the *schmoozing* and the pressing of the flesh. Carr was the Creative Director, who designed and built the offers that Wilson sold. He was the one who ensured customers got what they were paying for. He and his wider team built the websites, built the processes needed inside the business, as well as the back-office systems used by online businesses to transact with their customers. His team also provided support to customers for any changes or new requirements needed. It was a very successful business. It had grown from just the two of them, to where it was now.

Wilson knew that Carr's lifestyle was gregarious and expensive, and from very early on, he exploited that for himself. Carr had wept again, when he told Cannon what Wilson had told him years before, about what he could expect as a gay man in prison.

Wilson had stated it repeatedly, then he had bullied him, abused him, threatened him, letting him know the implications if Carr, or anyone else, ever opened their mouths about the murder. Wilson had used that hold over every one of them, and all were complicit in accepting it.

"But there is one thing I have over him, this time," he had said, as he rubbed his face with his necktie. He seemed emboldened by what he was going to share.

"And what's that?" Cannon had asked.

"That he had lied to the police, and I expect to you too."

"What do you mean?"

"You must understand Mr. Cannon", Carr had said, "that being gay has some advantages, especially with the ladies."

Cannon had smiled inwardly at this. "Go on" he had urged.

"Alex's PA, Janet, who I know you met the other day, told me that Alex had asked for some details to give to you about his recent travel arrangements. Is that right?"

Cannon responded, nodded, affirming the question.

"Well, what you got was all lies."

"What do you mean?" he had responded.

"He wasn't where he claimed to be."

Cannon's interest piqued.

"Where was he then?" he had asked, not expecting the explosive response he received.

"He was at his other house. His hideaway, in Bourton-on-the Water, about an hour's drive from here…..*screwing* Rachel Crabb!"

Cannon drove home, his mind spinning like a gyroscope.

As he sped through the darkness, he barely saw the rain that slashed across the car, nor noticed the wind sending showers of dark, moist leaves flying through the air.

Wilson and Rachel Crabb? How was that possible?

Something about Carr's assertions niggled him. It didn't fit with where his instincts were leading him. He couldn't challenge Carr, but there was something Cannon had noticed a while ago that could verify it, one way or the other. *What was it….?*

The darkened sky and the teeming rain seemed to make the surroundings of empty fields and narrow lanes more sinister than normal. Cannon understood that it was his imagination playing games with him, as he continued to wrestle internally with what he had heard from Carr.

The lights of his car hit the wall of the stables, then rolled across the front of the house, as he turned into his short driveway and parked. The incessant rain had meant that the barn and stable doors had needed to be firmly shut, particularly given the strength of the wind, which had whipped and howled its way throughout the building. There was no one around, and only a small light above the main barn door gave any indication of any sign of life. The house lights were on, but the curtains downstairs were drawn. Clearly, Cassie and Michelle wanted to keep the filthy night at bay.

Cannon turned off the ignition and the lights of the car and jumped out of his seat, his head bowed against the breeze and the cold rain. He pressed the button on his car fob, and the side lights blinked twice, the sound of the doors locking drifted away on the wind.

He began a quick walk around the back of the car, head bent and his hands holding his coat around himself. As he walked alongside the car's boot, a dark shape moved rapidly behind him. The crack of the baseball bat on Cannon's shoulders, sent him flying forward onto the wet ground.

He rolled onto his back, but before he knew it, another blow rained into his ribs. The pain shot through him like electricity. He lifted his hands to protect himself from the next hit, opening his eyes despite the agony in his chest, to try and see who his attacker was, but the falling rain blurred his vision. All he could see was the bulk of what he thought was a man, silhouetted against the barn, dressed completely in dark clothing, including across the face. Cannon kicked out with his legs, just as a third blow was struck. The attacker's aim was deflected slightly, and the bat hit the ground, just beside Cannon's head.

Cannon rolled over to his left, the searing pain from his chest making breathing difficult. He tried to call out. The attacker took another swing across Cannon's legs, the full force being felt on his thigh. As Cannon waited for the next blow, he covered his head with his hands, before realizing that apart from the rain and the wind, he was alone.

For a minute or so, he just lay on the floor. His breathing laboured. His heart, racing. His clothes soaked, the water around him seeping into every pore.

He tried to roll over and begin an inexorable journey to get to his feet, but the pain in his chest and leg, made him gasp, and he collapsed onto his back. With his eyes closed and the rain on his face, he mentally worked his way through all his limbs, thankfully concluding that nothing was broken. He realized however that if he hadn't kicked out, his head may not be in one piece. As it was, when he touched his face, he wasn't sure if he was touching blood or water, but he felt a deep graze just above his left eye. The roughness against his fingers made him realize that he had left some skin somewhere on the floor. He tried again to stand up when suddenly an ever-widening ray of light cut across the ground towards him.

"Mike? Mike?" came the cry

It was Michelle.

Then she saw him sprawled on the floor. "Mike! Oh my God, what happened?" she called out.

He rolled over to be able to see her. As he did so, she ran out into the rain and across to him. Within seconds he was on his feet, her arm around his waist and his around her shoulder, and the pair limped across into the house, the pain beginning to get worse as the initial shock within him, wore off.

Once inside, she made him lie on the couch in the living room and went to collect a towel and some clean clothes. Upon her return, she began to undress him, throwing the wet and dirty items into a pile. As she did so, he winced in pain when she removed his shirt.

"Did you fall?" she asked.

Before he answered, he asked, "Where's Cassie?"

"She's in her room."

"OK, I don't want her to see me like this," he said. "I don't want her to be scared. But to answer your question, I was attacked."

Michelle stopped for a second, not quite comprehending, "When?"

"Just now," he replied, "just near the barn."

"By who?"

"I don't know," he said, "but I have an idea who it could be. I must be getting close to finding out what's going on, as someone is getting anxious."

"Anxious enough to almost kill you," she said. "We must call the police" she insisted.

"No!" he said, trying to sit up, as he put on a new pair of jeans.

She looked at him as if he was mad, a worried expression creasing her face

"Look, please trust me on this. I know what I'm doing."

For a second, she looked into his eyes. Her own almost pleading with him to do as she asked. Finally, she acquiesced saying, "OK, but please be careful. I couldn't handle losing you."

He leant forward to kiss her mouth, then suddenly yelped in pain as the muscles around his cracked ribs went into spasm. He collapsed back onto the couch.

"I'll get you some bandages, and something for that graze on your face," she said.

"Better get some Panadol or something else, perhaps a whisky," he joked as she walked off into the kitchen taking his wet clothes with her, to drop them into the washing machine.

While Michelle was away, Cannon thought about what had happened out in the yard. He realized he had been fortunate not to have suffered more physical damage than he had. He tried to recreate in his mind the size and shape of his attacker. He believed it was a man, the power in the blows suggested that. Unfortunately, he had not been able to grab his assailant, so he had no concept of the person's height. Lying on the floor had distorted his perception, plus with the darkness around him and the rain falling, he had no real opportunity to see the person's face.

'The face, the face,' he thought. Then he realized that there had been no face for him to look into anyway. There had only been blackness, where the face should have been. Why was that?

It took him a few seconds, and then he realized what it was. His attacker had *NO* face. Whoever it was, had been wearing a full-body, black latex suit. The kind you see people wearing at places like cricket or rugby matches, or on stag nights. When he had kicked out with his foot, the sensation of the shoe on latex had seemed odd at the time, but now he realized why.

He was confused. The theory he had been constructing in his mind as he drove home, now wasn't adding up.

They had told Cassie when she had come down for dinner that he had fallen, having tripped when running from the car to the house.

"Too much to drink at lunch, Dad?" she had said, her face glowing at the dig she was having. She loved to tease him when she could.

"Not quite love, I didn't drink at all. Well, just the one beer!" he had smiled.

They ate dinner and talked more than they had done for months. They talked like a *normal* family. There was no animosity between Cassie and Michelle at all. They made small talk, shared jokes, mostly at his expense. It was as if what had happened over the past week or so, had somehow unlocked the door to their relationship.

As he lay in bed wide awake, with Michelle fast asleep beside him, his ribs and the side of his head throbbed, despite all the painkillers he had taken. He was sure that the pain dulling effects of the tablets had worn off by now.

Michelle and he had talked until almost twelve, discussing what he had found out so far. He had been light on with the details, telling her only the things that he thought that she should know. The less she knew, the less danger she would be in. He didn't underestimate what could occur, but reassured her that he thought what had happened to him earlier in the evening, was just a warning. A warning to him, about his investigation. He didn't believe Cassie or Michelle were in any danger. At least that was the message he wanted to get across to her. He didn't want her worrying.

Eventually, just after midnight, his body had sought relief and they had both fallen asleep. However, within an hour, the ghosts had come to visit and he had woken with a start, a cry of pain as a bullet passed through him. As he lay there, his conscious mind rationalizing what he had experienced, he realized that the pain from the bullet was the pain in his ribs. He knew then that he hadn't been shot, but it was just a dream. Another dream to add to the others, and what he had experienced in his confused state, as he had slept, was not real.

Once his heartbeat had returned to normal, he listened to Michelle's steady breathing as she lay next to him. Her chest rising and falling rhythmically, in time with the steady rain hitting the window pane of the bedroom.

Over the following few hours, his mind drifted in and out of sleep, his thoughts jumping from one thing to another. Eventually, the alarm went off at 6 am, a luxurious treat he was now becoming used to.

During the hours that he was awake, however, he thought of his horses and he thought about his Investigation. He thought of a young girl trying to run away from a pack of men hungrily chasing her. He thought of fences that his horses needed to contend with on the racetrack, and if they were ready to do so. He knew *Belle o' the Ball* was due to run at Southwell soon and hoped she was ready for it. He thought of the barriers being put up, that HE himself, had to clear, in order to find the truth. He wondered if he was still capable, or had he lost it? He questioned himself. Was all of this chasing around in his old world, really worth it?

He knew where he wanted to be. He knew why. He needed to check with Rich how the horses were doing. He realized that he was losing touch with the rest of his team, indeed he was starting to feel too far removed from what was going on more broadly with his current crop of horses. He needed to get back to being a trainer again.

His final thought before he had fallen into a troubled sleep around 3 am, was that he believed he knew who the murderer of Simon Crabb and Graham Jefferson was. Tomorrow at the funeral, he would be able to prove it.

Chapter 18

The rain had stopped just before dawn.

The clouds had begun to break up, and pockets of clear sky began to emerge as the night sacrificed itself on the sun's watery rays. It remained cold, and the forecast was for a maximum temperature in single figures.

The funeral parlour and the small chapel were on Oxford road in Kidlington. The service for Simon Crabb was to start at 11:30 and was expected to last for 45 minutes. The body was to be taken afterwards to the Oxford crematorium, just over 6 miles away to the east.

For the attendees, a wake, starting at 1 pm, had been organized at the nearby Bicester Hotel and Spa, not too far up the road.

Before he had left home, Cannon had made a couple of phone calls and asked a few questions, the answers to which he hoped would prove his theory about the murderer. He arrived for the funeral service, an hour early. His face had swollen slightly overnight on the left-hand side, leaving his eye partially closed. While his vision was fine, it felt uncomfortable and it looked unsightly. His ribs still hurt, but Michelle had bandaged him up tightly and the painkillers he had taken, had kicked in. With his shirt, a jumper, and his coat on, no one would notice the damage to his chest.

He remained in his car in the parking lot across the road from the building, where he had stopped and parked. It was from here that he could observe people entering the funeral parlour. He noticed that there was no hearse in front of the building, so assumed that the coffin would be taken from the chapel through a back entrance, then transported to the crematorium.

He was hoping to see Rachel Crabb and Alex Wilson together, expecting at some point that he would be able to take them aside and let them know that he was aware of their affair and that he was aware of their role in Crabb's death.

He wanted to do this so that he could let Joe Crabb know afterwards that his work was done, his *obligation* met. It was then up to the police to get a conviction. He would provide them all the evidence he could.

His initial hopes of being able to get either Wilson or Rachel Crabb alone before the service started, however, were dashed, when Wilson and Greg Carr arrived in one car together.

Rachel, dressed as all grieving widows were expected to. All in black. She arrived in a group, with her parents in law, Joe and Irene Crabb, along with Wendy, followed immediately by several people who Cannon recognized from the golf club, Tony Book, Dale Simpson, and Jack Winton. They mingled outside the building for a while, before they collectively turned and walked inside.

Others walked solemnly towards the Funeral Directors' front door, heads bowed against the wind, walking almost in reverence to the occasion. Cannon did not recognize many of them, but it was clear to him that Crabb had attracted a large turnout. He was obviously very popular.

As he was about the extract himself and head across the road, Skinner and Quick pulled into the parking lot in Quick's car, stopping about three car lengths away from where Cannon sat.

Cannon groaned to himself. He could see where this was likely to end. The confrontation he had expected to have, may now not be, with who he had hoped it would be with. He remained in his car and watched the two policemen exit their vehicle, cross the road and enter the building. He was sure they had not seen him.

He waited for a further five minutes and watched several stragglers hurry towards the building, just as the service was about to begin. He entered the small chapel himself, just as the celebrant began proceedings. Sitting at the very back of the fifteen rows in the chapel, he observed the various members of the congregation. A few rows in front of him, Quick and Skinner sat together, effectively doing the same thing as he was, observing.

At one point during the service, Skinner turned around and noticed Cannon at the back. Skinner's face changed almost immediately from focus to anger. He looked at Cannon, with eyes that seemed to say, *'what the fuck are you doing here?'*

Cannon knew that once proceedings were over and they were outside, Skinner would be all over him like a rash. He noticed the policeman elbow his colleague and nod his head in Cannon's direction, making Quick turnaround to look towards him. Cannon was prepared for any confrontation now, so it didn't concern him. The earlier *contretemps* he had experienced at the police station and at the pub proved to him yet again, that Skinner was a *prick* and was past his use-by date. A fact Cannon already knew from prior experience.

He would have preferred not to have any argument at all but he knew that it was inevitable.

Once the hymns had been sung, the eulogies read and the service concluded, the coffin was then taken through a trap door at the front of the chapel. He followed the family out through the entrance to the chapel to where Rachel and Joseph stood at the door accepting condolences and best wishes.

Irene had taken poor Wendy, who had sobbed quietly throughout the service, away from her mother and Grandfather, and sat quietly with her in their car.

Cannon stood in a short queue before he was able to shake Joe Crabb's hand, and then holding that of Rachel, he gave her a short peck on her cheeks, softly offering his condolences. As he moved his face away from her own, she noticed for the first time the graze on his face and the swelling around his eye. She gasped sympathetically. Cannon did not believe it was a genuine reaction, just a ruse. He stared deeply into her eyes for a couple of seconds before he was required to move on as other mourners hurried him away, so that they too, could offer their own sympathies.

Cannon walked away towards his car, quickly turning around after he had crossed the road. Rachel was staring at him. Then, hoping he hadn't noticed, she quickly turned away to accept the best wishes of another funeral attendee.

The wind had died a little while the service was conducted. The sun still struggled to provide any warmth and while the breaks in the clouds were lasting longer, the temperature had not risen at all. Standing at his car, leaning against the bonnet, he waited for Skinner and Quick.

Eventually, they arrived. Skinner sauntering over to him, his demeanour aggressive. Quick walked behind his boss by a couple of yards.

"Didn't expect you here," Skinner said, looking down at his shoes.

"I was invited," Cannon responded, "were you?"

Cannon knew that Skinner and his colleague had not been asked to attend. He wanted to make the point that he, Cannon, did have a reason to be there. He still had an ongoing personal involvement in trying to solve the murder of Crabb, even if the police didn't like it.

Ignoring the question posed, Skinner pointed at Cannon's face. "Slip did we?" he asked sarcastically.

"You could say that."

"An improvement I must say. You should do it more often." Skinner smiled sardonically, turning to Quick and putting his tongue firmly in his cheek as he did so. Quick remained impassive, looking past Skinner and straight at Cannon.

"So what do you want?" asked Cannon.

"I *WANT* you to stay out of this!" exclaimed Skinner, "this is not your game anymore."

"Is that what it is to you Skinner, a game?"

"You know what I mean."

"Yes, I do. I know that you think you have all the answers, but from where I am standing," he looked Skinner up and down, showing his contempt, "you've got nothing so far. Otherwise, you wouldn't be here sniffing around. You would be dragging people in for questioning. From what I can see, you're still digging around in the weeds somewhere. I think...."

Cannon was cut short as Skinner launched himself, aiming to grab Cannon by the throat.

"You smug bastard!" Skinner screamed. "You fucking cunt!"

Cannon reacted by moving backwards, then launching his own attack. Hitting Skinner in the stomach, the soft flesh absorbing the impact, doubling Skinner over as he felt the impact of the blow and expelling his breath.

Quick moved to hold up his boss as he stumbled against the car next to them. Skinner retched as he tried to gulp oxygen into his lungs. Tears flowed down his cheeks. Cannon took a further step away, his own breathing slightly laboured. His heart beating rapidly, as the adrenaline coursed through his veins.

"I told you before Skinner, not to touch me again."

Skinner retched again, gasping for air.

Quick interjected saying, "Mike, I think this has gone too far. This is personal now and it needs to stop."

"You better tell your boss that," he replied nodding towards Skinner, "in the meantime, I have a wake to attend."

Cannon then opened his car door and slowly climbed inside. His ribs were hurting now, the impact of his punch and the recoil on his shoulder, had jarred his chest. "Fuck," he muttered as the pain crisscrossed his upper body.

Starting the car, he noticed that Skinner was now upright, pushing Quick away from him.

Cannon wound down his window as he put the vehicle into gear, and before he drove off said, "If you weren't so arrogant Skinner, I would share with you what I know, but until I have proof about Crabb's death, I'm going to keep it to myself. It's not the first time you've tried to keep me out of a case for your own selfish or political reasons, so for now, you can piss off and find your own answers to all of this!"

He then wound up his window and drove out of the car park.

He had some questions to ask.

Chapter 19

The feeling of someone constantly watching him made Cannon very unsettled.

The room where the wake was being held, was very Art Deco, rather like much of the hotel interior. It was somewhat surprising given the age of the building, however, it was clear from the quality of the finishes and the lack of any signs of age, that a major renovation had taken place a few years prior. The exterior looked almost Victorian, but inside, it was quite garish. The carpet was a pattern of red and black geometric diamond shapes. Triangles touching at their bases and their apex's, point-to-point.

On the wall's, upturned shell-shaped light fittings spread the light towards the ceiling, giving a subtle hue to the room. The wallpaper, giving the impression of a glamourous black and silver-lined envelope, which surrounded everyone in its embrace.

There were a dozen or so tables in the room, each covered with freshly starched white tablecloths, and each fully laid for the three-course meal that was to be served to the attending guests. Each table could seat eight people, and while not everyone had attended the service at the chapel, a large number had come to pay their respects at the wake itself. It was evident within twenty minutes of him arriving at the venue, that the room would soon be full.

He stayed close to Joe Crabb and his wife Irene, for most of the afternoon. At times, he discretely moved away, trying to get Rachel Crabb on her own. As he did so, he received the odd jibe about his damaged face and jokes about *having been hit by a bus* from those he interacted with. It was not easy to isolate Rachel however, as most of the time there was a huddle of bodies around her. Most offering their sympathies, others sharing anecdotes with her about her late husband. Cannon watched when he could, to see how she reacted during such conversations. She played the dutiful wife, nodding when she needed to, smiling wanly when expected to. Cannon admired her acting, but he felt he could see right through her now.

He kicked himself for falling for her charm, and the ease at which he was duped by her. For having got himself as deep as he did and for supporting her during her interview with the police. He thought back to the conversation they shared in the tearoom and realized how stupid he had been.

Cannon waited for his opportunity. He knew that what was starting off as a solemn occasion would, as the attendees imbibed more and more during the afternoon, eventually transcend into a celebration of life for those living today, and would over time, become less of a celebration of the late Simon Crabb's life.

As the afternoon wore on and the numbers thinned out, Joe Crabb and Irene having left to go home with Wendy, he found Rachel sitting alone at one of the tables, a drink in her hand. On the other side of the table, an elderly couple were talking quietly to themselves. Cannon took them to be long-standing golf club members. She was watching Alex Wilson who was at the bar, talking with some of his golfing friends. Her attention being distracted, she did not notice him quietly slip into the seat next to her.

He introduced himself to the elderly couple.

"Dale Simpson," the man said, "Club Chairman, Kirtlington Golf Club, and this is my wife Brenda."

Cannon stood and shook hands with them, introducing himself as a family friend.

"Simon was our club professional," Simpson continued, nodding in deference to Rachel. "Such a tragedy to lose him. Terrible business, so sad, so very sad."

Cannon nodded in agreement, then said, "Excuse me, I need to speak with Mrs. Crabb alone, would you mind if we do?"

"Not at all," came the reply, "we'll leave you to it."

Simpson and his wife stood up from the table, wishing her all the best and indicating they would say goodbye before they left.

For a few seconds, Rachel watched them go. Cannon sensed in her a level of discomfort in being alone with him. Her eyes seemed to darken and her body language reflected internal tension. Cannon got the impression she was desperate for someone to join them.

"Penny for your thoughts," he said.

She turned to him and gave him an embarrassed smile.

"Isn't it obvious?" she replied.

Cannon considered this. She hadn't really answered his question. Her answer was open to interpretation.

"I'm not sure."

"I'm thinking about how hypocritical people can be," she went on. She looked around the room slowly and then turning back to him, said, "Everyone knows that Simon was a bastard," the venom in her comments was clear even though she spoke quietly. "And yet all I hear, is how *'great'* he was, and *'how devastated'* I must be. It's just a game!"

"And are you also playing that game?" he asked, looking straight into her eyes.

"What do you mean?"

Cannon sighed inwardly. It was always the same. He knew that the guilty, the wrongdoer, could always find a reason in their own mind as to why what they did was right, and everyone else was wrong.

"I know the truth," he continued.

She looked at him quizzically, not understanding where he was coming from.

"I know what happened," he said.

"What?" she answered, her eyes showing both a lack of understanding and fear, "You know who killed Simon?"

He put his hand on her arm. "I think we should find a place to talk. When I came in, I saw there was another small room, possibly a reading room just up the corridor. It was empty, hopefully, it still is."

Cannon stood up from the table. Slowly Rachel did the same, and she followed him out into a corridor that led towards the hotel reception.

The room that Cannon had observed earlier, was still vacant. It was about fifteen yards away from the function room where the wake was being held. Once inside he closed the door, remained standing, and leant with his back against it. Rachel sat down on a brown leather high-back chair, with long curved wing armrests, the style very much in tune with the rest of the hotel.

"So what have you found out?" she asked.

"I know about you and Alex Wilson, and I know where you were on the day of Simon's murder?" he answered.

Rachel remained impassive. She looked down at her hands that she kept folded on her lap. For a few seconds, the silence between them was palpable. Muffled sounds of voices from the wake echoed through the walls. Eventually, she looked up.

"I'm not sure what you think you have discovered," she said, "but you don't know anything about me."

Cannon remained stony-faced. "Perhaps not," he replied, "but I know you killed your husband…."

Before he could continue, she was out of her seat, the chair pushed away behind her, toppling over onto its side.

Her face was red with rage. "What the hell are you talking about?" she screamed.

"There has been something bothering me ever since the day we first met in the school car park," he went on, ignoring her outburst, "and it's taken me a while to piece things together, eventually though, it all fell into place."

"And you think I killed Simon do you?" she answered.

"If not you directly, then you and Alex Wilson."

She shook her head and gave out a cry of frustration. "I think Mr. Cannon that my father-in-law made a big mistake asking you to help us with Simon's murder. He should have left it to the police!"

She moved towards the door to try to leave, but he stood his ground.

With her face almost to his she said, "Get out of my way, this conversation is over!"

"I'm afraid it's not," he replied.

Suddenly and without warning, Cannon felt himself falling. He stretched out his arms to protect himself as he fell towards her as the door behind his back was forced open. Cannon and Rachel hit the ground together almost side by side. The hard landing expelling the air in Cannon's chest, his damaged ribs screaming in pain.

He turned his head as he fell, looking to see how the door had opened so dramatically. Alex Wilson stood in the opening, almost completely filling the door frame.

"What the fuck is going on here?" he shouted, walking into the room, slamming the door behind him.

Rachel and Cannon lifted themselves simultaneously off the floor, Rachel to sit on another chair, while Cannon remained standing, his left arm holding his chest.

Struggling to breathe, Cannon gestured towards Rachel. "I was about to explain to your lover here," he said evocatively, "who killed her husband. But I think you know who already, don't you?"

Wilson turned to Rachel, his head tilted towards Cannon, "What's he said so far?" he asked.

"He thinks we killed Simon."

Turning to Cannon, Wilson said, "And why would we do that, Mr. Cannon? What possible motive would we have?"

"To keep him quiet," responded Cannon.

"About what?" sneered Wilson.

Cannon looked over at Rachel.

He wasn't completely sure if she knew the full story, or indeed if she knew anything of the history of her late husband, Greg Carr, Graham Jefferson, and Wilson himself. Nor was he certain if she knew of Peter Grey, and what they had done years ago to the young girl that Wilson ultimately murdered. He decided to play his cards cautiously.

Facing Wilson again he said, "When I came to see you, you gave me some information about your travel plans and where you were the day that Simon Crabb was murdered."

"That's right, I was in the US."

Turning to Rachel, Cannon said, "And you were in Edinburgh at a conference?"

She nodded her head slightly, but with less conviction than Cannon would have expected. He knew she was lying.

"Well," he went on, "I know you are both lying."

Wilson and Rachel looked at each other surreptitiously. Wilson's ego got the better of him, and he responded aggressively, trying to intimidate Cannon. "That's a ballsy statement, Mr. Cannon. I hope you can back it up?"

Turning to Rachel, Cannon continued. "Before you arrived at the school on the day we met, your father-in-law told me about the arguments that Wendy had heard you having with your husband," he said. "Joe wasn't sure if they were serious or not and didn't want to get involved. He thought Wendy may have been exaggerating. But from what I can guess, it was likely to be much more than that." He said, pausing, waiting for a response.

"Go on," she said.

"I think that the arguments *were* real and that they were based on Simon's continued cheating on you. Somehow, eventually, you ended up playing the same game as he did, and he found out."

"So you think I killed him?" she replied.

"Yes," answered Cannon, "I do, or at least you both arranged for him to be killed."

"You're fucking crazy!" shouted Wilson.

Looking at Rachel, Cannon went on. "When you arrived at the school, you had supposedly been unable to contact Simon the previous evening, and after speaking to your father-in-law dashed to the school to be there before Wendy arrived back from the school trip."

"That's right," she said.

Cannon smiled, saying, "Well this is what I've been struggling with since that day. I noticed it at the time, but couldn't recall what I had been missing until last night. Overnight it came to me."

"And what is that?" interjected Wilson.

"That there was no luggage in the boot of the car. It was empty!"

He let his statement sink in for a few seconds, then continued.

"If you had been away at a conference for two to three days, I would have expected there to be some luggage in your car, even just a small overnight bag, and especially given your claim that you had driven straight from the conference to the school. But there was nothing! It was only when I found out about you and Wilson that the missing pieces began to fit. You weren't in Edinburgh at all, were you?" He pointed an accusatory finger in her direction. "During those three days, you were at Wilson's other home in Gloucestershire, in Bourton-on-the-Water to be precise, weren't you?!"

Rachel's mouth hung open, she clearly wanted to speak, but the truth, as outlined by Cannon, stunned her into silence.

"I think you're guessing," Wilson replied, trying desperately not to acknowledge what had been revealed to him, but wondering inwardly where Cannon had gotten his information from. Trying to bluff his way out of the hole that he was falling into, he said, "And what does that prove? That we are lovers? So what? It proves NOTHING!" he spat.

"It proves you were lying," responded Cannon. "So if you were lying about where you were, what else have you been lying about?"

He left the question hanging before continuing. "I also did some checking this morning and you did fly to Europe as you said you did, a day or so before Crabb was killed, but instead of transiting via Heathrow to the US, you cancelled your flight and re-entered the country." He paused for effect. "Your PA's details were very thorough. But the PA of the US representative that you were supposed to see there, was just as thorough. I called them yesterday and they told me by way of email response, that you had *cancelled* your visit due to *unforeseen circumstances*." He smiled before saying, "It's amazing what a British accent and knowledge of police protocol can extract from young assistants in America you know."

"You bastard!" said Wilson, veins in his neck bulging.

Letting his comments sink in, Cannon continued, lowering his tone to ensure he held their attention and to emphasize the gravity of the situation. "I have a contact in the police who I spoke with this morning and who already knew about your so-called trip. They are going to speak with you shortly I believe, so I hope you both have got your stories straight?"

Rachel eventually found her voice.

Staring into Cannon's eyes, she said, "OK, Mr. Cannon, Mike. Yes you are right, I wasn't in Edinburgh nor was Alex in the US, but we didn't kill Simon. Why would we?"

Cannon laughed, then turned towards Wilson and pointing at his own face asked, "And I suppose *YOU* didn't try to kill me last night either?"

"You are a bloody nutcase," responded Wilson, "why the fuck would I do that, I'm not a murderer," he said.

Contemplating what he had just heard, Cannon knew it was time. Pointing his index finger at Wilson he said, "I think you had better sit down and shut up," he said.

Wilson's anger remained unabated, but looking towards Rachel, he saw the uncertainty in her eyes. He stood his ground for a second before eventually picking up the overturned seat, and sat down in it.

Cannon remained standing. He was aware that the sounds in the room next door had abated. It was likely that most of the guests were slowly drifting away.

"Let me tell you what I think," he said, looking at Rachel. "I don't think you know the full truth about this man," he nodded in Wilsons' direction, "so let me explain something to you."

"What do you mean?" she asked, confused.

"Peter Grey," he said, looking at Wilson, who flinched almost as soon as the words had left Cannon's mouth.

She looked totally lost, "Who is he?" she asked.

Cannon's eyes never left Wilson's face. They stared at each other like gunfighters about to draw in a duel at sundown. Neither blinked.

"What's he talking about Alex?" Rachel said, leaning to grab him by the arm.

"I have no idea," came the stoic reply, "let him tell us."

Cannon shrugged his shoulders, hiding the pain from his cracked ribs as he did so.

"I gather from that comment, Alex," he deliberately used Wilsons' Christian name to show that contempt had now moved to familiarity, "that Rachel here does not know the secret you forced her husband and others to keep all these years?"

"What secret is that then?" sneered Wilson.

"One that you thought you had buried, but due to a strange twist of fate had inadvertently resurfaced," Cannon went on, "resulting in the need for you to kill those who you had previously intimidated into silence, for fear that they would reveal the full story."

Wilson remained silent, hiding behind a veneer of strength, but to Cannon's mind was hiding behind his arrogance.

"Let's return to Peter Grey and his death some years ago," went on Cannon. "I managed to find out that he did indeed commit suicide, but I think you knew that didn't you Alex?"

Wilson remained passive, nonchalant, non-committal.

"I can't prove anything, but I think you may have had something to do with it," continued Cannon.

Turning to Rachel, Cannon slowly relayed to her the story that Greg Carr had revealed to him. He was careful not to reveal his source but was able to provide her with all the detail and to leave her in no doubt what had happened all those years ago.

As he told the story, she seemed to shrink further and further into her chair. At one point, she drew her legs underneath her and wrapped her arms around herself. Steady tears ran down her cheeks. He realized at that point that she was not involved in her husband's murder.

"You have no proof to all this," shouted Wilson angrily. "It's all nonsense, crap!" he said. "Why would I want to kill my friends anyway, after all these years?"

"Because of a slip of the tongue."

Wilson laughed, "What are you on about?"

"On the night you killed that girl, you were at a concert. That band recently announced it was reforming, and that came out in a casual conversation at the golf club one night. I figure you realized that your friends talking about it was a risk. A risk that maybe would bring up the past."

Cannon stared into Wilson's eyes, conscious that the man's anger could explode at any time.

"You tried to shut it down. But I think you soon realized that despite your secret having been buried for so long, the hold you had over your *friends* was no longer strong enough, so you decided to resolve the problem yourself."

"What hold was that Mr. Cannon?" answered Wilson smugly.

"Firstly," he answered, "you were screwing Simon's wife, and while he may have been a bastard himself, I guess he still loved her." Turning to Rachel and noticing her embarrassment, he continued. "Is that what the arguments were about? Did he want you to stop sleeping with Alex? Did he promise he would stop his affairs as well?"

Rachel didn't answer.

"I think Simon wanted you back," he said to Rachel. "He may have promised you the world, I don't know, but I think he genuinely loved you."

He turned to Wilson and pointed, "He may not have been able to convince Rachel to stop seeing you, but he did have one card over you that I think he finally needed to play to get her back, and I think during some pillow talk Rachel here may have talked to you about it," he went on. "I think he may not have told Rachel any of the details. In fact, I think that's apparent now, but when she mentioned to you that Simon had told her that he had a *secret* that he could use against you, that set in motion your plan to kill him before he was able to contact the police."

Rachel looked at Wilson, fear, and loathing in her eyes. She began to sob. "What have I done?" she said softly to herself.

Cannon having seen this film many times before in his former life, had no sympathy for either of them. He went on. "As for Jefferson, he was dying anyway so your hold on him was lost. You couldn't be sure if he was another one of your group that was wavering, so you killed him too."

Wilson laughed, "Oh you are so funny," he said, "so funny and so very wrong."

"When I came to see you at your office, you knew I wasn't with the police. Someone had tipped you off. I'm not sure if it was Rachel here or someone else. Perhaps it was Jefferson himself, but whoever it was, you knew at the time who I was, and why I was asking questions. I think I started to unsettle you, and so you reacted by killing Jefferson as well. After all, you didn't know what he had told me and you couldn't be sure that your secret wasn't yet out. Getting rid of another witness was the best way to save your arse."

Cannon noticed that Wilson had become like a tightly sprung coil, ready to explode with threatening force. "And that's why," he went on, *"YOU,* tried to kill me last night."

"You have no idea," Wilson sneered, his chest heaving and his hands flexing with rage, "how much I would love to smash your head in right now, but...."

"STOP IT!" shrieked Rachel, "Stop it, both of you!"

Both men seemed to freeze where they were, despite the adrenaline coursing through their veins, and the testosterone fuelling their anger.

The two men looked at her. She took a few seconds to compose herself, to get herself back under control.

"Mike, I don't know if what you have said is true, but I've heard enough to know that I've been a bloody fool. I will deal with that in due course," she said looking at Wilson. "If you have any evidence about what happened years ago, then I strongly suggest you go to the police and let them do what they must."

"It's all a fucking lie," pleaded Wilson, realizing instantly that his relationship with her was now over.

"I'm not sure it is," she responded, "however time will tell. What I can say though Mike, is that you are wrong about Alex or myself being involved in Simon's or Graham Jefferson's murders."

"Why?" answered Cannon, cynically.

"Because," she said, "despite what you may think of me, I am telling you the truth. Alex *was* with me on the night Simon was murdered, and he *was* likewise with me the night that Jefferson was killed. We spent both nights together."

Cannon tried to comprehend what he was hearing. It didn't compute. Was she really telling the truth?

"And last night," she went on, "Alex and I spent the night here in the hotel. We never left the building after six o'clock. We ate dinner in the restaurant, which the staff can confirm, and then went back to our room. I'm sure the CCTV can corroborate that we never left the building. So whoever attacked you last night, it wasn't Alex."

Cannon thought back to last night. He believed he knew who had attacked him and why. Was he wrong?

While he had doubted her initially, he now began to doubt himself.

If it wasn't Wilson who attacked him, then who was it and why?

He slowly realized that his world was coming apart.

Chapter 20

"I can't believe I got it so wrong," he said.

"Maybe you didn't," came the reply. "When I get back to the station, I'll inform Skinner, and he can decide how he wants to play it. While he hasn't covered himself in glory so far, perhaps he can go out on a high? A conviction for a murder from so long ago is just the thing he would love. He could live in retirement for months, on the accolades he would get."

They were sitting at the bar at the Punchbowl Inn, on Oxford Street in Woodstock. Literally a two-minute walk from the King's Head, where Skinner would be drinking.

Dusk had already been come and gone. The rain that had been on and off during the afternoon, had decided to stay for a while. The bar was only about half full because of it. Various hats and coats, including their own, were stacked on top of each other on the backs of chairs near an open fire, in an attempt to get them dry. The flickering of the flames and the heat from the hearth, made the bar area warm, inviting, relaxing.

"Has he said anything about that? About retiring?" asked Cannon.

"No, not really," answered Quick, "it's just an impression I'm getting. He's too set in his ways to change, and I think he's finding it hard now to operate with all the new systems and protocols. All the *newbie* stuff as he calls it." Following a slight pause, he said, "He and I had a real blow-up yesterday. I can't work with him anymore, so I've been to see the Superintendent today to lodge a complaint, and I've told him I want a transfer out."

Cannon considered this. "Probably for the best," he said sighing, his voice dull. He felt for Quick but was mindful of his own errors, his failures. His demeanour reflected his negative mood. He raised the glass containing his almost untouched beer and took a sip, ruminating on what Quick had said, and on what had happened a short while earlier.

After he had walked out from the room at the hotel, leaving Wilson and Rachel together, he had called Quick and asked him to meet him, if possible, within the hour. Cannon had indicated he had some information that he wanted to share but didn't want Skinner around. They had agreed to meet where Skinner was unlikely to be.

He had then called Michelle and told her of his plans. He had indicated to her, that he would be home in a couple of hours. He also told her that he had made a huge mistake in his thinking, and therefore despite what he had thought previously, he was now unsure who had been in the yard the previous evening. He asked her to be vigilant but indicated that he now thought that it was someone who was trying to get to the horses, rather than anything to do with his investigation of the Crabb murder. After he had finished talking with Michelle, he spoke with Rich to ask him if he could stay around at the stables until he arrived back, just to be there in case anyone tried to break in and do any damage.

"*No problem at all Boss,*" had been the reply.

Putting his glass back down on the countertop, and waving his hand slightly to indicate the pub's interior, Cannon said, "Thanks for coming here anyway."

"Given my day, I think I should be thanking you," replied Quick, a smile of resignation on his face.

"No problem at all. As I said before. I can't prove what I've told you, but hopefully, Carr will provide *Queen's* evidence against Wilson and the others, and you can get a result. I think it's something you will need to push hard on. See if you can get him to open up, as he is vulnerable enough, scared enough. Hopefully, he will crack. Especially if he still thinks Wilson killed the others, and would eventually have come for him."

"Thanks," answered Quick. Then asking in a more conciliatory tone, he said, "Mike, there is something I want to know, so I'll come right out and ask it straight."

"Sure, go ahead."

"Why the animosity between you and Skinner?" he inquired. "It borders on hate, and it's so palpable, that anyone can see it. Whenever you are together or when your name comes up in any conversation he is involved in, Skinner just reacts like a lunatic. It's bizarre!" he went on. "So what happened, for it to be so bad?"

Cannon took a long gulp of his beer before answering.

"It goes back about 15 years or so," he said, his mind's eye recalling what he had experienced so long ago. "We were both working on the same case, quite high profile. We'd been drafted in to work undercover on a matter involving a series of armed robberies in the Midlands. Jewellery shops, cash in transit vans, banks. It seemed the gang or gangs would hit any target they wanted, at any time."

"And?"

"Well through sheer luck, we were able to turn someone in the gang, who was able to get one of our own on the *inside*. That turned out to be Skinner. His sole job was to work as a mechanic at one particular garage, near Birmingham airport. He had told the lead investigating officer on the case, a DCI, that in his younger days he had driven stock cars, motorbikes and had raced them as well. He convinced him that what he didn't know about cars wasn't worth knowing."

Quick sat impassively, listening carefully as Cannon continued.

"The intelligence we had, suggested that this particular garage was where the getaway cars were taken after each robbery. After each job, the car would be driven there, emptied of the cash or jewels or whatever was stolen. After that, it was almost completely dismantled, a new engine put in, new chassis, etcetera, and then the whole lot re-sprayed. They even had genuine number plates ready for use, and this would all be done in less than 12 hours."

"Some operation," interjected Quick.

"Yes," he agreed. "Once completely overhauled, that car was driven hundreds of miles away and torched somewhere remote. The engine and other parts that were removed from the original car were put into other vehicles or just dumped into the canals around the area. This had been going on for a couple of years, and nobody on the investigation had any idea what to do."

Before continuing, Cannon looked around and noticed the bar was filling up with more customers. The rain had eased again and had brought out more revellers. He picked up his drink, nodded towards a remote table that was unoccupied because it was furthest away from the fire, and they moved away to where they could not be overheard, taking their coats with them.

"Anyway," he continued once they had sat down again, "my job in the team was to be Skinner's liaison and act as a lookout for him. Anything relevant to the investigation, any small detail we could use that he found out, he would pass on to me. I, in turn, would pass it back to the investigating team, as Skinner couldn't be seen to be engaging with anyone outside of the small circle of people associated with the gang. We would meet in pubs, at service stations in the area, or a local McDonalds, wherever it was that seemed safe and innocuous. If anyone asked him, we wanted the gang to think that I was his mate, and my cover was that I was a small-time drug dealer."

"And?" Quick asked.

"After a while," he went on, "I noticed Skinner becoming more and more distant. It was becoming clearer as the operation continued that he was falling victim to the Stockholm Syndrome. He continuously *denied* it to me and to our superiors, but he couldn't *hide* it from me, as I had seen what he did during that last raid."

"So what went down?"

"Intelligence received a tip-off that a heist was to take place on a transit van that was to be delivering over £2million in cash, to a particular bank. We had the date, the time, everything we needed. We set a trap for when the robbers got back to the garage in order to catch those that had hit the van, and those already waiting at the garage."

Quick sat quietly, intrigued, desperate to hear what the outcome was from the investigation, all those years ago.

"Well the operation went tits up," stated Cannon, as his mind recalled the events of that day. "What should have been a mass arrest of the perpetrators, ended up being a bloody shoot-out, a blood-bath. Six people were killed including two of our own," he said. "One of those killed was shot by Skinner. That victim was the very man we had been able to turn. He was shot in the back, and I saw Skinner do it!"

Cannon looked across the table at Quick, who looked gobsmacked. Cannon could see that his companion was trying to rationalize what he had just heard. Eventually, he asked, "But didn't anyone expect there to be violence, after all these were experienced hard men, armed robbers?"

"Well this is where the rubber hit the road," he answered. "Skinner had told me that the garage was gun-free, to give the impression of a legitimate business and was *clean*, so as not to be caught out by any of the spot raids on garages that we were undertaking across the area. In addition, he told me that after any robbery the guns used, shotguns, small arms, were disposed of on route to the garage using a sophisticated network of drop-off points. In fact, he said from the moment the cash was taken, another car involved in the hold-up, was used to spirit all the firearms away, to be destroyed and dumped somewhere. I relayed this information back to our superiors."

Cannon took another drink from his glass, emptying it as he did so.

"But it was untrue," he went on, "Skinner had lied to me!"

"And so the firefight," said Quick nodding, understanding.

"Yes."

"I assume there was an internal inquiry after the event, plus the court case. Wouldn't all this have come out?"

"The internal inquiry took several months to complete. The court case to get the convictions, even longer. Leading up to both, Skinner and I, plus a couple of others were given suspensions from duty for a while. At the inquiry, Skinner said that his cover was somehow blown. He implied that it could have been me, which was absolute nonsense." Cannon revealed. "I think he found out that I had expressed concern about his own behaviour, and he used that to deflect from his own actions, his own greed. Eventually, he was cleared of any wrongdoing, due to insufficient evidence. It was concluded that he had been lied to by the gang about the weapons and that what he had told me, he had believed to be true."

"But your evidence about him killing the insider, what happened to that?"

"Skinner claimed it was in self-defence, that in the chaos, he had no choice."

"But *you* said you saw him do it," said Quick.

"I did. But it was my word against his. The inquiry concluded that I was wrong. Case closed."

"And so…?"

"Well, eventually the team was split up and both of us went our separate ways. To different departments. For a while, I worked in the drug squad around the Chelmsford area and I believe Skinner joined the CID in Northampton. Skinner was always ambitious, but he became known for cutting corners, putting others at risk. Eventually, we met up again here in Oxfordshire, in the Thames Valley Force. Skinner had hit a ceiling and knew he would never be promoted again above his existing rank. He blamed me for that, for making him go through the inquiry, and for him, having to defend his actions. He believed it put a black mark against his name. In reality, it was his attitude that prevented him from any further promotions. You have seen yourself, how belligerent he can be." Cannon paused for a second, noting Quick nodding in agreement. "You can also see how he hates those who have come along and gone up the ladder above him. Those younger men and women that he despises so much."

"That explains his *couldn't give a shit* attitude."

"Exactly," went on Cannon. "So the upshot of all this is that we kept our distance from each other until eventually, I left the Force. He still bears that grudge though."

"If we get the conviction of Wilson and Carr, for what essentially is a cold case it will be ironic that you would have helped him do that," Quick said.

"I guess so," replied Cannon, a half-smile on his face. He picked up his empty glass, trying to extract the last drop.

"Another?" asked Quick.

"No, but thanks anyway. I'm driving."

The two men sat in silence for a little while, watching and listening to those around them enjoying the evening.

Cannon looked at his watch. He would be heading off home shortly. Michelle would be making dinner now, he thought, and the horses already put away for the night. He was looking forward to *Belle o' the Ball's* upcoming race at Southwell, and he wanted to get back into his old routine as soon as possible.

"What I don't understand though," commented Quick, his words bringing Cannon back from his reverie, "is…. if you believe Rachel that Wilson was with her the night her husband was killed, and she's telling the truth, then who *did* murder him and why?"

"To be honest," answered Cannon, "I haven't a clue," he acknowledged. He shrugged his shoulders. "A complete bloody mystery I'm afraid. Do you have a view?"

"No, we've checked everything we can. DNA. CCTV, everything. So far all we have has been bloody useless to us."

Cannon could sense the frustration in Quick's tone.

"Plus we have interviewed everyone we could, that was there on the night. No one saw a thing," went on Quick.

"And what about the mysterious phone calls?"

"What about them?"

"Well, did they come to anything?" Cannon enquired.

"No, nothing, nada! They don't seem to mean anything to anyone. Just the same snippet of a song, left several times on Crabb's phone."

"Yes, I'm aware of that."

"Oh," answered Quick, "so you knew about them?"

"Yes. Jefferson, Wilson, and Carr all told me about the calls, but I have no idea about the music. I've not even heard it," he said.

"It's by a band called *Everyman*."

"Never heard of them," answered Cannon.

"They were quite big about twenty-odd years ago."

"Oh, fair enough" he shrugged.

"I've got the song on my phone here," Quick said, "have a listen."

Cannon was slightly put out, he was ready to go home. It had been a big day and his ribs were still hurting from his earlier fall when Wilson had pushed open the door while he was questioning Rachel.

"It's a bit noisy in here, do you have any earphones?"

Quick took a set from out of his pocket, then found the song on the phone. He passed the phone over the table for Cannon to insert the earpieces into the jack and for him to push the *play* button.

The music began. Cannon listened intently for about twenty seconds, then talking one earpiece out, said to Quick, "I thought there was only a short snippet of the music on the phone?"

"Yes, there was," he said, "but we were able to track down the band and get a full version of it. It's called, *'Took you Away.'*"

Cannon put the loose earpiece back into his ear, closed his eyes to concentrate on the song, and listened for a further half a minute. Quick watched.

Suddenly, Cannon's eyes flew open!

He sat bolt upright. "Fuck!" he shouted, not realizing he couldn't hear himself speak. Some of the patrons turned around to stare at him. "FUCK!" he said again, tearing the earphones away from his face.

"What? What is it?!" asked Quick, totally bewildered.

Cannon stumbled over his words. In his excitement, he couldn't get the words out quick enough. "Fuck me," he said again, "I know this tune. I've heard it before!" he yelled.

"So, what does it mean?"

Cannon gathered himself together, "It means I know who the killer is. Damn, how could I have missed it? How could I have been so blind?" he admonished himself.

"What? Who?" queried Quick.

Before he could answer, Cannon's phone rang. From the screen, he could see it was Michelle.

"Hi," he said, "just about to...."

Michelle replied, but he couldn't hear her properly. The noise in the bar and the noise against which Michelle was shouting, nearly drowned her out. "Fi...," he heard her say, "The house...."

"What's that darling?" he asked, placing a finger in one ear while pressing his phone firmly to the other.

"The house Mike, get here quickly," she shouted again down the line, "the house, it's on fire!"

Chapter 21

The short drive home seemed to him, to be the longest journey he had ever undertaken.

While the rain had now totally abated, the roads were wet and the cars ahead of him seemed to move in slow motion. His mind was frantic, trying to understand what was going on, what he was going to find. Inside, his stomach churned and fear tore at his heart.

They had left the bar together, running to their cars, like two cheetahs chasing gazelles on the African savannah. Neither of them knew that they could move so fast.

As they had left the bar, Cannon had shouted at Quick to call 999, and to get the fire brigade, and all the other services, to his farm as soon as possible. Driving out of the parking lot of the pub, Quick followed Cannon in his own car. After having gotten through to the emergency services, he called Cannon on his mobile.

"Fire brigade are on their way, as is an ambulance. I'll call Skinner shortly," he shouted into the phone, "and Mike, I'm about a minute or two behind you."

"Thanks," answered Cannon.

Once clear of the traffic, having turned off Oxford Road onto the A4095 and headed towards home, he gunned his car for all it was worth. As he turned into Combe Road, he could see a red glow in the distance, lighting up the night sky.

"Shit," he said out loud, his mind churning with anxiety for Cassie and Michelle.

As he pushed the car harder into the turns, his mobile rang again. It was Michelle. "Mike, where are you. How far away are you?" she asked, the panic in her voice rising with every passing second.

"I'm about two minutes away," he replied. "Are you ok? How's Cassie?"

"She's here with me," she answered. "Mike, my God, get here quickly," she pleaded. "The house it's…it's…."

"Ok, nearly there," he shouted back into the phone. "Get away from the house as far as you can!" he screamed, "I'll meet you at the driveway entrance."

As he drove closer to the house, he could see flames spewing from the roof. Thick tongues of red and yellow, licking at the dark sky. The one end of the building was ablaze, that closest to the road, but furthest from the stables. One of the windows had blown out from the heat, glass, and pieces of the window frame lay strewn beneath the window cavity, and partially onto the road.

His car wheels crunched across the debris, and he could feel the heat through the car door as he passed that end of the house and turned into his driveway. There were several cars already parked there.

Michelle and Cassie were waiting. They were both in tears, in shock.

Cannon jumped out of his car. As he did so, he could hear sirens coming up behind him. He saw flashes of blue and red from the fire engines, ambulance, and police vehicles light up the darkness of the road that snaked away behind him. They looked like a wagon train as they came up the road, each astern of the other.

"Are you alright?" he shouted to Cassie and Michelle.

"Yes," they said in unison. Then Cassie hugged him, holding him tightly to her, "Oh Dad," she cried through her tears. "What's happening to us?"

He held her tight, as he did so Michelle said, "Mike, this is deliberate. Someone did this to us. It's NOT an accident." Cannon looked at her, her eyes wide with fear. He tried to be positive for Cassie's sake.

He stood up straight, uncoupling himself from Cassie.

"The horses, what's happening to the horses?"

"Rich is with them," Michelle said. "Thank goodness he was still here when the fire started. He's called some of the lads already. Some are already here," she pointed towards the other cars in the driveway.

"Okay," he said, "you stay here! I'll go and see what I can do. We may need to move them out of their stables into the field up top if Rich hasn't started that already."

With that, he ran towards the stables, looking all the time at the house as it continued to burn. He noticed how the sound of the fire grew with intensity, but was still only at the one end of the building.

Please God, the fire brigade can save most of the building he thought, hearing the fire truck's airbrakes scream, as they stopped on the road.

Noise and chaos began to assail his senses, as shouts of firefighters, policemen, and paramedics all joined together in a cacophony of sound as they tried to organize themselves in fighting the fire while asking about the number of residents and trying to see who was accounted for, and who was not.

Cannon reached the stables just as a couple of the lads were each bringing out a few of their charges. Where possible they had leads and bridles to keep the horses under control. The fire was still twenty-five or thirty yards away from the entrance to the stable door, but the noise and the smoke had begun to agitate the highly-strung animals. Some were significantly distressed. Their instinct to flee and run needing strong arms and calming words, to try and keep them under a semblance of control.

Cannon found Telside, as he too, brought a few of the animals out from the stable block.

"Mike!" exclaimed Rich, "Thank God you're here."

"Are you alright? The lads?"

"Yes, we're fine. Looks like the fire started in the bedroom, at the back of the house near the road," he said. "We're bloody lucky it's the furthest part away from the stables."

"Yes, I agree," answered Cannon, "and lucky you were still here."

"We're just taking them up the hill onto the gallops for safety," Rich answered, nodding in the general direction. "Some of the lads are up there already. We've managed to get about twelve of them up there so far, this lot, and those over there," indicating the two lads who had passed Cannon as he neared the stables, "means that we just have a few more left inside," he tilted his head towards the interior of the barn. "I managed to get one of the vets up top as well," he went on, "so I hope we've got enough hands to keep them all together and calm those that are a bit upset. Fortunately, once they are away from here, and can't see the flames, hopefully, they will settle down quickly enough."

"Okay," said Cannon. "I'll get the others out. When you get back up top can you send a couple of lads to take them up? I'll wait for the lads to come down, but I'll need to get back to Michelle, Cassie, and the police as soon as possible."

Telside led off his charges. Flickers of flame flashed on the hindquarters of the horses as they walked away. Cannon looked back at the house. He noticed some of the firemen with their yellow helmets and their dark overalls on, were unravelling hoses from their trucks, while others began spraying water from already connected pipes, onto the flames. The electricity in the house was still on, and in the lower part of the house, lights shone through the windows. Cannon noticed the glow reflect off the luminous strips on the firemen's overalls.

"What a fucking mess," he muttered to himself. As he turned to run into the barn to retrieve the last of the equine inhabitants, he realized that he hadn't shared with Quick his conclusions about who had killed Crabb and Jefferson. '*Shit!*' he thought to himself. Suddenly, as he realized what he was confronted with and where he was standing, it struck him that what had happened to him the previous night, less than twenty hours before, was connected to the fire. In an instant, all the pieces fell into place. It was as if he had received another blow to the ribs. The fire *was* linked to the murders!

The final three horses still in their boxes, had become even more agitated. Their snorts and whinnies, were both loud and frequent, indicating their nervousness. *Aeon's Ago* who was due to race the following week was banging a hoof against the bottom of his stable door. His ears were pricked and his eyes were beginning to show signs of the red mist of fear coursing through his veins. It was clear how unsettled he was feeling.

"There, there, fella," said Cannon as he slipped a halter over the horse's head, patting him on the neck. "Easy boy."

He led the horse from his box, just as a couple of lads came rushing in. He handed over *Aeon's Ago* to one of them, and the other lad calmly opened the last couple of doors and in a coordinated move was able to take hold of the two remaining animals.

"Thanks," said Cannon, "looks like that's all of them now. Let's hope we can keep the fire away from this stable block."

Cannon then ran back to where had left Cassie and Michelle. He couldn't see them.

The fire had spread further along the roofline and part of the roof had already collapsed. Flames and sparks shot into the dark sky, embers thrown up by the wind rose upwards then disappeared, as the cool air dimmed their glow.

The fire crews worked furiously, ladders raised from the back of fire trucks allowed the men to reach higher into the night and aim their jets of water more accurately into the blaze. Rivers of water began to form around the base of the house and on the driveway. The puddles, remnants of the water aimed at the flames, flowed in multiple directions, ash and wood fibres littering them as the darkened water spread.

"Looks like you may lose most of upstairs, Sir," one of the firemen said to Cannon, "but downstairs, it will likely be the water damage that will be your biggest problem."

Cannon watched as the torrents of water continued flowing downwards from the roof, through the ceiling, and into the ground floor rooms. He looked down at his wet and dirt-covered shoes, the filth picked up from when he had walked through the detritus the water had left behind on the driveway. The noise of the fire, which was previously deafening, like an angry dragon's roar, slowly began to dim. It was clear that man was winning the fight over the flames.

As he stood beside the fireman, Quick walked over to Cannon. The heat from the flames was still intense, the colours still vibrant, but now containing more blue and purple tongues, rather than just red and orange.

"I'm so sorry Mike," he said, his voice sympathetic.

Cannon looked at the building. Taking in what he could, then saying, "Looks like we haven't lost everything and the horses are all okay, thank goodness. Plus no one was hurt, which is something to be thankful for."

He looked around, the blue flashing lights, and the floodlights set up by the fire brigade, casting eerie shadows on the walls of the house and the stable block. He noticed the ambulance drive off, its lights no longer indicating a sense of urgency. It seemed like with the fire being brought under control, there was no real immediate danger to life, so the ambulance crew had been despatched to attend to another crisis elsewhere.

"Have you seen Michelle or Cassie?" he asked Quick.

Quick thought for a second. "Last I saw of them, they were being taken to the fire truck to get some thermal blankets, despite this heat." He pointed towards the fire, which was progressively getting smaller, the water devouring the flames with a slithering, hissing noise, grey smoke now billowing out, but barely visible against the night sky.

"Thanks," he said, "I need to find them."

He walked off, Quick followed a few yards behind.

As they walked, Quick caught up with him, "Mike! Mike!" he said.

"What?" Cannon stopped dead in his tracks turning to face Quick.

"The music, the song?" he queried. "You said it identified the killer of Crabb and Jefferson. Who is it?" he pleaded.

"Sorry, I should have said," answered Cannon. "That tune, yes I *have* heard it before, and you are absolutely sure that it was the tune that Wilson, Jefferson, and Carr, heard on Crabb's phone?" he questioned.

"Yes I am, 100% sure" came the reply.

"Then our killer is Sam Painter!"

"Who?" responded Quick.

"Sam Painter, the Aussie barman at the golf club."

Quick looked confused, "But how…?"

"When I first went to the clubhouse I met him in the bar," Cannon said. "He was busy cleaning up if I recall. He didn't notice me, as he had his back turned to me. He was whistling away. It was a tune I had never heard before, but it was quite distinctive. I didn't think much of it at the time, but given it was not a well-known tune, when you played it to me at the pub, it struck me immediately." He went on. "I realized how unlikely it was, how much of a coincidence it was, that such an unknown tune could be on Crabb's phone, and yet the barman was able to whistle it so easily?"

"Maybe he knew it?" asked Quick.

"No, I think it was a warning to them. He's probably done it before. Possibly whistled it in front of all of them, but they weren't listening. I think he was teasing them, right under their noses."

Quick still could not see the connection. "If it is him, the barman," he said, "what's the motive?"

"It's obvious isn't it?" answered Cannon, "Revenge!"

Chapter 22

Cannon reached the fire engine, where Michelle sat with a silver-coloured thermal blanket held tightly across her shoulders.

She was sitting on a step, on the opposite side of the vehicle, away from the flames.

Cannon reached her, she stood up and he held her tightly against him. He kissed her head, and stroked her hair, offering words of encouragement and sympathy. It was a significant ordeal for anyone to experience. She wasn't injured at all and had suffered no smoke inhalation, but she was definitely suffering from shock.

Quick stood about ten yards away, and watched, desperate to get more information from Cannon. He would need to contact Skinner, once he was satisfied that Cannon was right.

Cannon looked around. "Where's Cassie?" he asked.

Michelle was confused for a second.

"She said she was going to find you after she went to the toilet," replied Michelle. "We couldn't go into the house obviously, so she said she was going to go around the back of the stables. She only went about five minutes ago."

Cannon turned around in a panic. "Cassie!" he shouted, "Cassie!"

His voice drifted off into the night, mixing with the still hissing fire and the growling of the fire engines.

"What is it?" asked Michelle.

"Mike?" queried Quick, walking towards him

"Cassie!" he shouted again, even louder than previously.

As he did so, a car shot out from behind the stables and careered towards, and through a hedge that separated Cannon's property from the road. As it did so, Cannon looked towards the driver's side of the car. All he could see was a dark silhouette, a head, no face, highlighted by the remaining flames from the house.

"Shit," screamed Cannon, "he's got her. The bastard has taken Cassie."

He ran towards his car, his ribs beginning to complain at the lack of respect he showed them. Quick ran beside him, they reached the car together.

"Get in!" shouted Cannon.

Quick jumped into the passenger seat, as Cannon rammed the car into first gear and they sped off. The car bounced, as it took with it another portion of the hedge that the other car had just crashed through. As the tyres hit the tarmac surface of the road, still damp from the rain and the water from the hosepipes that partially snaked onto it, it twitched left and right. Cannon fought the wheel, the back end slewing and gyrating like a novice on an ice rink for the very first time. The two men were thrown around in unison, against the doors and the side windows, both cracking their heads against the glass. For a few seconds, it felt like they would crash into a ditch on the other side of the road, but fortunately, Cannon was able to right the car, just in time. He crunched through the gears, reaching speeds way beyond what was safe, on the narrow roads.

"Where does he live?" he shouted at Quick.

"I'm not sure, can't remember," came the answer.

"Well, call someone!" Cannon indicated the mobile that Quick was holding.

They continued chasing the car directly ahead of them. It was between a quarter to a half a mile in front of them. The distance was difficult to tell. The road twisted and turned. The car they were chasing had driven away from the farm, and away from the village of Stonesfield, itself. Once on the A4095 heading south-east, it could reach the A40 and then be gone from sight very quickly. At that point, it could go all points West or East, and they would lose it.

Quick called Mason. He knew he would have the detail he needed. Without any formality or context of explanation to Mason, he said, "Sam Painter. On your DB, what's his address?"

"Just a minute," came the reply, "let me open my laptop."

"Hurry man," replied Quick. "We're chasing a car which we believe is occupied by the killer of Crabb and Jefferson. We need to know where Painter lives, and quickly!" His appeal making Mason all the more nervous, as he waited for his computer to boot up.

Cannon looked across at Quick, his eyes urging, his facial expression grim. His mind praying that he would get the detail they needed. Time was of the essence. He feared for Cassie. He would never be able to forgive himself if she was hurt in any way.

"It's a caravan park," said Mason down the phone line. "It's at Standlake, the Lincoln Farm Caravan Park, on Standlake Road."

"Thanks," replied Quick. Turning to Cannon he said, "I know where it is. It's about fifteen minutes from where we are now."

"Okay," replied Cannon. "I hope that's where he is heading as I have lost him now. I can't see him anymore!"

Quick looked ahead, but all he could see was the darkness, the car's rear lights that they had seen ahead of them previously, had now disappeared.

"You don't think he just stopped or turned off into a field do you?"

"I don't know, but I hope to Christ you're wrong," answered Cannon. "If he harms a single hair on Cassie's head, I'll kill him!"

Quick turned to look at Cannon, whose face was lit up by the dashboard, his eyes focused on the road ahead, he looked full of concentration and anger as he speared the car through the night.

Finally, as the road became narrower, twisting like a wet snake and flanked by tall hedges on both sides of the road, they needed to slow down to maintain a safe driving speed. Quick called Skinner, filling him in on what had happened and where they were heading. He told him that he would provide all the details later, but that he needed back up at the caravan park. While he spoke, he gave Cannon directions using hand signals.

"He's livid," said Quick, after he had finished speaking with his boss.

"Serves the bastard right."

"He's arranging a couple of cars to meet us out there. He'll be there too."

Cannon groaned. "Great, that's all I need."

"Look," said Quick, "let's get Cassie back safe and sound first. We can worry about personal fights after that. I think we both have the same view of Skinner, but let's address that issue once this is all over."

They stopped the car in front of the office, at the entrance to the caravan park.

The office was closed for the night, as they expected it would be.

Being a long-term residential park, as well as a camping site, but it being out of season, there were very few visitors around. The notice at the entrance said that the office was only open between ten am and four pm Monday, Wednesday, and Friday, otherwise by appointment. The park itself was situated at the end of a long road, deep into the woods. Unless you knew the area, most people would not have readily known of the place's existence.

The facilities as advertised on a large billboard at the entrance to the park, illuminated by a single spotlight looked modern. Swimming pool, onsite shop, leisure centre, play area for children. Certainly a place for a family summer holiday, but not a place to visit during a cold, grey, and wet November.

Cannon and Quick exited the car having switched off the ignition and plunging the area into semi-darkness. They looked around at the dimly lit gravel laneways that went off in three different directions. Their eyes initially struggling with the darkness that enveloped the small roads, each of which stretched away, into the deeper recesses of the park.

The clouds that held the rain in its grasp, strolled across the moonless sky. They were dark shapes in the air, moved on by a chilly wind. Other than the cracking engine noise from Cannon's car as it cooled, there was silence all around them.

Immediately ahead of them, dark shapes, outlines of silent caravans, park homes, and empty tent stands, gave the impression of giant sleeping animals that lay snoring in a field. The barely lit *streets* disappeared into the distance, bending as they did so, following unseen contours. Somewhere amid this *jungle* was Cassie.

"Which way?" whispered Cannon, his breath forming clouds that quickly disappeared on the breeze swirling all around them. It was cold, but not freezing. Damp, but not wet.

"Not sure," came the answer.

"Do you have an exact address for him?"

"No, just the park itself."

Cannon looked around for anything that would indicate names of occupants anywhere. There were no combined post boxes, like those in apartment blocks often found on ground floors. Nothing to distinguish who lived where.

Cannon assumed that all normal mail, and that delivered by couriers, would be dropped off at the office for safekeeping. The long-term occupants collecting it, as and when they could. He walked towards the *street* that led off to the right and checked the ground for any numbers. He used the torch *app* on his phone to light up small areas on the ground.

Eventually, he noticed small-stenciled plot numbers, running along the *roadside* kerb, indicating which plot was which.

Walking about twenty yards along the street immediately ahead of him, he noticed some of the numbers were prefixed with a 'P', others with a 'T', the empty lots having no prefix at all. He assumed this meant which sites were for permanent and which were for temporary caravans, and that those without a prefix, were for tents only.

What they needed was the permanent area. Quick had recalled from the interviews, that Painter had been living at the same address for at least 18 months.

Cannon ran back twenty yards to the office, his heart beginning to beat faster. His concern for Cassie growing each minute. On the window of the office was a map of the park that he had noticed earlier. He shone the light from the phone onto it, the sharp light reflecting back at him from the glass, partially blinding him for a second.

"Shit," he cried out, as the glare stole his vision, stars flashing across his eyes. He blinked as rapidly as he could, to banish the slowly diminishing lights. As he did so, he stood to one side at an angle to the window, squinted, and shone the light back onto the map.

Finding the entrance and then tracing the map with his finger, he found a section on the map with a large 'P' watermarked into the page, this showed a more distinct section of the park, the area he was looking for. From his reckoning, it started about 400 yards along the *street* to the right-hand side.

"Come on," he said to Quick, rushing ahead at a rapid jog in the direction indicated on the map.

As they approached the permanent section of the site, Cannon slowed from a run to a walk. Quick was a few yards behind him. Both men were gasping for breath, Cannon's ribs complaining at the exertion.

The area was eerily quiet.

From what they could see in the dim light, there was a row of about seven caravans on one side of the *street*, with a further row or two behind them. On the other side of the *street,* were what appeared to be park homes sitting on cement bases, these being much more permanent arrangements, than a normal caravan.

Slowly they walked along the *street,* an occasional flicker of a TV could be seen through closed curtains or blinds in a few of the park homes. Lights in some of the caravans indicated that the occupants were likewise, at home.

"Which way?" whispered Quick.

"Not sure," said Cannon, looking at the occasional car that was parked beside the caravans, indicating that someone lived there. "Are you sure he lived in a caravan?" he asked.

"Yes, positive."

As they reached the end of the *street* it made a curve to the left, turning back on itself towards the entrance. Effectively the *street* was now the middle of the three that they had been facing when they first stood at the office.

The light from the small street lamps was less effective here. The poor illumination in this particular stretch, coming from the lamp atop the pole on the *street* that they had just walked along and turned left and away from.

The first caravan they came across was dark, appearing empty. It was large, at least a six-berth, the white exterior glistened in places as condensation formed on its exterior. Drops of water fell from the sides of the van, and down the windows. It was at an angle to the last one that they had passed. The shadow from the bulk of the caravan standing in front of it blocked some of the light from the streetlamp, making it seem darker on the one side, more forbidding than some of the others.

As they walked past, Cannon noticed a car in the deeper recesses of the shadow next to the caravan. He wasn't sure if it was the one they were after. He put a finger to his lips and pointed towards it.

For a few seconds, they waited. The silence around them seemed to magnify Cannon's heartbeat as it pounded in his chest.

He crept slowly towards the car, bending his back to stay low, his ribs crying out for relief as he did so.

Quick stayed on the *street,* waiting for Cannon to indicate if the car was the one they had seen. The one they were looking for.

Cannon moved behind the car, careful to stay out of sight. He was worried that anyone could have been inside the caravan, watching him through the tiny gaps between the curtains and the window frame. He was aware that their night sight would be much better than his own, as the caravan was in total darkness.

He crept slowly from the back of the vehicle on the driver's side, towards the front of the car. As he reached the front wheel, he felt the heat from the engine. Suddenly, and without warning, a cat shot out from underneath the vehicle where it had been lying enjoying the warmth radiating from the engine. Cannon fell backwards with a thud, the unexpected movement of the cat, scaring him. He cracked his head on the ground.

"Shit," he cried in exasperation, his hand automatically reaching for the back of his head. He felt the wetness but wasn't sure if it was damp from the ground he had fallen onto, or blood. It felt cold. *'Thank God,'* he thought, *'it's not blood.'*

As he regained his feet and moved into a crouch to peer through the driver's side window of the car, looking towards the caravan door, ten feet to his left, a spotlight attached to the caravan came on, filling the area with bright luminosity.

Cannon noticed Quick move out of sight, keeping in the shadows near the *street.*

A curtain twitched in one of the windows, and he saw Painter glare through the gap he had created, looking out into the darkness. For a split second he saw Cassie being held close to him, his arms around her shoulders.

Cannon jumped up, revealing himself from his hiding place, and ran to the caravan door.

He pulled hard at the handle, but it was locked.

He banged on the door in frustration, shouting out Cassie's name as he did so.

"Cassie! Cassie! Are you alright?"

He heard a faint cry from inside the caravan. This was quickly followed by a shout, and then what sounded like a thump as if someone had fallen onto the floor.

He banged again on the door and then tried to smash a window with his hands. The double glazing made it impossible. He looked around for something, anything, to attack the door handle with, but could find nothing. He couldn't even see Quick, he had no idea where he had gone.

Cannon began to panic. Even with all the noise he made, there was no movement from any of the other caravans. He banged again on the window, then suddenly the caravan door opened.

Painter almost completely filled the door, silhouetted against the light coming from inside the caravan. His shoulders almost touched both sides of the entrance. He stood with legs apart, still dressed all in black, a mono-suit. The mask and head cover was still hanging from a ring at his waist. It was this outfit that had made it impossible to see any of his features when he had attacked Cannon the previous night, and when he had kidnapped Cassie earlier.

"Get in!" he shouted at Cannon, "If you want to see her alive again."

"If you've harmed….." Cannon started to say.

"You'll do what? Kill me?" he mocked. "I've been dead for twenty years already," Painter continued, "so nothing you can do, can hurt me anymore, now GET IN!"

Cannon looked into Painters eyes. He saw both anger and sadness.

Slowly, Cannon walked towards the door, *'where is Quick?'* he thought to himself.

He couldn't see any sign of the policeman.

Painter moved aside, as Cannon entered the vehicle. He walked straight into a well-equipped kitchen. Looking to the right, Cannon saw Cassie lying on the floor towards the other end of the caravan, about halfway along, in a kind of sitting area. He rushed towards her. As he did so, Painter slammed the door, double locking it behind him.

"Cassie!" shouted Cannon, as he moved through the caravan towards her. When he reached her, he noticed that she was drifting in and out of consciousness. She had black masking tape wound around her wrists and ankles. Across her mouth was another strip of tape.

Cannon picked her up, moved her onto a small fold-down couch attached to the side of the 'van. He ripped off the tape that covered her mouth. She cried out as she did so.

"It's ok," he said. "I'm here baby, I'm here." He held her close, her arms useless, because of her bindings. Her mind was still confused after fainting from fear. She gladly accepted his hug. In his arms, she felt like a rag doll.

Cannon turned towards Painter, who was now only about six feet away. His anger rising, his muscles tensing. He believed he could take Painter, despite his damaged ribs, but until Cassie was clear and away from danger, he knew he needed to be patient.

"You bastard," he shouted, "you fucking bastard. She's done nothing to you. So let her go!" he demanded.

Painter looked at the pair of them, sitting prone, in front of him.

"And neither had you," he said, "until you got in the way!" he emphasized.

Cannon was confused. "What?"

Painter remained where he was. "You had done nothing to me either *until* you got in the way," he said. "But now your investigation has stopped me from doing what I have spent half my life trying to do. What I have been trying to put right," a sad weariness clear in his voice. "So let's see how you feel when something you love is taken away from you!"

"You mean your sister, right?" Cannon said.

Painter stopped dead, immobilized by what he had just heard.

"How? How do you know about that?" he asked, the wind taken from his sails. All aggression stripped from him. His soul laid bare. All in just a few words.

Cannon stood up to his full height. He was a couple of inches taller than Painter. He lifted Cassie by her arm, then put his arm around her waist. She stood unsteadily on her still bound feet against him, her head digging into his side, his ribs. He winced but tried to show he hadn't felt anything.

Cannon looked around him, noticing cupboards at eye level, built-in furniture, other chairs, and a TV on a bracket against the far wall. Further to his right were a couple of bedrooms and a bathroom. The kitchen and all the utensils, including knives were to the left, behind where Painter now stood.

Cannon knew there was only one way out. The door that he had been told by Painter, to enter through. It was back along the narrow passage that he had walked along to get to Cassie, and which ran along the one side of the caravan.

"You were the missing piece," he said, "once I heard the story of how a girl was murdered about twenty-odd years ago, and who was involved, I knew the deaths of Crabb and Jefferson needed to be linked. What I couldn't understand was why. At first, I thought it was Wilson that…"

"That bastard," interrupted Painter with venom, "It was him. He was the one who killed her, he was the instigator. I wanted to leave him until the end. To see the fear grow in his eyes, just like it must have been for Kylie! I wanted him to suffer, wonder, to be on edge, always wondering when I would come for him."

"Was that her name?" asked Cannon gently, trying to lower the tension between them. He needed to keep Painter talking so that he could work out a way to try and escape, get past him. To get to the door.

With the door locked, and the space to move in the caravan limited, he would need to somehow get him off guard long enough, to get Cassie and himself free.

"Yes, and you're right, *SHE* was my sister."

"What happened?" he asked. Lowering Cassie back onto the couch. He sat down making himself smaller and less threatening, trying to give himself time to think and space to move.

Painter thought for a second, not sure that he wanted to waste time. He wasn't sure if Cannon had been alone or not. Either way, he no longer cared.

"My names not really Sam Painter," he said finally, "nor am I Australian, though I lived there for about fourteen years. My real name is Clarkson, Sam Clarkson."

"Oh?" answered Cannon, not sure what else to say.

"I was born in Swindon, grew up there. Later we moved to Oxford when I was about twelve. We were happy as a family until my mother died from ovarian cancer. Our father couldn't handle being without our mother. He was lost, started drinking, becoming abusive, *the whole world was against him,* was how he put it."

Cannon nodded, listening.

"As Kylie got older, she turned quite rebellious. Dad and she clashed continuously, but he still loved her. He held *me* accountable, responsible, to keep her *on the straight and narrow.* He couldn't do it himself, he didn't have the will. He had relied on our mother in the past, but once she was gone, he relied on me."

Cannon noticed that Painter's eyes were glazing over, his memories stirring emotions within him, visions of the past swimming through his brain. Sadness filled his very being. Painter began to weep.

"We went to the concert that night at Kylies' insistence," he went on. "She was determined to have a good time, to party, to get *picked up,* as she put it. During the concert we fought, she told me she would find her own way home. I lost sight of her in the crowd. Afterwards, despite trying to find her, spending hours searching, I gave up," Painter said, the pitch of his voice rising as his emotions became stronger with every word he uttered. "We didn't have mobiles in those days, so I guessed she had found a lift, and that I would find her back at home. When I got there she hadn't returned."

They stared at each other in silence for a few seconds. Cannon looked at Cassie, who was now awake, lying still but her eyes open. He looked at her and smiled. "It's okay," he said, "everything will be just fine." He hoped his reassuring words would help her stay calm.

"She never came home." Painter said softly, bowing his head as if in prayer, before repeating, "she never came home."

Cannon slowly looked around the caravan for anything he could use as a weapon, careful to be seen to be doing nothing more, than listening to his captor.

"And you were held responsible for that?" enquired Cannon.

Without warning, Painter gave out an almighty scream, his voice a wail. "Do you know what it's like!" he shouted, "to be told that I had failed her, had failed my father, that I was useless, that I was not worthy of his love? That if she didn't come home, then I should leave his house and never come back. That I was lower than an insect? Do you know what that feels like?" he screamed, walking aggressively towards Cannon and Cassie, tears streaming from his eyes, mucus dripping from his nose, and spittle around the mouth.

Cassie closed her eyes, Painters aggression scaring her, she lay trembling next to Cannon, who stood up, anxious to protect her. They were now only a few feet apart.

"And she never did come home did she?" he said.

"No," answered Painter, "and soon, I had no home myself. My father's behaviour became so aggressive, his temper so bad, that I couldn't take it anymore. He beat me continuously, cursed me. Couldn't bear to be in the same room with me. So finally, I left."

"And went to Australia?"

"Eventually yes. I thought I could get away from him and the past," he said. "I tried though to keep in touch with what was going in regarding the investigation. I tried to find out what the police were doing to find her, but nothing happened. Despite all the information I could provide, had provided, there was nothing," he repeated. The despair in Painter's voice saddened Cannon. He knew himself, how much those he loved, meant to him.

Continuing, Painter said, "Eventually I heard my father had died. He went to his grave not knowing what had happened to Kylie. That was about three years ago." he said sadly.

"So what brought you back?"

"From the day I left, until the day I found out what had happened to her, I never stopped searching for answers," answered Painter. "While my father may have felt that I was useless, I knew I wasn't. I have lived every day since that night with a sense of guilt that has never gone away. A sense of guilt that can only be removed once justice has been done."

"So how did you find out about Wilson and the others?"

Painter smiled sardonically. "You hear a lot in a bar," he said. "But with social media, you can find out a lot more." He stopped for a second, pleased that he could tell his story. Pleased that in his own mind he had vindicated himself, shown his father that he was wrong about his son.

"It's easy to pretend to be someone you are not. When I saw on Facebook, that the band *Everyman* was reforming, and would be playing concerts again in the next year, I knew that this was the band whose concert we went to on the night Kylie disappeared," he said.

"So I joined lots of Facebook groups that 'liked' the band. I followed a trail of comments from many people in that Facebook group until I found one from Simon Carr that Graham Jefferson had responded to, about *'that night'*. I looked at their profiles, their pictures, their ages, the area where they lived and searched online for old photographs of them. Eventually, in an old newspaper article that I came across, I found a picture from the school that they had all attended. It was a final year party. They must have been about seventeen or eighteen. I recognized Wilson's face from the night of the concert. A face that has been imprinted on my brain since that night. After that, it was a matter of finding out what they did today, where they worked. The easiest was Crabb, being a golf pro, his face was on the club's website. I applied for a job as a barman there and got it. Over the following few months or so I watched them. Listened to them, when they thought no one could hear them."

"And you were able to conclude that you had the right men? After twenty years?"

Painter seemed to take exception to Cannons' comments, his body language changed. He became tense, taught.

"I'm not stupid," he said, "I watched, I listened, then I tested them."

"With the phone calls?"

"Yes."

"Why so elaborate?" asked Cannon, suddenly aware of sounds emanating from outside the caravan. Painter became aware of the movement outside as well. He knew it was likely the police but now that he had told his story, he didn't care anymore.

"I wanted them to shit themselves. I wanted them to be unable to sleep at night. To stay awake, wondering what each sound in the darkness meant. Just like I did, waiting for Kylie to come home. Scared to sleep. I wanted them to wonder what the music that I had left on Crabb's phone meant to them." he said. "I used a system that I had found out about when I was in Australia, about routing calls through different countries. It's easy once you know how," he went on. "Anyway, I knew that one of the band members had emigrated to South Africa somewhere, so I diverted my calls through Johannesburg so that they couldn't be traced to where the phone calls were actually coming from. But where they were really from, was from right here." he pointed at his surroundings. "At least two of them knew the tune and what it meant. At least Crabb and Wilson did," he said. "They may have told you otherwise, but they DID know, Mr. Cannon, they DID!" he shouted.

"So why try and implicate me in all this? Why attack me? Why set my house on fire?" retorted Cannon angrily, "What have we done to you?"

Painter looked into Cannon's eyes. The emotion of the past and Painter's actions of the evening ripped at the very fabric of the man. Cannon could see that he was torn between what was right, and the wrong that he had endured, for over two decades.

"You were getting in my way," he said. "I didn't want to hurt you, that's why I only beat you the other night, not killed you, I could have if I had wanted to," he said. Cannon knew that to be true, he had wondered why he hadn't been struck around the head initially, just in the back. Now he knew.

"When I used the bridle with a metal plate attached, to strangle Jefferson, it was because I wanted you to stop focusing on what I was trying to, needing to, do," he said. "I needed your focus elsewhere."

"I was curious about that," responded Cannon. "I didn't have anything missing of my own gear, so how did you do that?" he asked.

Painter smiled to himself, "It's amazing what a camera on a smartphone can take pictures of at the races, especially when you are standing next to the parade ring as a horse is led by," he answered. "The zoom facility on the phone, and a little bit of metalwork. Easily done."

"And the house? Why set the house on fire tonight?"

"The police had let you go, you were still investigating. I needed something more dramatic to keep you away. When I came at you the other night, I'd hoped that was enough, but it wasn't. You're a persistent bugger, Mr. Cannon, I'll give you that."

He wasn't sure how to take that, so Cannon stayed silent, letting Painter carry on.

"I set the house on fire at the furthest end from where I knew your lady and daughter were. I had watched the place from the time it had gone dark this afternoon. I didn't want to hurt them, just scare them, and you too," he pointed at Cannon. "I had hoped that the fire brigade would get there quickly and limit the damage. I thought it would keep you focused on sorting that out, and looking after your own business, not continuing to mess in mine" he said.

"And kidnapping my daughter?"

"Desperate measure, I ….."

As Painter spoke, Cannon turned to look at Cassie, and as he did so the whole of the caravan lit up in a bright light that streamed through the nylon curtains at the windows. Light from arc lights, set up around the caravan which had suddenly burst into life, temporarily blinding them all.

"Police!" came a voice through a loud hailer. *Skinner* thought Cannon.

"Come out Mr. Painter, we know you are in there," continued the disembodied sound. "We don't want anyone hurt, so please give yourself up and let Mr. Cannon and his daughter go."

Painter looked at Cannon, both men's vision now having returned to normal. Cannon could see that Painter had not thought of an escape plan for himself if he was ever caught or cornered. Painter's eyes filled again with tears. His shoulders slumped. His hands fell to his sides.

Cannon knew that it was just a matter of time. The police just needed to wait it out. He didn't believe that Painter had ever intended to harm Cassie. From what Painter had confessed to him, it was clear that Painter had wanted his revenge only on those that had destroyed his life. Unfortunately, Cannon had got in the way of that. Cannon realized that by doing so, he had likely saved two lives, those of Wilson and Carr, while at the same time had negated a reason *for* living, in Painter himself.

Painter, who had lived with guilt for over twenty years and had probably had no real life of his own. He had been trying for most of his life to make right that which could not be put right. Softly, beneath his breath and between sobs, Painter said, "Get out. Go on, go!" he urged.

Cannon looked at his captor. Looked at Cassie. "Sam, it doesn't have to be this way," he said.

"Go on, get out!" was the repeated response.

Painter moved aside, showing Cannon the way to the door. As he did so, he reached into a cupboard, bringing out a pair of scissors. He leaned over and cut the tape from Cassie's hands and feet. She briefly flexed her arms before Painter leant forward and pushed them towards the door. "Go on, out!" he shouted for the third time.

Cassie and her father reached the door in a matter of strides, Painter not far behind them.

Cannon undid the locks, and as he did so the door flew open, the breeze catching it, and it banged against the side of the caravan. The artificial light enveloped them. Putting hands to their eyes, they ran to where they could hear a loudspeaker issue a further instruction. "Okay, Mr. Painter, now come out yourself, please. Let's do this nice and….shit!"

As the last syllable echoed into the night sky, Cannon turned around to see the caravan door slam shut.

A woman police officer ran over to them quickly, from about thirty yards down the *street* where an ambulance now waited. She took Cassie by the left hand, Cassie's other hand still held tightly by Cannon.

"Come with me to the ambulance love, let's get you checked over," she said.

Cassie looked up and Cannon nodded at his daughter. "Go on, it's ok I'll see you in a minute," he said.

"Are you okay Mike?" asked Quick, who was standing close to Skinner.

"Yes we're fine," he said, "he had no intention of hurting us."

"I'll be the judge of that!" answered Skinner.

Cannon looked around him. He saw at least four police cars and a dozen or so men in dark jackets with body armour, black masks upon their faces, holding Heckler and Koch semi-automatic rifles all lined up around the caravan.

He judged that Quick had been able to contact Skinner while he and Cassie had been detained inside and direct him, along with the support that was now dispersed around the immediate vicinity, towards the caravan.

"What's this?" he said to Skinner, pointing at all the activity around him.

"Isn't it obvious? The man's a killer," he nodded towards the caravan. "We needed support to set you free. Now we need support to get him out of there."

"He's not going to hurt anyone," said Cannon, "just give him a minute to compose himself. He's told me the full story. I know why he did what he did. I'm convinced he'll be out soon."

Skinner looked at Cannon with disgust. "That's as maybe," he said, "but I'm in charge here and this is a Police matter. If you get in my way again I will have you arrested. So for fuck's sake stay out of my business!"

Cannon took a slight step back, watching the happenings around him. He hoped to God that he had gotten through to Painter.

They stood around for a few minutes. The cold began to seep into Cannon. The adrenaline of the chase, the fear he held for Cassie's safety had all dissipated now. He felt the chill of the night.

Skinner spoke into the loud hailer again, "One more time Mr. Painter, please come out with your hands up where we can see them. We'll give you a few more minutes to think about it, then we are coming in."

Skinner turned to Quick having lowered the loud hailer. "Get the men ready," he said, pointing towards a couple of the armed men. Quick walked away towards the firearms officers.

"What's that smell?" shouted one of the policemen standing a few yards in front of Cannon and Skinner, closer to the caravan.

"Gas!" someone else shouted, "it's coming from inside."

"Shit," exclaimed Skinner, "he's trying to kill himself."

"Move away," exclaimed Cannon, "get out of the way it's dangerous!"

Quick ran the few yards back towards his boss, having heard the shouts. "What do you want to do, should we evacuate the area?" he asked.

"No," said Skinner, "let's find the gas valve quickly. It should be around the base of the 'van. We can turn it off there. Hurry!"

"But I don't know where to look," replied Quick.

"Oh, for Christ's sake," answered Skinner, "I'll do it myself."

Quick and Cannon watched as Skinner ran towards the caravan. He was only ten to fifteen yards away from them, and about three yards away from the caravan when an explosion ripped through the air. The blast wave knocking Quick, Cannon, and many others off their feet. Shrapnel flew out from the caravan in all directions, upwards and outwards. A fireball lit up the sky, engulfing Skinner and two other armed policemen. They were dead before their bodies hit the ground, molten metal shards and spears of wood and glass piercing their bodies, face, and legs in hundreds of places, fire from the flame, melting skin, and incinerating flesh.

Fire raged through what was left of Painter's caravan and car. The two caravans standing immediately next door and to the front of Painter's home were also destroyed in the blast. Fortunately, these had been empty of occupants.

Cannon got to his feet. He couldn't hear properly. He had burst eardrums in both ears. Blood trickled down the side of his face. He watched in horror at the scene before him. His face lit by the dancing flames, sound diminished to dull crackles and thuds. All around him people scampered, trying to make sense of the chaos, sense of what they had just witnessed. He reached down to help Quick to his feet.

They stood together, as paramedics ran towards them from the ambulance where Cassie had been receiving treatment.

Smoke billowed into the night sky, the smell of burnt flesh, wood, and rubber reached them. Quick doubled over, vomiting onto the ground.

Cannon closed his eyes. He knew this scene like others from the past, would come back to haunt him as they always did. He turned away from the flames that continued to lick the night and walked towards where Cassie was waiting. His ribs hurt, he was physically tired, emotionally drained.

He just wanted to collect her and take her home.

END